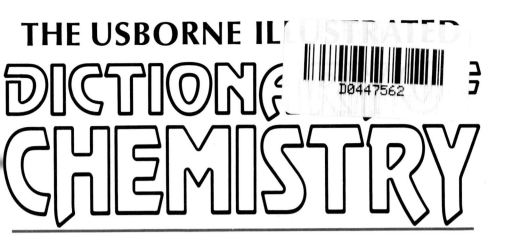

THE USBORNE ILLUSTRATED
DICTIONARY OF
CHEMISTRY

Jane Wertheim, Chris Oxlade and
Dr. John Waterhouse

Edited by Tony Potter and Corinne Stockley

Scientific advisors:
J. Raffan, MA, R. Michaelis, B.Sc. and A.Alder, B.Sc.

Designed by:
Anne Sharples, Roger Berry,
Sue Mims and Simon Gooch.

Illustrated by:
Kuo Kang Chen, Kim Blundell,
Guy Smith, Chris Lyon, Jeremy
Gower and Mark Franklin.

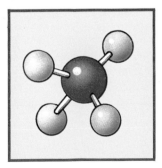

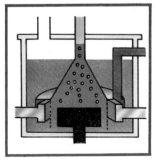

Contents

First published in 1986 Usborne Publishing Ltd, Usborne House 83-85 Saffron Hill, London EC1N 8RT, England

© Copyright 1986 Usborne Publishing Ltd

The name Usborne and the device 🐝 are Trade Marks of Usborne Publishing Ltd.

Printed in Great Britain

About this book

Chemistry is the study of substances – what they are made of and how they react under various conditions. It is divided into three main branches – physical chemistry, inorganic chemistry and organic chemistry. The first three colour-coded sections of this book deal with these three areas. The book also covers environmental chemistry and has a section of general information.

Red section Physical chemistry – the structure and properties of substances, and the laws of chemistry.

Blue section Inorganic chemistry – the chemical elements and their compounds.

Green section Organic chemistry – the carbon-chain compounds.

Yellow section Environmental chemistry – e.g. air, water and pollution.

Black and white section A section of general information, relating to such things as units, apparatus and chemical methods. It includes charts of information on the properties of elements, and a glossary of non-specific scientific words.

How to use this book

This book can be used as a dictionary or as a revision handbook. The definitions are arranged thematically, that is, all the words to do with the same subject are grouped together, in most cases on two facing pages. These subjects are listed as contents on page 2. The two indexes (pages 116-128) form the dictionary reference section. They are alphabetical lists of all the individual definitions in the book, giving page numbers for both main entries and supplementary entries. See pages 116 and 122 for more about the use of the indexes.

Key to use of the book

1. Every main definition is preceded by a dot, the entry word is printed in bold type, and any symbols or formulae follow immediately afterwards, e.g.:

●**Lithium (Li).**

2. Any singulars or plurals (which are not simply the addition of a letter s) follow straight after an entry, e.g.:

●**Nucleus** (pl. **nuclei**).

3. Any synonyms of the word also follow immediately, e.g :

●**Sodium chloride** or **salt.**
(only one synonym)

●**Electron shell**. Also called **shell** or **energy level.**
(more than one synonym)

4. Many other words are also printed in bold. These are either defined where they appear, or the bold type is a sign that their own definitions can be found elsewhere on the same two pages.

5. If a word is in bold type and has an asterisk (*), it is defined elsewhere in the book and is in the footnote at the bottom of the page.

6. This is a typical footnote:

* **Complex ion**, 40 (**Complex salt**); **Charles' law**, 28; **Ductile**, 114; **Nucleus**, 12.

a) The term **complex ion** can be found inside the text of the main definition entry **Complex salt** on page 40.

b) **Nuclei*** (the plural) may have been what appeared in the text, rather than **nucleus***. The singular is given since this is the entry word on page 12.

Physical chemistry

Physical chemistry is the study of the patterns of chemical behaviour in **chemical reactions** under various conditions, which result from the **chemical** and **physical properties** of substances. Much of physical chemistry involves measurements of some kind. It covers the following:

1. Solids, liquids and gases, the changes between these states and the reasons for these changes in relation to the structure of a substance (see **states of matter**, pages 6-7, **kinetic theory**, page 9 and **gas laws**, pages 28-29).

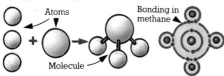

Liquid

Gas

2. The physical and chemical composition of substances – their particles and bonding (see **elements, compounds and mixtures**, pages 8-9, **atoms and molecules**, pages 10-11, **bonding**, pages 16-20 and **crystals**, pages 21-23).

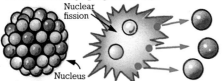

Atoms

Molecule

Bonding in methane

3. The structure of the atom and its importance in the structure of substances (see **atomic structure** and **radioactivity**, pages 12-15).

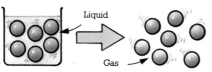

Nuclear fission

Nucleus

4. The measurement of quantities and the relationship between amounts of liquids, gases and solids (see **measuring atoms**, pages 24-25).

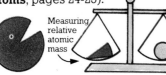

Measuring relative atomic mass

5. Special types of ▶ chemical behaviour (see **acids and bases**, pages 36-38 and **salts**, pages 39-41).

Acid   Base

Salt

6. Representing chemicals and chemical reactions (see **representing chemicals**, pages 26-27).

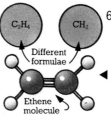

C_2H_4 CH_2

Different formulae

Ethene molecule

7. How substances mix (see **solutions and solubility**, pages 30-31).

Solution

8. Changes during chemical reactions (see **energy and chemical reactions**, pages 32-33 and **rates of reaction**, pages 46-47) and special reactions (see **oxidation and reduction**, pages 34-35 and **reversible reactions**, pages 48-49).

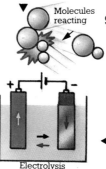

Molecules reacting

9. The action of electricity on substances and the production of electricity from reactions (see **electrolysis**, pages 42-43 and ◀ **reactivity**, pages 44-45).

Electrolysis

10. The different levels ▶ of reactivity shown by substances and the reasons for this (see **reactivity**, pages 44-45).

Forming ions

4

Properties and changes

●**Physical properties**. All the properties of a substance except those which affect its behaviour in **chemical reactions**. There are two main types – **qualitative properties** and **quantitative properties**.

●**Qualitative properties**. Descriptive properties of a substance which cannot be given a mathematical value. They are such things as smell, taste and colour.

Qualitative properties are used in the description of a substance.

Solid   Liquid   Gas

Smell   Taste   Colour

●**Quantitative properties**. Properties which can be measured and given a specific mathematical value, e.g. melting point, boiling point, **mass***, hardness and **density***.

Density* (depends on the **mass*** of the particles and how they are packed together)

Hardness (depends on **bonding*** and structure)

Malleability* and ductility* (depend on **bonding*** and structure)

Melting point (depends on **bonding*** and structure)

Boiling point (depends on **bonding*** and structure)

Conductivity* (depends on whether charged particles can move)

Solubility*

●**Physical change**. A change which occurs when one or more of the **physical properties** of a substance is changed. It is usually easily reversed

A **physical change** from liquid to solid is caused by removing energy from the particles of the substance (see **kinetic theory**, page 9).

●**Chemical properties**. Properties which cause specific behaviour of substances during **chemical reactions**.

Chemical properties depend on **electron configuration***, **bonding***, structure and energy changes.

●**Chemical reaction**. Any change which alters the **chemical properties** of a substance or which forms a new substance. During a chemical reaction, **products** are formed from **reactants**.

●**Reactants**. The substances present at the beginning of a **chemical reaction**.

●**Products**. The substances formed in a **chemical reaction**.

The **rusting*** of iron is a **chemical reaction**.

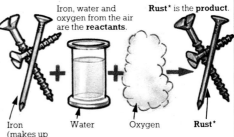

Iron, water and oxygen from the air are the **reactants**.

Rust* is the **product**.

Iron (makes up nearly all of steel)

Water

Oxygen

This reaction is quite slow - many reactions are much faster.

Rust*

●**Reagent**. A substance used to start a **chemical reaction**. It is also one of the **reactants**. Common reagents in the laboratory are hydrochloric acid, sulphuric acid and sodium hydroxide.

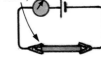

*Bonding, 16; Conductivity, 114 (Conductor); Density, 114; Ductility, 114 (Ductile); Electron configuration, 13; Malleability, 115 (Malleable); Mass, 115; Rust, 60; Rusting, 95 (Corrosion); Solubility, 31.

States of matter

A substance can be **solid**, **liquid** or **gaseous**. These are the **physical states** or **states of matter** (normally shortened to **states**). Substances can change between states, normally when heated or cooled to increase or decrease the energy of the particles (see **kinetic theory**, page 9).

•**Solid state**. A state in which a substance has a definite volume and shape.

Solid state - volume and shape stay the same.

•**Gaseous state**. A state in which a substance has no definite volume or shape. It is either a **vapour** or a **gas**. A vapour can be changed into a liquid by applying pressure alone; a gas

Gaseous state - volume and shape will alter.

must first be turned into a vapour by reducing its temperature to below a level called its **critical temperature**.

•**Liquid state**. A state in which a substance has a definite volume, but can change shape.

Liquid state - volume stays the same, but shape alters.

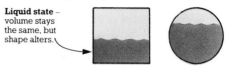

•**Phase**. A separate part of a mixture of substances with two or more states. A mixture of sand and water contains two phases – the **solid** phase (sand) and the **liquid** phase (water).

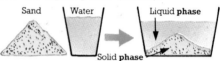

Sand   Water   Liquid **phase**   Solid **phase**

•**Fluid**. A substance that will flow, i.e. is either in the **gaseous** or **liquid state**.

Changes of state

A **change of state** is a **physical change*** of a substance from one state to another. It normally occurs because of a change in the energy of the particles, caused by heating or cooling (see **kinetic theory**, page 9).

•**Melting**. The change of state from **solid** to **liquid**, usually caused by heating. The temperature at which a solid melts is called its **melting point** (see also pages 98-99), which is the same temperature as its **freezing point** (see **freezing**). At the melting point, both solid and liquid states are present. An increase in pressure increases the melting point. All pure samples of a substance at the same pressure have the same melting point.

•**Molten**. Describes the **liquid** state of a substance which is a **solid** at room temperature.

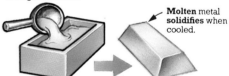

Molten metal solidifies when cooled.

•**Solidification**. The change of state from **liquid** to **solid** of a substance which is a solid at room temperature and atmospheric pressure.

Ice (**solid** form of water) **melts** at 0°C or 273K.

• **Freezing**. The change of state from **liquid** to **solid**, caused by cooling a liquid. The temperature at which a substance freezes is the **freezing point**, which is the same temperature as the **melting point** (see **melting**).

Water **freezes** at 0°C or 273K.

• **Fusion**. The change of state from **solid** to **liquid** of a substance which is solid at room temperature and pressure. The substance is described as **fused** (or **molten**). A solid that has been fused and then solidified into a different form is also described as fused.

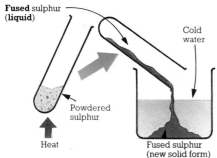

Fused sulphur (**liquid**)

Cold water

Powdered sulphur

Heat

Fused sulphur (new solid form)

• **Boiling**. A change of state from **liquid** to **gaseous** (**vapour**) at a temperature called the **boiling point** (see also pages 98-99). It occurs by the formation of bubbles throughout the liquid. All pure samples of the same liquid at the same pressure have the same boiling point. An increase in pressure increases the boiling point.

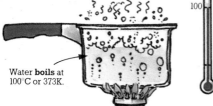

100

Water **boils** at 100°C or 373K.

• **Evaporation**. A change of state from **liquid** to **gaseous** (**vapour**), due to the escape of molecules from the surface. A liquid which evaporates readily is described as **volatile***.

A solution of a **salt*** eventually forms crystals if left standing. The water **evaporates** and **crystallization*** takes place.

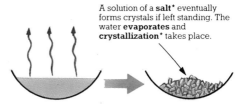

• **Liquefaction**. A change of state from **gaseous** (**gas**) to **liquid**, of a substance which is a gas at room temperature and pressure. It is caused by cooling (to form a **vapour**) and increasing pressure.

Some **gases** are **liquefied** for transport.

• **Condensation**. A change of state from **gaseous** (**gas** or **vapour**) to **liquid**, of a substance which is a liquid at room temperature and pressure. It is normally caused by cooling.

Water **vapour condenses** on cold mirror.

• **Sublimation**. The change of state from **solid** to **gaseous** (**gas**, via **vapour**) on heating, and from gaseous directly to solid on cooling. At no stage is a **liquid** formed. See picture, page 48.

• **Vaporization**. Any change resulting in a **gaseous state**, i.e. **boiling**, **evaporation** or **sublimation**.

Elements, compounds and mixtures

Elements, **compounds** and **mixtures** are the three main types of chemical substance. All substances are made of elements, and most are a combination of two or more elements.

- **Element**. A substance which cannot be split into simpler substances by a chemical reaction. There are just over 100 known elements, classified in the **periodic table** (see pages 50-51). Elements are the building blocks of all chemicals, combining to form **compounds**. Most elements are solids or gases at room temperature.

Hydrogen atom

Oxygen atom

Chemical symbol H

Chemical symbol O

- **Compound**. A combination of two or more **elements**, bonded together in some way. It has different physical and chemical properties from the elements it is made of. The proportion of each element in a compound is constant, e.g. water is always formed from two parts hydrogen and one part oxygen. This is shown by its chemical **formula***, H_2O. Compounds are often difficult to split into their elements and can only be separated by chemical reactions.

- **Binary**. Describes a **compound** composed of two **elements** only, e.g. carbon monoxide.

- **Chemical symbol**. A shorthand way of representing an **element** in **formulae** and **equations** (see pages 26 and 27). It represents one atom and usually consists of the first one or two letters of the name of the element, occasionally the Greek or Latin name. See page 98 for a list of elements and their symbols, and pages 116 onwards to match symbols to elements.

Silver atom

Nitrogen atom

Chemical symbol Ag – Argentum is Latin for silver

Chemical symbol N

- **Mixture**. A blend of two or more **elements** and/or **compounds** which are not chemically combined. The proportions of each element or compound are not fixed, and each keeps its own properties. A mixture can usually be separated into its elements or compounds fairly easily by physical means.

- **Synthesis**. The process by which a **compound** is built up from its **elements** by a sequence of chemical reactions, e.g. iron(III) chloride is made by passing chlorine gas over heated iron.

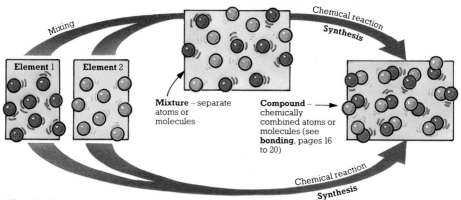

Mixing

Chemical reaction
Synthesis

Element 1

Element 2

Mixture – separate atoms or molecules

Compound – chemically combined atoms or molecules (see **bonding**, pages 16 to 20)

Chemical reaction
Synthesis

* Formulae, 26.

- **Homogeneous.** Describes a substance which is the same throughout in its properties and composition, e.g. solutions (the particles of the **solute*** and **solvent*** are molecules or ions).

- **Heterogeneous.** Describes a substance which varies in its composition and properties from one part to another, e.g. **suspensions*** (the particles are groups of atoms, molecules or ions).

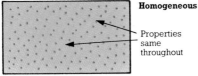

Homogeneous

Properties same throughout

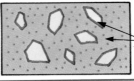

Heterogeneous

Properties differ from place to place

- **Pure.** Describes a sample of a substance which consists only of one **element** or **compound**. It does not contain any other substance in any proportions. If the substance does contain traces of another then it is described as **impure** and the other substance is called an **impurity**.

Kinetic theory

The **kinetic theory** explains the behaviour of solids, liquids and gases, and **changes of state*** between them, in terms of the movement of the particles of which they are made (see diagram below).

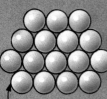

According to the **kinetic theory**:

Heat gives particles enough energy to break the bonds keeping them together.

Eventually, heat gives particles enough energy to escape from the surface of a liquid to form gas.

The greater the speed and frequency with which molecules of a gas hit surfaces, the higher its pressure.

Particles in solids are closely packed together. They vibrate, but do not move about.

Particles in a liquid are quite close together, but are free to move about.

A gas consists of widely spaced particles moving at high speed.

- **Brownian motion.** The random movement of small particles in a **fluid***, e.g. smoke particles in air. Particles are hit by molecules of the fluid, so keep changing direction.

- **Diffusion.** The process by which two **fluids*** mix without mechanical help. The process supports the kinetic theory, since the particles must be moving to mix and gases can be seen to diffuse faster than liquids. Only **miscible*** liquids diffuse.

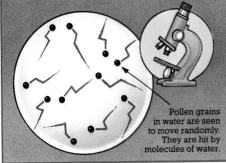

Pollen grains in water are seen to move randomly. They are hit by molecules of water.

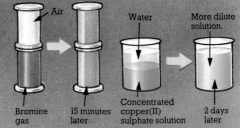

Air

Water

More dilute solution.

Bromine gas

15 minutes later

Concentrated copper(II) sulphate solution

2 days later

*Change of state, Fluid, 6; Miscible, 31; Solute, Solvent, 30; Suspension, 31.

Atoms and molecules

Over 2000 years ago, the Greeks decided that all substances consisted of small particles which they called **atoms**. Later theories extended this idea to include **molecules** – atoms joined together. **Inorganic*** molecules generally only contain a few atoms, but **organic*** molecules can contain hundreds of atoms.

●**Atom**. The smallest particle of an element that retains the chemical properties of that element. The atoms of many elements are bonded together in groups to form particles called **molecules** (see also **covalent bonding**, page 18). Atoms consist of three main types of smaller particles – see **atomic structure**, page 12.

●**Molecule**. The smallest particle of an element or compound that normally exists on its own and still retains its properties. Molecules normally consist of two or more **atoms** bonded together – some have thousands of atoms. **Ionic compounds*** consist of ions and do not have molecules.

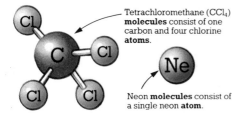

Tetrachloromethane (CCl₄) **molecules** consist of one carbon and four chlorine **atoms**.

Neon **molecules** consist of a single neon **atom**.

●**Atomicity**. The number of **atoms** in a **molecule**, calculated from the **molecular formula*** of the compound.

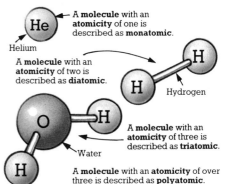

A **molecule** with an **atomicity** of one is described as **monatomic**.

Helium

A **molecule** with an **atomicity** of two is described as **diatomic**.

Hydrogen

A **molecule** with an **atomicity** of three is described as **triatomic**.

Water

A **molecule** with an **atomicity** of over three is described as **polyatomic**.

●**Dalton's atomic theory**. John Dalton's theory, published in 1808, attempts to explain how **atoms** behave. It is still generally valid. It states that:

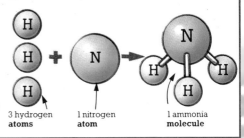

4. **Atoms** of different elements have different properties and different masses.

1. All matter is made up of tiny particles called **atoms**.

2. **Atoms** cannot be made, destroyed or divided (now disproved – see **radioactivity**, page 14).

5. When compounds form, the **atoms** of the elements involved combine in simple whole numbers (now known to be untrue for large **organic*** molecules containing hundreds of atoms).

3. All **atoms** of the same element have the same properties and the same mass (now disproved – see **isotope**, page 13).

| 3 hydrogen **atoms** | 1 nitrogen **atom** | 1 ammonia **molecule** |

10 *Inorganic chemistry, 52; Ionic compound, 17; Molecular formula, 26; Organic chemistry, 76.

- **Dimer**. A substance with **molecules** formed from the combination of two molecules of a **monomer***.

Nitrogen dioxide (**monomer***) combines to form dinitrogen tetraoxide (**dimer**).

$$NO_2\,(g) \;+\; NO_2\,(g) \;\rightarrow\; N_2O_4\,(g)$$

Nitrogen dioxide   Nitrogen dioxide   Dinitrogen tetraoxide

- **Trimer**. A substance with **molecules** formed from the combination of three molecules of a **monomer***.

- **Macromolecule**. A **molecule** consisting of a large number of **atoms**. It is normally an **organic*** molecule with a very high **relative molecular mass***.

Basic laws of chemistry

Three laws of chemistry were put forward in the late 18th and early 19th centuries. Two pre-date **Dalton's atomic theory** and the third (the **law of multiple proportions**) was developed from it. These laws were of great importance in the development of the atomic theory.

- **Law of conservation of mass**. States that matter can neither be created nor destroyed during a chemical reaction. It was developed by a Frenchman, Antoine Lavoisier, in 1774.

Chemical reaction

Reactants   Products

- **Law of constant composition**. States that all pure samples of the same chemical compound contain the same elements combined in the same proportions by mass. It was developed by a Frenchman, Joseph Proust, in 1799.

All **molecules** of methane contain four hydrogen **atoms** (**relative atomic mass*** 1) and one carbon atom (relative atomic mass 12).

Proportion of carbon to hydrogen by mass = 12 : 4 = 3 : 1

H (1)
H (1)
H (1)
H (1)
C (12)

All pure samples of a substance contain a whole number of **molecules** (i.e. parts of molecules do not exist in compounds).

So all samples of methane contain carbon and hydrogen in the ratio 3:1 by mass.

- **Law of multiple proportions**. States that if two elements, A and B, can combine to form more than one compound, then the different masses of A which combine with a fixed mass of B in each compound are in a simple ratio. It is an extension of **Dalton's atomic theory**.

For one nitrogen **atom**:

Nitrogen dioxide, NO_2

Nitrogen monoxide, NO

Dinitrogen oxide, N_2O

Number of **atoms** of oxygen per atom of nitrogen are 2, 1 and ½.

Masses of oxygen in ratio 4:2:1

***Monomers**, 86; **Organic chemistry**, 76; **Relative atomic mass**, **Relative molecular mass**, 24.

11

Atomic structure

Dalton's atomic theory (see page 10) states that the atom is the smallest possible particle. However, experiments have proved that the atom contains smaller particles, or **subatomic particles**. The three main subatomic particles are **protons** and **neutrons**, which make up the **nucleus**, and **electrons**, which are arranged around the nucleus.

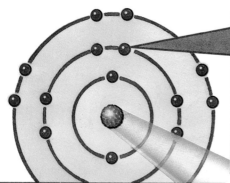

●**Electron**. A **subatomic particle** (see introduction) which moves around the **nucleus** of an atom within an **electron shell**. Its mass is very small, only $\frac{1}{1836}$ that of a **proton**. An electron has a negative electrical charge, equal in size but opposite to that of a proton. There are the same number of electrons as protons in an atom.

●**Neutron**. A **subatomic particle** (see introduction) in the **nucleus** of an atom. It has a **relative atomic mass*** of 1 and no electrical charge. The number of neutrons in atoms of the same element can vary (see **isotope**).

●**Nucleus** (pl. **nuclei**) or **atomic nucleus**. The structure at the centre of an atom, consisting of **protons** and **neutrons** (usually about the same number of each) packed closely together, around which **electrons** move. The nucleus makes up almost the total mass of the atom, but is very small in relation to the total size.

●**Proton**. A **subatomic particle** (see introduction) in the **nucleus** of an atom. It has a **relative atomic mass*** of 1 and a positive electrical charge equal in size but opposite to that of an **electron**. An atom has the same number of protons and electrons, making it electrically neutral.

●**Electron shell**. Also called a **shell** or **energy level**. A region of space in which **electrons** move around the **nucleus** of an atom. An atom can have up to seven shells, increasing in radius, and each can hold up to a certain number of electrons. The model on the right is a simplified one – in fact, the exact positions of electrons cannot be determined at any one time, and each shell consists of **orbitals**.

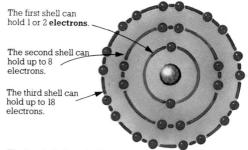

The first three **electron shells**.

The first shell can hold 1 or 2 **electrons**.

The second shell can hold up to 8 electrons.

The third shell can hold up to 18 electrons.

The fourth shell can hold up to 32 electrons.

* Relative atomic mass, 24.

- **Orbital**. A space in which there can be either one or two **electrons**. Each **electron shell** consists of one or more orbitals of varying shapes.

- **Outer shell**. The last **electron shell** in which there are **electrons**. The number of electrons in the outer shell influences how the element reacts and which **group** it is in (see **periodic table**, pages 50-51).

- **Electron configuration**. A group of numbers which shows the arrangement of the **electrons** in an atom. The numbers are the numbers of electrons in each **electron shell**, starting with the innermost.

A sodium atom has an **electron configuration** of 2.8.1

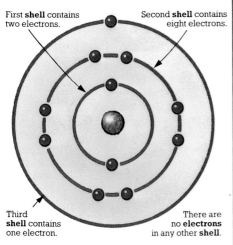

First **shell** contains two electrons.

Second **shell** contains eight electrons.

Third **shell** contains one electron.

There are no **electrons** in any other **shell**.

- **Octet**. A group of eight **electrons** in a single **electron shell**. Atoms with an octet for the **outer shell** are very stable and unreactive. All **noble gases*** (except helium) have such an octet. Other atoms can achieve a stable octet (and thus have an **electron configuration** similar to that of the nearest noble gas) either by sharing electrons with other atoms (see **covalent bonding**, page 18) or by gaining or losing electrons (see **ionic bonding**, page 16).

- **Atomic number**. The number of **protons** in the **nucleus** of an atom. The atomic number determines the element of the atom, e.g. any atom with six protons is carbon, regardless of the number of **neutrons** and **electrons**.

- **Mass number**. The total number of **protons** and **neutrons** in one atom of an element. The mass number of an element can vary because the number of neutrons can change (see **isotope**). The mass number is usually about twice the **atomic number**.

The **atomic number** and **mass number** are often written with the symbol for the element.

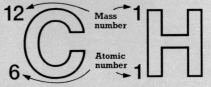

Mass number

Atomic number

Number of **protons** = **atomic number** = 6

Number of **electrons** = 6 (to balance number of **protons**)

Number of **neutrons** = **mass number** – **atomic number** = 6

Number of protons = 1

Number of neutrons = 0

Mass number and **atomic number** the same. **Nucleus** of hydrogen is a single **proton**.

- **Isotope**. An atom of an element in which the number of **neutrons** is different from that in another atom of the same element. Isotopes of an element have the same **atomic number** but different **mass numbers**. Isotopes are distinguished by writing the mass number by the name or symbol of the element.

Carbon has three **isotopes**.

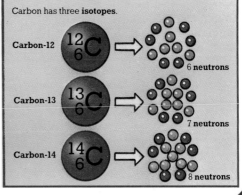

Carbon-12 — 6 neutrons

Carbon-13 — 7 neutrons

Carbon-14 — 8 neutrons

* **Noble gases**, 75.

Radioactivity

Radioactivity occurs when the **nucleus*** of an atom splits up, producing rays or particles (**radiation**), and forms the nucleus of a different element. A radioactive element is one whose nuclei are gradually splitting up in this way. Such nuclei are unstable, usually because they have either very high **mass numbers*** or an imbalance of **protons*** and **neutrons***. Radiation in large doses is lethal.

●**Radioisotope** or **radioactive isotope**. The general term for a radioactive substance, since all are **isotopes***. There are several naturally-occurring radioisotopes, such as carbon-14 (see **radiocarbon dating**, page 15), and others are formed in a variety of ways.

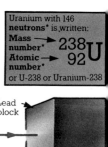
Uranium with 146 **neutrons*** is written:
Mass → ^{238}U
number*
Atomic → 92
number*
or U-238 or Uranium-238

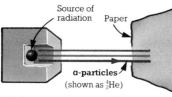
Source of radiation   Paper
Aluminium sheet
Lead block
α-particles (shown as $^4_2$He)
β-particles
γ-particles

●**Alpha particle (α-particle).** One type of particle emitted from the **nucleus*** of a radioactive atom. It is like a helium nucleus, consisting of two **protons*** and two **neutrons***, has a **relative atomic mass*** of 4 and a charge of plus 2. It moves slowly and has a low penetrating power.

●**Beta particle (β-particle).** A fast-moving particle emitted from a radioactive **nucleus***. It can be either an **electron*** or a **positron** (which is like an electron, but positively charged), and can penetrate objects with low density and/or thickness, e.g. paper.

●**Gamma rays (γ-rays).** Rays generally emitted after an **alpha** or **beta particle** from a radioactive **nucleus***. They take the form of waves (like light and x-rays) and have a high penetrating power, going through aluminium sheet. They are stopped by lead.

●**Radioactive decay.** The process whereby the **nuclei*** of a radioactive element undergo a series of disintegrations (a **decay series**), eventually resulting in the formation of a new stable element.

●**Disintegration.** The splitting up of an unstable **nucleus*** into two parts, usually another nucleus and an **alpha** or **beta particle**. The **atomic number*** changes, so an atom of a new element is produced. If this is a stable atom, then no further disintegrations occur. If it is unstable, it disintegrates in turn and the process continues as a **decay series** until a stable atom is formed.

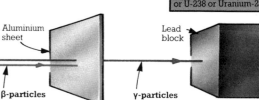
Disintegration of uranium-238 to thorium-234
New nucleus **mass number*** = 238 − 4 = 234
$^{238}_{92}$U
$^4_2$He
$^{234}_{90}$Th
Atom of U-238
α-particle (mass number* 4, atomic number* 2) emitted.
New **atomic number*** = 92 − 2 = 90 so new element is thorium.

Disintegration is shown by a **nuclear equation**.

$$^{238}_{92}U \rightarrow\ ^{234}_{90}Th + ^4_2He$$

 * Atomic number, 13; Electron, 12; Isotope, Mass number, 13; Neutron, Nucleus, Proton, 12; Relative atomic mass, 24.

- **Decay series** or **radioactive series**. The series of **disintegrations** involved when a radioactive element decays, producing various elements until an element with stable atoms is formed.

Decay series for plutonium-242 to uranium-234

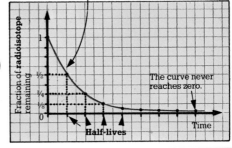

Alpha particle emitted

Uranium-238

Thorium-234

Beta particle emitted

Protactinium-234

Uranium-234

- **Becquerel**. A unit of **radioactive decay**. One becquerel is equal to one nuclear **disintegration** per second. A **curie** equals 3.7×10^{10} becquerels.

- **Half-life**. The time taken for half of the atoms in a sample of a radioactive element to undergo **radioactive decay**. The amount of radiation emitted is halved. The half-life varies widely, e.g. uranium-238, 4.5 thousand million years; radium-221, 30 seconds.

Radioactive decay curve

The curve never reaches zero.

Fraction of radioisotope remaining

Half-lives

Time

Uses of radioactivity

- **Nuclear fission**. The division of a **nucleus***, caused by bombardment with a **neutron***. The nucleus splits, forming neutrons and nuclei of other elements, and releasing huge amounts of energy. The release of neutrons also causes the fission of other atoms, which in turn produces more neutrons – a **chain reaction**. An element which can undergo fission is described as **fissile**. Controlled nuclear fission is used in nuclear power stations, but uncontrolled fission, e.g in atom bombs, is extremely explosive.

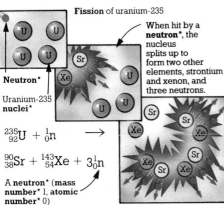

Fission of uranium-235

When hit by a **neutron***, the nucleus splits up to form two other elements, strontium and xenon, and three neutrons.

Neutron*

Uranium-235 nuclei*

$$^{235}_{92}U + ^{1}_{0}n \longrightarrow$$

$$^{90}_{38}Sr + ^{143}_{54}Xe + 3^{1}_{0}n$$

A neutron* (mass number* 1, atomic number* 0)

- **Nuclear fusion**. The combination of two **nuclei*** to form a larger one. It will only take place at extremely high temperatures and releases huge amounts of energy. Nuclear fusion takes place in the hydrogen bomb.

- **Radioactive tracing**. A method of following a substance as it moves by tracking radiation from a **radioisotope** introduced into it. The radioisotope used is called a **tracer** and the substance is said to be **labelled**.

- **Radiocarbon dating** or **carbon dating**. A method used to calculate the time elapsed since a living organism died by measuring the radiation it gives off. All living things contain a small amount of carbon-14 (a **radioisotope**) which gradually decreases after death.

Radiocarbon dating of organic remains

- **Radiology**. The study of radioactivity, especially with regard to its use in medicine (**radiotherapy**). Cancer cells are susceptible to radiation, so cancer can be treated by small doses.

---

* Atomic number, Mass number, 13; Neutron, Nucleus, 12.

Bonding

When substances react together, the tendency is always for their atoms to gain, lose or share electrons so that they each acquire a stable (full) **outer shell*** of electrons. In doing so, these atoms develop some kind of attraction, or **bonding**, between them (they are held together by **bonds**). The three main types of bonding are **ionic bonding**, **covalent bonding** (see pages 18-19) and **metallic bonding** (see page 20). See also **intermolecular forces**, page 20.

●**Valency electron.** An electron, always in the **outer shell*** of an atom, used in forming a bond. It is lost by atoms in **ionic bonding** and **metallic bonding***, but shared with other atoms in **covalent bonding***.

Ions

An **ion** is an electrically charged particle, formed when an atom loses or gains one or more electrons to form a stable **outer shell***. All ions are either **cations** or **anions**.

●**Cation.** An ion with a positive charge, formed when an atom loses electrons in a reaction (it now has more **protons*** than electrons). Hydrogen and metals tend to form cations. Their atoms have one, two or three electrons in their **outer shells***, and it is easier for them to lose electrons (leaving a stable shell underneath) than to gain at least five more.

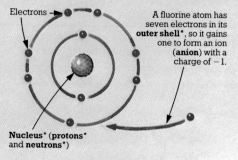

Electrons →

A fluorine atom has seven electrons in its **outer shell***, so it gains one to form an ion (**anion**) with a charge of −1.

Nucleus* (**protons*** and **neutrons***)

A fluoride ion (**anion**) is written F⁻.

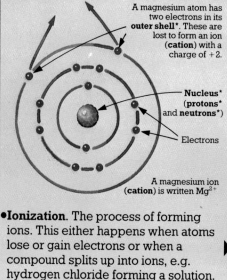

A magnesium atom has two electrons in its **outer shell***. These are lost to form an ion (**cation**) with a charge of +2.

Nucleus* (**protons*** and **neutrons***)

Electrons

A magnesium ion (**cation**) is written Mg^{2+}

●**Anion.** An ion with a negative charge, formed when an atom gains electrons in a reaction (it now has more electrons than **protons***). Non-metals tend to form anions. Their atoms have five, six or seven electrons in their **outer shells***, and it is easier for them to gain electrons (and acquire a stable shell) than to lose at least five. Some anions are formed by groups of atoms gaining electrons, e.g. **acid radicals***.

●**Ionization.** The process of forming ions. This either happens when atoms lose or gain electrons or when a compound splits up into ions, e.g. hydrogen chloride forming a solution.

Ionization of hydrogen chloride in water, forming hydrogen ions and chloride ions.

▶

$$HCl\,(g) \quad \rightarrow \quad H^{+}(aq) + Cl^{-}(aq)$$

Covalent compound* of hydrogen chloride

Separate ions produced in solution

---

* **Acid radical**, 39; **Covalent bonding, Covalent compounds**, 18; **Metallic bonding**, 20; **Neutron, Nucleus**, 12; **Outer shell**, 13; **Proton**, 12.

Ionic bonding

When two elements react together to form ions, the resulting **cations** and **anions**, which have opposite electrical charges, attract each other. They stay together because of this attraction. This type of bonding is known as **ionic bonding** and the electrostatic bonds are called **ionic bonds**. Elements far apart in the periodic table tend to exhibit this kind of bonding, coming together to form **ionic compounds**, e.g. sodium and chlorine (sodium chloride) and magnesium and oxygen (magnesium oxide).

•**Ionic compound.** A compound whose components are held together by ionic bonding. It has no molecules, instead the **cations** and **anions** attract each other to form a **giant ionic lattice***. Ionic compounds have high melting and boiling points (the bonds are strong and hence large amounts of energy are needed to break them). They conduct electricity when **molten*** or in **aqueous solution*** because they contain charged particles (ions) which are free to move.

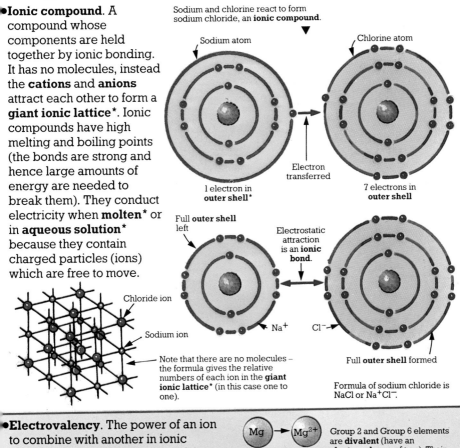

Sodium and chlorine react to form sodium chloride, an **ionic compound**.

Sodium atom

Chlorine atom

Electron transferred

1 electron in **outer shell***

7 electrons in **outer shell**

Full **outer shell** left

Electrostatic attraction is an **ionic bond**.

Na^+ Cl^-

Full **outer shell** formed

Formula of sodium chloride is NaCl or Na^+Cl^-.

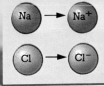

Chloride ion

Sodium ion

Note that there are no molecules – the formula gives the relative numbers of each ion in the **giant ionic lattice*** (in this case one to one).

•**Electrovalency.** The power of an ion to combine with another in ionic bonding. It is equal to the size of the charge on the ion. The ions combine in such proportions that the total charge of the compound is zero.

$Mg \rightarrow Mg^{2+}$

$O \rightarrow O^{2-}$

Group 2 and Group 6 elements are **divalent** (have an **electrovalency** of two). Their ions each have a charge of $+2$ or -2.

$Na \rightarrow Na^+$

$Cl \rightarrow Cl^-$

Group 1 and Group 7 elements are **monovalent** (have an **electrovalency** of one). Their ions each have a charge of $+1$ or -1

$Al \rightarrow Al^{3+}$

$N \rightarrow N^{3-}$

Some Group 3 and Group 5 elements are **trivalent** (have an **electrovalency** of three). Their ions each have a charge of $+3$ or -3

* **Aqueous solution**, 30; **Giant ionic lattice**, 23; **Molten**, 6; **Outer shell**, 13.

17

Covalent bonding

Covalent bonding is the sharing of electrons between atoms so that each atom acquires a stable **outer shell***. Electrons are shared in pairs called **electron pairs** (one pair being a **covalent bond**). Covalent bonds between atoms are strong. However, **covalent compounds** (compounds with covalent bonds) are usually liquids or gases at room temperature (see also **molecular lattice**, page 23). The melting and boiling points are low because the attraction between the molecules is small and hence little energy is needed to overcome it. They do not conduct electricity because there are no charged particles (ions) present.

●**Single bond**. A covalent bond formed when one pair of electrons is shared between two atoms.

A chlorine molecule has a **single bond**.

Chlorine atoms (each with seven electrons in **outer shell***)

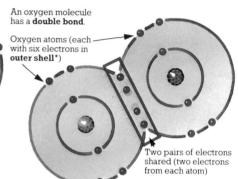

Pair of electrons shared (one electron from each atom)

A **single bond** is shown in a formula by a single line: Cl-Cl

Each atom now has a stable **outer shell*** of eight electrons (see **octet**, page 13).

●**Double bond**. A covalent bond formed when two pairs of electrons are shared between two atoms.

An oxygen molecule has a **double bond**.

Oxygen atoms (each with six electrons in **outer shell***)

Two pairs of electrons shared (two electrons from each atom)

A **double bond** is shown in a formula by a double line: O=O

Each atom now has a stable **outer shell*** of eight electrons (see **octet**, page 13).

●**Triple bond**. A covalent bond formed when three pairs of electrons are shared between two atoms.

A nitrogen molecule has a **triple bond**.

Nitrogen atoms (each with five electrons in **outer shell***)

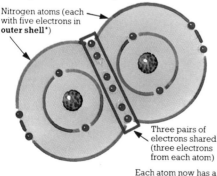

Three pairs of electrons shared (three electrons from each atom)

Each atom now has a stable **outer shell*** of eight electrons (see **octet**, page 13).

A **triple bond** is shown in a formula by a triple line: N≡N

●**Dative covalent bond** or **coordinate bond**. A covalent bond in which both electrons in the bond are provided by the same atom. It donates a **lone pair**.

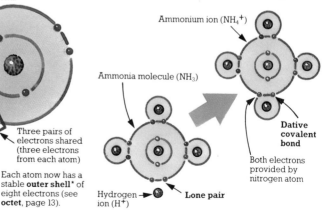

Ammonium ion (NH_4^+)

Ammonia molecule (NH_3)

Dative covalent bond

Both electrons provided by nitrogen atom

Hydrogen ion (H^+) **Lone pair**

●**Covalency**. The maximum number of covalent bonds an atom can form. It is equal to the number of hydrogen atoms which will combine with the atom. The covalency of most elements is constant, but that of **transition metals*** varies.

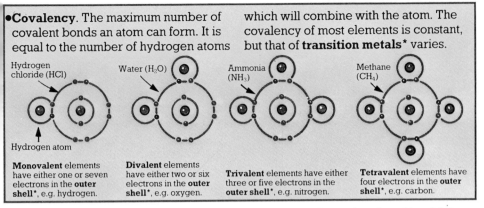

Hydrogen chloride (HCl)

Water (H_2O)

Ammonia (NH_3)

Methane (CH_4)

Hydrogen atom

Monovalent elements have either one or seven electrons in the **outer shell***, e.g. hydrogen.

Divalent elements have either two or six electrons in the **outer shell***, e.g. oxygen.

Trivalent elements have either three or five electrons in the **outer shell***, e.g. nitrogen.

Tetravalent elements have four electrons in the **outer shell***, e.g. carbon.

●**Lone pair**. A pair of electrons in the **outer shell*** of an atom which is not part of a covalent bond (see ammonia picture on previous page).

●**Electronegativity**. The power of an atom to attract electrons to itself in a molecule. If two atoms with different electronegativities are joined, a **polar bond** is formed. Weakly electronegative atoms are sometimes called **electropositive** (e.g. sodium) as they form positive ions fairly easily.

●**Polar bond**. A covalent bond in which the electrons are nearer to one atom's **nucleus*** than the other. This effect is called **polarization**. It is caused by a difference in **electronegativity** between the atoms, the electrons being more attracted to one than the other.

●**Polar molecule**. A molecule with a difference in electric charge between its ends, caused by an uneven distribution of **polar bonds**, and sometimes by **lone pairs**. Liquids with polar molecules may be **polar solvents*** and may dissolve **ionic compounds***. A **non-polar molecule** has no difference in charge at its ends.

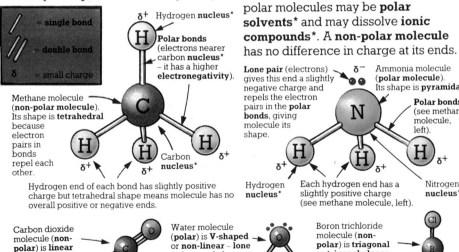

= single bond

= double bond

δ = small charge

$δ^+$ Hydrogen **nucleus***

Polar bonds (electrons nearer carbon **nucleus*** – it has a higher **electronegativity**).

Methane molecule (**non-polar molecule**). Its shape is **tetrahedral** because electron pairs in bonds repel each other.

Carbon **nucleus***

$δ^+$

Hydrogen end of each bond has slightly positive charge but tetrahedral shape means molecule has no overall positive or negative ends.

Lone pair (electrons) gives this end a slightly negative charge and repels the electron pairs in the **polar bonds**, giving molecule its shape.

$δ^-$ Ammonia molecule (**polar molecule**). Its shape is **pyramidal**.

Polar bonds (see methane molecule, left).

Hydrogen **nucleus***

Each hydrogen end has a slightly positive charge (see methane molecule, left).

Nitrogen **nucleus***

$δ^+$

Carbon dioxide molecule (**non-polar**) is **linear** (atoms in straight line).

Water molecule (**polar**) is **V-shaped** or **non-linear** – lone pairs repel electron pairs in bonds.

Boron trichloride molecule (**non-polar**) is **triagonal** or **trigonal planar** – electrons in bonds repel each other.

●**Isomerism**. The occurrence of the same atoms forming different arrangements in different molecules. The arrangements are **isomers***. They have the same **molecular formula*** but different **graphic formulae***.

Metallic bonding

Metallic bonding is the attraction between particles in a **giant metallic lattice*** (i.e. in metals). The lattice consists of positive ions of the metal with **valency electrons*** free to move between them. The free or **delocalized** electrons form the bonds between the metal and, because they can move, heat and electricity can be conducted through the metal. The forces between the electrons and ions are strong. This gives metals high melting and boiling points, since relatively large amounts of energy are needed to overcome them. For more about other types of bonding, see pages 16-19.

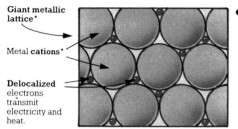

Giant metallic lattice*

Metal **cations***

Delocalized electrons transmit electricity and heat.

●**Delocalization**. The sharing of **valency electrons*** by all the atoms in a molecule or **giant metallic lattice***. Delocalized electrons can belong to any of the atoms in the lattice and are able to move through the lattice, so the metal can conduct electricity and heat.

Intermolecular forces

●**van der Waals' forces**. Weak attractive forces between molecules (**intermolecular forces**) caused by the uneven distribution and movement of electrons in the atoms of the molecules. The attractive force is approximately twenty times less than in **ionic bonding***. It is the force which holds **molecular lattices*** together, e.g. iodine and solid carbon dioxide.

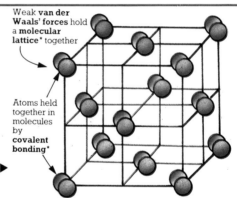

Weak **van der Waals' forces** hold a **molecular lattice*** together

Atoms held together in molecules by **covalent bonding***

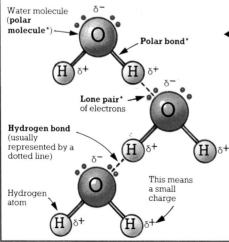

Water molecule (**polar molecule***)

δ⁻

Polar bond*

H δ⁺   H δ⁺

δ⁻

Lone pair* of electrons

Hydrogen bond (usually represented by a dotted line)

δ⁻

H δ⁺   H δ⁺

This means a small charge

Hydrogen atom

H δ⁺   H δ⁺

◄●**Hydrogen bond**. An attraction between a **polar molecule*** containing hydrogen and a **lone pair*** of electrons in another molecule. The **polar bonds*** mean that each hydrogen atom has a slightly positive charge and is therefore attracted to the electrons. Hydrogen bonding accounts for high melting and boiling points in water in relation to other substances with small, but **non-polar molecules***. Both the hydrogen bonds and the **van der Waals' forces** must be overcome to separate the molecules.

* **Cation**, 16; **Covalent bonding**, 18; **Giant metallic lattice**, 23; **Ionic bonding**, 17; **Lone pair**, 19; **Molecular lattice**, 23; **Non-polar molecule**, 19 (**Polar molecule**); **Polar bond**, 19; **Valency electron**, 16.

Crystals

Crystals are solids with regular geometric shapes, formed from regular arrangements of particles. The particles can be atoms, ions or molecules and the bonding of any type or mixture of types. The edges of crystals are straight and the surfaces flat. Substances that form crystals are described as **crystalline**. Solids without a regular shape (i.e. those which do not form crystals) are described as **amorphous**.

●**Crystallization**. The process of forming crystals. It can happen in a number of ways, e.g. cooling **molten*** solids, **subliming*** solids (solid to gas and back), placing a **seed crystal** in a **supersaturated*** solution or placing a seed crystal in a **saturated*** solution and cooling or evaporating the solution. The last method is the most common. Either cooling or evaporating means that the amount of soluble **solute*** decreases, so particles come out of solution and bond to the seed crystal, which is suspended in the solution. Crystallization can be used to purify substances – see page 107.

Methods of **crystallization**

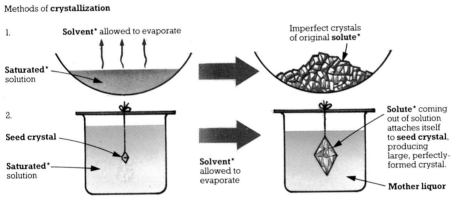

1. Solvent* allowed to evaporate

Saturated* solution

Imperfect crystals of original solute*

2. Seed crystal

Saturated* solution

Solvent* allowed to evaporate

Solute* coming out of solution attaches itself to **seed crystal**, producing large, perfectly-formed crystal.

Mother liquor

●**Seed crystal**. A small crystal of a substance placed in a solution of the same substance. It acts as a base on which crystals form during **crystallization**. The crystal which grows will take on the same shape as the seed crystal.

●**Water of crystallization**. Water contained in crystals of certain **salts***. The number of molecules of water combined with each pair of ions is usually constant and is often written in the chemical **formula*** for the salt. The water can be driven off by heating. Crystals which contain water of crystallization are **hydrated***.

●**Mother liquor**. The solution left after **crystallization** has taken place in a solution.

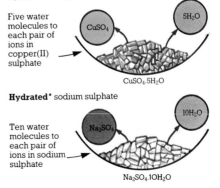

Hydrated* copper(II) sulphate

Five water molecules to each pair of ions in copper(II) sulphate

$CuSO_4$

$5H_2O$

$CuSO_4.5H_2O$

Hydrated* sodium sulphate

Ten water molecules to each pair of ions in sodium sulphate

Na_2SO_4

$10H_2O$

$Na_2SO_4.10H_2O$

* Formulae, 26; Hydrated, 41 (Hydrate); Molten, 6; Salts, 39; Saturated, Solute, Solvent, 30; Sublimation, 7; Supersaturated, 31.

Crystals continued - shapes and structures

Crystals (see page 21) exist in many different shapes and sizes. This is due to the arrangement and bonding of the particles (atoms, molecules or ions). The arrangement in space of the particles and the way in which they are joined is called a **crystal lattice**. The shape of a particular crystal depends on its crystal lattice and how this lattice can be split along **cleavage planes**. The main crystal shapes are shown below.

Basic shapes from which large crystals are built.

Tetragonal **Monoclinic** **Triclinic** **Hexagonal**

Cubic

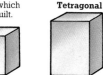

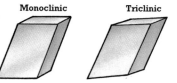

●**Polymorphism**. The occurrence of two or more different crystals of the same substance, differing in shape and appearance. It is caused by different arrangements in the separate types. Changes between types often take place at a certain temperature called the **transition temperature**. Polymorphism in elements is called **allotropy**.

●**Allotropy**. The occurrence of certain elements in more than one crystalline form. It is a specific type of **polymorphism**. The different forms are called **allotropes** and are caused by a change in arrangement of atoms in the crystal.

●**Monotropy. Polymorphism** in which there is only one stable form. The other forms are unstable and there is no **transition temperature**.

●**Enantiotropy. Polymorphism** in which there are two stable forms of a substance, one above its **transition temperature**, and one below.

Sulphur exhibits **enantiotropy** – it has two **allotropes**.

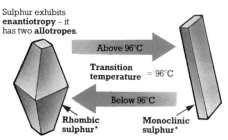

Above 96°C

Transition temperature = 96°C

Below 96°C

Rhombic sulphur* **Monoclinic sulphur***

●**Transition temperature**. The temperature at which a substance exhibiting **enantiotropy** changes from one form to another.

●**Isomorphism**. The existence of two or more different substances with the same crystal structure and shape. They are described as **isomorphic**.

●**Cleavage plane**. A plane of particles along which a crystal can be split, leaving a flat surface. If a crystal is not split along the cleavage plane, it shatters.

●**X-ray crystallography**. The use of X-rays to work out crystal structure. Deflected X-rays produce a **diffraction pattern** from which the structure is worked out (see below).

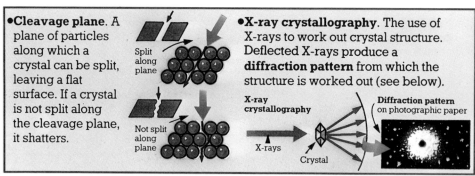

Split along plane

Not split along plane

X-ray crystallography

Diffraction pattern on photographic paper

X-rays

Crystal

* Monoclinic sulphur, Rhombic sulphur, 70.

Crystal lattices

●**Giant atomic lattice**. A **crystal lattice** ▶ consisting of atoms held together by **covalent bonding***, e.g. diamond. Substances with giant atomic lattices are extremely strong and have very high melting and boiling points.

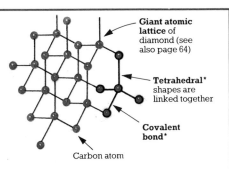

Giant atomic lattice of diamond (see also page 64)

Tetrahedral* shapes are linked together

Covalent bond*

Carbon atom

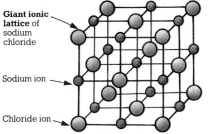

Giant ionic lattice of sodium chloride

Sodium ion

Chloride ion

●**Giant ionic lattice**. A **crystal lattice** consisting of ions held together by **ionic bonding***, e.g. sodium chloride. The ionic bonds are strong, which means the substance has high melting and boiling points. ◀

●**Giant metallic lattice**. A **crystal** ▶ **lattice** consisting of metal atoms held together by **metallic bonding***, e.g. zinc. The **delocalized*** electrons are free to move about, making a metal a good conductor of heat and electricity. The layers of atoms can slide over one another, making metals **malleable*** and **ductile***.

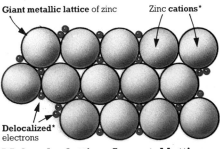

Giant metallic lattice of zinc

Zinc **cations***

Delocalized* electrons

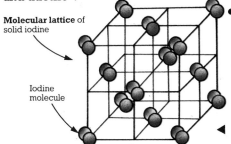

Molecular lattice of solid iodine

Iodine molecule

●**Molecular lattice**. A **crystal lattice** consisting of molecules bonded together by weak **intermolecular forces** (see page 20), e.g. iodine. The intermolecular forces are overcome when the crystal is broken, not the **covalent bonds*** in the molecules, so the crystal has low melting and boiling points compared with **ionic compounds***. ◀

In crystals where the particles are all the ▶ same size, e.g. in a **giant metallic lattice**, various arrangements of the particles are possible. The most common are shown here.

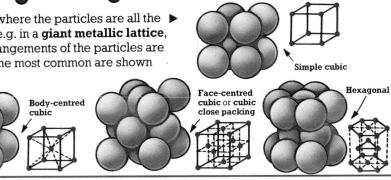

Simple cubic

Body-centred cubic

Face-centred cubic or **cubic close packing**

Hexagonal

* **Cation**, 16; **Covalent bond**, **Covalent bonding**, 18; **Delocalization**, 20; **Ductile**, 114; **Ionic bonding**, **Ionic compound**, 17; **Malleable**, 115; **Metallic bonding**, 20; **Tetrahedral**, 19.

Measuring atoms

With a diameter of about 10^{-7} millimetres and a mass of about 10^{-22} grams, atoms are so small that they are extremely difficult to measure. Their masses are therefore measured in relation to an agreed mass to give them a manageable value. Because there are many millions of atoms in a very small sample of a substance, the **mole** is used for measuring quantities of particles. The masses of atoms and molecules are measured using a machine called a **mass spectrometer**.

• **Relative atomic mass** or **atomic weight**. The average mass (i.e. taking into account **relative isotopic mass** and **isotopic ratio**) of one atom of a substance divided by one twelfth the mass of a carbon-12 atom (see **isotope**, page 13). It is stated in **unified atomic mass units** (**u**). See also pages 98-99.

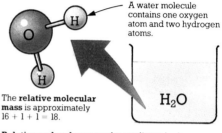

A water molecule contains one oxygen atom and two hydrogen atoms.

The **relative molecular mass** is approximately $16 + 1 + 1 = 18$.

$$H_2O$$

Relative molecular mass also applies to **ionic compounds***, even though they do not have molecules.

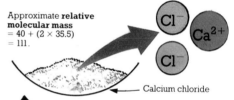

Approximate **relative molecular mass**
$= 40 + (2 \times 35.5)$
$= 111$.

Calcium chloride

$1/12$ mass of a carbon-12 atom

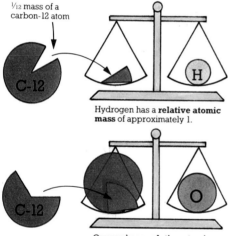

Hydrogen has a **relative atomic mass** of approximately 1.

Oxygen has a **relative atomic mass** of approximately 16.

• **Relative molecular mass**. Also called **molecular weight, relative formula mass** or **formula weight**. The mass of a molecule of an element or compound divided by one twelfth the mass of a carbon-12 atom (see **isotope**, page 13). It is the sum of the **relative atomic masses** of the the atoms in the molecule.

• **Relative isotopic mass**. The mass of an atom of a specific **isotope*** divided by one twelfth the mass of a carbon-12 atom. It is nearly exactly the same as the **mass number*** of the isotope.

• **Isotopic ratio**. The ratio of the number of atoms of each **isotope*** in a sample of an element. It is used with **relative isotopic masses** to calculate the **relative atomic mass** of an element.

Natural sample of chlorine contains about three times as many atoms of Cl-35 as Cl-37.

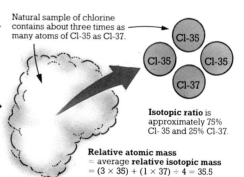

Isotopic ratio is approximately 75% Cl-35 and 25% Cl-37.

Relative atomic mass
= average **relative isotopic mass**
$= (3 \times 35) + (1 \times 37) \div 4 = 35.5$

* Ionic compound, 17; Isotope, Mass number, 13.

- **Mole (mol).** The **SI unit*** of the amount of a substance. One mole contains the same number of particles as there are atoms in 12 grams of the carbon-12 **isotope***.

| Each **mole** of copper contains the **Avogadro constant** of atoms. | Each **mole** of oxygen contains the **Avogadro constant** of molecules. | A **mole** of sodium chloride contains 1 mol Na$^+$ ions and 1 mol Cl$^-$ ions. |

- **Avogadro constant (L).** The number of particles per **mole**, equal to 6.02×10^{23} mol^{-1}.

- **Molar mass.** The mass of one **mole** of a given substance. It is the **relative atomic** or **molecular mass** of a substance expressed in grams.

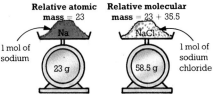

Relative atomic mass = 23

Relative molecular mass = 23 + 35.5

1 mol of sodium — 23 g

1 mol of sodium chloride — 58.5 g

Molar mass 23 g   **Molar mass** 58.5 g

- **Molar volume.** The volume of one **mole** of any substance, measured in cubic decimetres (dm^3). Molar volumes of solids and liquids vary, but all gases under the same conditions have the same molar volume. The molar volume of any gas at **s.t.p.*** is 22.4 dm^3 and at **r.t.p.** (**room temperature and pressure**, i.e. 20°C and 101325 **pascals***) it is 24 dm^3.

In solids and liquids, **molar volume** depends on size and arrangement of particles. ▼

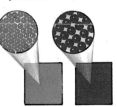

All gases (at same ▲ temperature and pressure) have same **molar volume**. Their particles are not bonded together.

- **Concentration.** A measurement of the amount of a **solute*** dissolved in a **solvent***, expressed in **moles** per dm^3 (mol dm^{-3}). **Mass concentration** is the mass of solute per unit volume, e.g. grams per dm^3 (g dm^{-3}).

4 **mol** of **solute***   2 dm^3 of **solvent***   **Concentration** of 2 mol dm^3

Concentration is the number of **moles** of **solute*** dissolved in each dm^3 of **solvent***.

- **Molarity.** A term sometimes used to describe the **concentration** when expressed in **moles** of **solute*** per dm^3 of **solvent***. The molarity is also expressed as the **M-value**, e.g. a solution with a concentration of 3 mol dm^{-3} has a molarity of 3 and is described as a 3**M** solution.

1 **mol** $CuSO_4$ each   1 dm^3 water   2**M** solution

A 2**M** copper(II) sulphate solution contains 2 **mol** of copper(II) sulphate in each dm^3.

- **Molar solution.** A solution that contains one **mole** of a substance dissolved in every cubic decimetre (dm^3) of solution. It is therefore a 1**M** solution (see **molarity**).

1 **mol** copper(II) sulphate   1 dm^3 water   1 dm^3 **molar solution** of copper(II) sulphate

A 1**M** or **molar solution** of copper(II) sulphate contains 1 **mol** of copper(II) sulphate in each dm^3.

- **Standard solution.** A solution of which the **concentration** is known. It is used for **volumetric analysis***.

* Isotope, 13; Pascal, SI units, 112; Solute, Solvent, 30; s.t.p., 29; Volumetric analysis; 108.

Representing chemicals

Most chemicals are named according to the predominant elements they contain. Information about the chemical composition and structure of a compound is given by a **formula** (pl. **formulae**), in which the **chemical symbols*** for the elements are used. A chemical **equation** shows the reactants and products of a chemical reaction and gives information about how the reaction happens.

Formulae

●**Empirical formula**. A formula showing the simplest ratio of the atoms of each element in a compound. It does not show the total number of atoms of each element in a **covalent compound***, or the **bonding** in the compound (see pages 16-20).

●**Molecular formula**. A formula representing one molecule of an element or compound. It shows which elements the molecule contains and the number of atoms of each in the molecule, but not the **bonding** of the molecule (see pages 16-20).

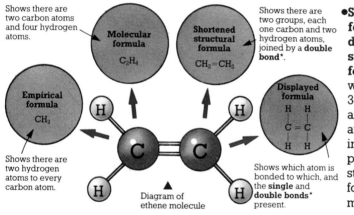

Shows there are two carbon atoms and four hydrogen atoms.

Molecular formula

C_2H_4

Empirical formula

CH_2

Shows there are two hydrogen atoms to every carbon atom.

▲ Diagram of ethene molecule

Shortened structural formula

$CH_2 = CH_2$

Shows there are two groups, each one carbon and two hydrogen atoms, joined by a **double bond***.

Displayed formula

H   H
| |
C = C
| |
H   H

Shows which atom is bonded to which, and the **single** and **double bonds*** present.

●**Stereochemical formula** or **3-dimensional structural formula**. A formula which shows the 3-dimensional arrangement of the atoms and **bonds*** in a molecule. See page 76 for the stereochemical formula of methane.

●**Shortened structural formula**. A formula which shows the sequence of groups of atoms (e.g. a **carboxyl group***) in a molecule and the **bonding** (see pages 16-20) between the groups of atoms (shown as lines).

●**Displayed formula** or **full structural formula**. A formula which shows the arrangement of the atoms in relation to each other in a molecule. All the bonds in the molecule are shown.

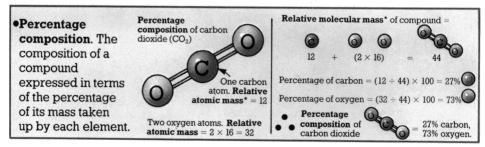

●**Percentage composition**. The composition of a compound expressed in terms of the percentage of its mass taken up by each element.

Percentage composition of carbon dioxide (CO_2)

One carbon atom. **Relative atomic mass*** = 12

Two oxygen atoms. **Relative atomic mass** = $2 \times 16 = 32$

Relative molecular mass* of compound =

$12 + (2 \times 16) = 44$

Percentage of carbon = $(12 \div 44) \times 100 = 27\%$

Percentage of oxygen = $(32 \div 44) \times 100 = 73\%$

Percentage composition of carbon dioxide = 27% carbon, 73% oxygen.

* Bonds, 16; Carboxyl group, 81 (Carboxylic acids); Chemical symbol, 8; Covalent compounds, Double bond, 18; Relative atomic mass, Relative molecular mass, 24; Single bond, 18.

Names

- **Trivial name.** An everyday name given to a compound. It does not usually give any information about the composition or structure of the compound. e.g. salt (sodium chloride), chalk (calcium carbonate).

- **Traditional name.** A name which gives the predominant elements of a substance, without necessarily giving their quantities or showing the structure of the substance. Some traditional names are **systematic names**.

- **Systematic name.** A name which shows the elements a compound contains, the ratio of the numbers of atoms of each element and the **oxidation number*** of elements with variable **oxidation states***. The **bonding** (see pages 16-20) can also be worked out from the name. In some cases the systematic name is simplified. Some systematic names are the same as **traditional names**. See also **naming simple organic compounds**, page 100.

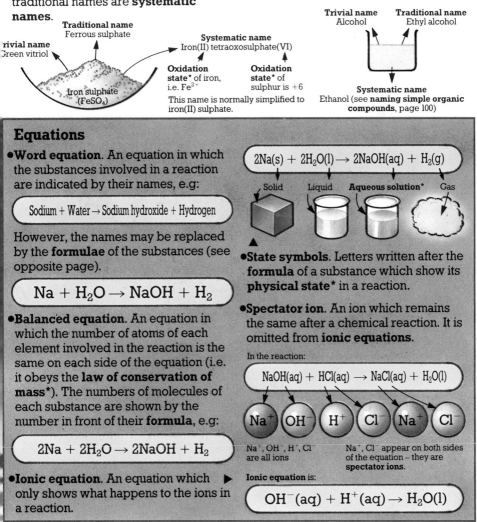

Traditional name
Ferrous sulphate

Trivial name
Green vitriol

Systematic name
Iron(II) tetraoxosulphate(VI)

Iron sulphate
(FeSO₄)

Oxidation state* of iron, i.e. Fe^{2+}

Oxidation state* of sulphur is $+6$

This name is normally simplified to iron(II) sulphate.

Trivial name
Alcohol

Traditional name
Ethyl alcohol

Systematic name
Ethanol (see **naming simple organic compounds**, page 100)

Equations

- **Word equation.** An equation in which the substances involved in a reaction are indicated by their names, e.g:

Sodium + Water → Sodium hydroxide + Hydrogen

However, the names may be replaced by the **formulae** of the substances (see opposite page).

$$Na + H_2O \rightarrow NaOH + H_2$$

- **Balanced equation.** An equation in which the number of atoms of each element involved in the reaction is the same on each side of the equation (i.e. it obeys the **law of conservation of mass***). The numbers of molecules of each substance are shown by the number in front of their **formula**, e.g:

$$2Na + 2H_2O \rightarrow 2NaOH + H_2$$

- **Ionic equation.** An equation which only shows what happens to the ions in a reaction.

$$2Na(s) + 2H_2O(l) \rightarrow 2NaOH(aq) + H_2(g)$$

Solid   Liquid   **Aqueous solution***   Gas

- **State symbols.** Letters written after the formula of a substance which show its **physical state*** in a reaction.

- **Spectator ion.** An ion which remains the same after a chemical reaction. It is omitted from **ionic equations**.

In the reaction:

$$NaOH(aq) + HCl(aq) \rightarrow NaCl(aq) + H_2O(l)$$

Na^+ OH^- H^+ Cl^- Na^+ Cl^-

Na^+, OH^-, H^+, Cl^- are all ions

Na^+, Cl^- appear on both sides of the equation – they are **spectator ions**.

Ionic equation is:

$$OH^-(aq) + H^+(aq) \rightarrow H_2O(l)$$

* **Aqueous solution**, 30; **Law of conservation of mass**, 11; **Oxidation number, Oxidation state**, 35; **Physical states**, 6.

27

Gas laws

The molecules in a gas are widely spaced and move about in a rapid, chaotic manner (see **kinetic theory**, page 9). The combined volume of the gas molecules is very much smaller than the volume the gas occupies and the forces of attraction between the molecules are very weak. This is true for all gases, so they all behave in a similar way. There are several **gas laws** that describe this common behaviour (see below).

Symbols used in **gas laws**	
P = pressure	T = temperature in **kelvins**
V = volume	k = a **constant***

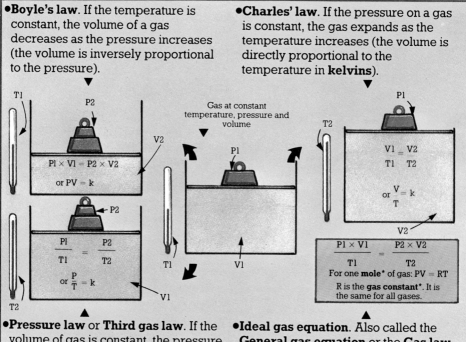

•**Boyle's law**. If the temperature is constant, the volume of a gas decreases as the pressure increases (the volume is inversely proportional to the pressure).

$$P1 \times V1 = P2 \times V2$$
or $PV = k$

$$\frac{P1}{T1} = \frac{P2}{T2}$$
or $\frac{P}{T} = k$

Gas at constant temperature, pressure and volume

•**Charles' law**. If the pressure on a gas is constant, the gas expands as the temperature increases (the volume is directly proportional to the temperature in **kelvins**).

$$\frac{V1}{T1} = \frac{V2}{T2}$$
or $\frac{V}{T} = k$

$\dfrac{P1 \times V1}{T1} = \dfrac{P2 \times V2}{T2}$
For one **mole*** of gas: PV = RT R is the **gas constant***. It is the same for all gases.

•**Pressure law** or **Third gas law**. If the volume of gas is constant, the pressure increases as the temperature increases (the pressure is directly proportional to the temperature in **kelvins**).

•**Ideal gas equation**. Also called the **General gas equation** or the **Gas law**. An equation that shows the relationship between the pressure, volume and temperature of a fixed mass of gas.

•**Ideal gas**. A theoretical gas that behaves in an "ideal" way. Its molecules have no volume, do not attract each other, move rapidly in straight lines and lose no energy when they collide. Many real gases behave in approximately the same way as ideal gases when the molecules are small and widely spaced.

Small, widely-spaced molecules

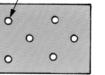

Behaves like an **ideal gas**.

Large molecules close together

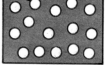

Does not behave like an **ideal gas**.

* Mole, 25; **Constant**, 114.

- **Partial pressure**. The pressure that each gas in a **mixture*** of gases would exert if it alone filled the volume occupied by the mixture.

- **Dalton's law of partial pressures**. The total pressure exerted by a **mixture*** of gases (which do not react together) is the sum of the **partial pressure** of each gas in the mixture.

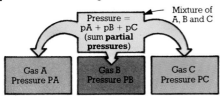

Mixture of A, B and C

Pressure = pA + pB + pC (sum **partial pressures**)

| Gas A Pressure PA | Gas B Pressure PB | Gas C Pressure PC |

- **Graham's law of diffusion**. If the temperature and pressure are constant, the rate of **diffusion*** of a gas is inversely proportional to the square root of its density. The density of a gas is high if its molecules are heavy and low if its molecules are light. Light molecules move faster than heavy molecules, so a gas with a high density diffuses more slowly than a gas with a low density.

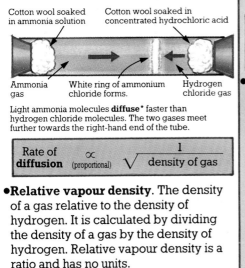

Cotton wool soaked in ammonia solution — Cotton wool soaked in concentrated hydrochloric acid

Ammonia gas — White ring of ammonium chloride forms. — Hydrogen chloride gas

Light ammonia molecules **diffuse*** faster than hydrogen chloride molecules. The two gases meet further towards the right-hand end of the tube.

$$\text{Rate of } \underset{\text{(proportional)}}{\text{diffusion}} \propto \sqrt{\frac{1}{\text{density of gas}}}$$

- **Relative vapour density**. The density of a gas relative to the density of hydrogen. It is calculated by dividing the density of a gas by the density of hydrogen. Relative vapour density is a ratio and has no units.

$$\text{Relative vapour density} = \frac{\text{Density of the gas}}{\text{Density of hydrogen}}$$

- **Gay-Lussac's law**. When gases react together to produce other gases and all the volumes are measured at the same temperature and pressure, the volumes of the reactants and products are in a ratio of simple whole numbers.

$$2CO(g) + O_2(g) \rightarrow 2CO_2(g)$$

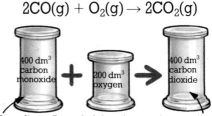

400 dm³ carbon monoxide + 200 dm³ oxygen → 400 dm³ carbon dioxide

According to **Avagadro's law**, these two jars contain the same number of molecules.

- **Avogadro's law** or **Avogadro's hypothesis**. Equal volumes of all gases at the same temperature and pressure contain the same number of molecules.

- **s.t.p.** An abbreviation for **standard temperature and pressure**. These are internationally agreed standard conditions under which properties such as volume and density of gases are usually measured.

s.t.p. =
temperature: 0°C or 273K (**kelvins**)
pressure: 101325 **pascals***

- **Kelvin (K)**. A unit of temperature on the **absolute temperature scale**. A kelvin is the same size as a degree **Celsius***, but the lowest point on the scale is zero kelvins or **absolute zero**. Absolute zero is equal to -273 degrees Celsius, a theoretical point where an ideal gas would occupy zero volume.

To convert degrees **Celsius** to **kelvins**, add 273.

To convert **kelvins** to degrees **Celsius**, subtract 273.

Degrees Celsius*		Kelvins
100°C	steam	373K
0°C	ice	273K
Absolute zero −273°C		0K

* **Celsius temperature**, 114; **Diffusion**, 9; **Mixture**, 8; **Pascal**, 112.

Solutions and solubility

When a substance is added to a liquid, several things can happen. If the atoms, molecules or ions of the substance become evenly dispersed (**dissolve**), the **mixture*** is a **solution**. If they do not, the mixture is either a **colloid**, a **suspension** or a **precipitate**. How well a substance dissolves depends on its properties, those of the liquid and other factors such as temperature and pressure.

●**Solvent**. The substance in which the **solute** dissolves to form a solution.

●**Solute**. The substance which dissolves in the **solvent** to form a solution.

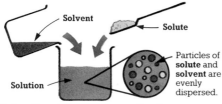

Solvent

Solute

Solution

Particles of **solute** and **solvent** are evenly dispersed.

●**Solvation**. The process of **solvent** molecules combining with **solute** molecules as the solute dissolves. When the solvent is water the process is called **hydration**. Whether or not solvation takes place depends on how much the molecules of the solvent and solute attract each other.

●**Polar solvent**. A liquid with **polar molecules***. Polar solvents generally dissolve **ionic compounds***. **Solvation** occurs because the charged ends of the solvent molecules attract the ions of the **giant ionic lattice***. Water is the most common polar solvent.

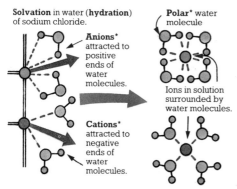

Solvation in water (**hydration**) of sodium chloride.

Anions* attracted to positive ends of water molecules.

Cations* attracted to negative ends of water molecules.

Polar* water molecule

Ions in solution surrounded by water molecules.

●**Non-polar solvent**. A liquid with **non-polar molecules***. Non-polar solvents dissolve **covalent compounds***. The **solute** molecules are pulled from the **molecular lattice*** by the solvent molecules and **diffuse*** through the solvent. Many organic liquids are non-polar solvents.

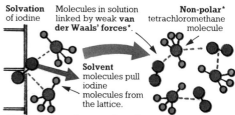

Solvation of iodine

Molecules in solution linked by weak **van der Waals' forces***.

Non-polar* tetrachloromethane molecule

Solvent molecules pull iodine molecules from the lattice.

●**Aqueous solvent**. A **solvent** containing water. Water molecules are **polar***, so aqueous solvents are **polar solvents**.

●**Aqueous solution**. A solution formed from an **aqueous solvent**.

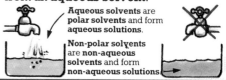

Aqueous solvents are **polar solvents** and form **aqueous solutions**.

Non-polar solvents are **non-aqueous** solvents and form **non-aqueous solutions**.

●**Dilute**. Describes a solution with a low **concentration*** of **solute**.

●**Concentrated**. Describes a solution with a high **concentration*** of **solute**.

●**Saturated**. Describes a solution that will not dissolve any more **solute** at a given temperature (any more solute will remain as crystals). If the temperature is raised, more solute may dissolve until the solution becomes saturated again.

* Anion, Cation, 16; Concentration, 25; Covalent compounds, 18; Diffusion, 9; Giant ionic lattice, 23; Ionic compound, 17; Mixture, 8; Molecular lattice, 23; Non-polar molecule, 19 (Polar molecule); van der Waals' forces, 20.

- **Solubility**. The amount of a **solute** which dissolves in a particular amount of **solvent** at a known temperature.

The **solubility** of a **solute** at a particular temperature is:

to produce a **saturated** solution.

The number of grams of **solute** which must be added to 100 grams of **solvent**

The solubility of a solid usually increases with temperature, while the solubility of a gas decreases.

Sugar dissolves better in hot tea than cold water.

Warm soft drinks have more bubbles than cold ones.

The change of solubility with temperature is shown by a **solubility curve**.

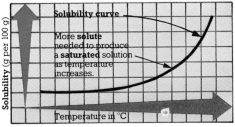

Solubility (g per 100 g)

Solubility curve

More solute needed to produce a saturated solution as temperature increases.

Temperature in °C

- **Soluble**. Describes a **solute** which dissolves easily in a **solvent**. The opposite of soluble is **insoluble**.

- **Supersaturated**. Describes a solution with more dissolved **solute** than a **saturated** solution at the same temperature. It is formed when a solution is cooled below the temperature at which it would be saturated, and there are no particles for the solute to **crystallize*** around, so the "extra" solute remains dissolved. The solution is unstable – if crystals are added or dust enters, the "extra" solute forms crystals.

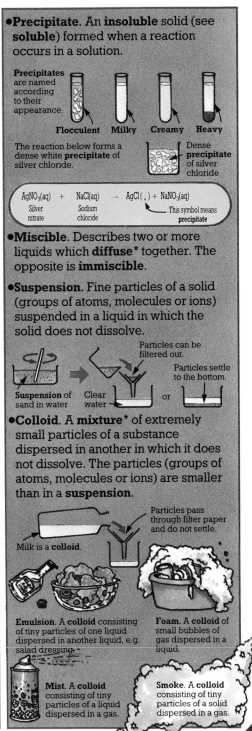

- **Precipitate**. An **insoluble** solid (see **soluble**) formed when a reaction occurs in a solution.

Precipitates are named according to their appearance.

Flocculent Milky Creamy Heavy

The reaction below forms a dense white **precipitate** of silver chloride.

Dense **precipitate** of silver chloride

$AgNO_3(aq)$ + $NaCl(aq)$ → $AgCl(\downarrow)$ + $NaNO_3(aq)$

Silver nitrate   Sodium chloride

This symbol means **precipitate**

- **Miscible**. Describes two or more liquids which **diffuse*** together. The opposite is **immiscible**.

- **Suspension**. Fine particles of a solid (groups of atoms, molecules or ions) suspended in a liquid in which the solid does not dissolve.

Particles can be filtered out.

Particles settle to the bottom.

Suspension of sand in water

Clear water   or

- **Colloid**. A **mixture*** of extremely small particles of a substance dispersed in another in which it does not dissolve. The particles (groups of atoms, molecules or ions) are smaller than in a **suspension**.

Particles pass through filter paper and do not settle.

Milk is a **colloid**.

Emulsion. A **colloid** consisting of tiny particles of one liquid dispersed in another liquid, e.g. salad dressing.

Foam. A **colloid** of small bubbles of gas dispersed in a liquid.

Mist. A **colloid** consisting of tiny particles of a liquid dispersed in a gas.

Smoke. A **colloid** consisting of tiny particles of a solid dispersed in a gas.

* **Crystallization**, 21; **Diffusion**, 9; **Mixture**, 8.

Energy and chemical reactions

Nearly all chemical reactions involve a change in energy. Some reactions involve electrical energy (see page 44) or light energy, but almost all involve heat energy. The change in energy in a reaction results from the different amounts of energy involved when bonds are broken and formed. The study of heat energy in chemical reactions is called **thermochemistry**.

• **Enthalpy change of reaction** or **heat of reaction** ($\triangle$**H** – pronounced "delta h"). The amount of heat energy given out or absorbed during a chemical reaction. It is the difference between the total **enthalpy** of the reactants and the total enthalpy of the products.

$$\begin{array}{c} \text{Enthalpy} \\ \text{change} \end{array} = \begin{array}{c} \text{total } \textbf{enthalpy} \\ \text{of products} \end{array} - \begin{array}{c} \text{total } \textbf{enthalpy} \\ \text{of reactants} \end{array}$$

The enthalpy change is written after the equation for a reaction and is measured using **calorimetry***. It is caused by the making and breaking of bonds during the reaction (see **bond energy**).

$$2H_2(g) + O_2(g) \rightarrow 2H_2O(g) \quad \triangle H = -488kJ$$

The value of $\triangle$**H** is only true for the number of **moles*** and the **physical states*** of the chemicals in the equation.

J stands for **joule***, a unit of energy. **kJ** stands for **kilojoule** (1000 **joules**).

• **Enthalpy (H)**. The amount of energy that a substance contains. It is impossible to measure directly, but its change during a reaction can be measured.

• **Energy level diagram**. A diagram which shows the **enthalpy change of reaction** for a reaction.

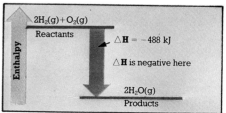

$2H_2(g) + O_2(g)$
Reactants
$\triangle H = -488 \text{ kJ}$
$\triangle H$ is negative here
$2H_2O(g)$
Products
Enthalpy

• **Standard enthalpy change of reaction** ($\triangle$**H**⁼). An **enthalpy change of reaction** measured under standard conditions, i.e. standard temperature and pressure (**s.t.p.***). If solutions are used, their **concentration*** is **1M***.

• **Enthalpy change of combustion** or **heat of combustion**. The amount of heat energy given out when one **mole*** of a substance is completely burnt in oxygen. The heat of combustion for a substance is measured using a **bomb calorimeter**.

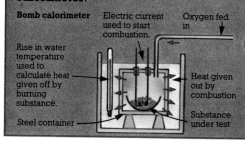

Bomb calorimeter

Electric current used to start combustion.

Oxygen fed in

Rise in water temperature used to calculate heat given off by burning substance.

Heat given out by combustion

Steel container

Substance under test

• **Enthalpy change of neutralization** or **heat of neutralization**. The amount of heat energy given out when one **mole*** of hydrogen ions (H⁺) is **neutralized*** by one mole of hydroxide ions (OH⁻). If the acid and alkali are fully **ionized***, the heat of neutralization is always -57 kJ. The **ionic equation*** for neutralization is:

$$H^+(aq) + OH^-(aq) \rightarrow H_2O(l) \quad \triangle H = -57kJ$$

Hydrogen ion · Hydroxide ion · Water molecule

When a **weak acid*** or a **weak base*** is involved, the heat produced is less. Some energy must be supplied to ionize the acid fully.

- **Exothermic reaction**. A chemical reaction during which heat is transferred to the surroundings.

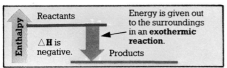

- **Endothermic reaction**. A chemical reaction during which heat is absorbed from the surroundings.

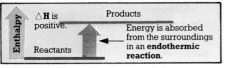

- **Bond energy**. A measure of the strength of a **covalent bond*** formed between two atoms. Energy must be supplied to break bonds and is given out when bonds are formed. A difference in these energies produces a change in energy during a reaction.

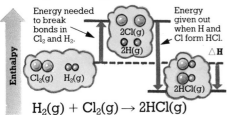

$$H_2(g) + Cl_2(g) \rightarrow 2HCl(g)$$

- **Law of conservation of energy**. During a chemical reaction, energy cannot be created or destroyed. In a **closed system*** the amount of energy is constant.

- **Hess's law**. This states that the **enthalpy change of reaction** that occurs during a particular chemical reaction is always the same, no matter what route is taken in going from the reactants to the products. Hess's law is illustrated by an **energy cycle**.

Energy cycle

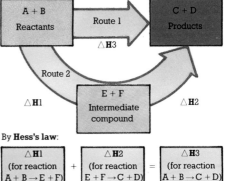

By **Hess's law**:

$\triangle$**H1** (for reaction $A + B \rightarrow E + F$)	+	$\triangle$**H2** (for reaction $E + F \rightarrow C + D$)	=	$\triangle$**H3** (for reaction $A + B \rightarrow C + D$)

Hess's law is used to find enthalpy changes of reaction which cannot be measured directly, e.g. the **enthalpy change of formation** of methane.

- **Enthalpy change of solution** or **heat of solution**. The amount of heat energy given out or taken in when one **mole*** of a substance dissolves in such a large volume of **solvent*** that further dilution produces no heat change.

- **Molar enthalpy change of fusion** or **molar heat of fusion**. The amount of heat energy required to change one **mole*** of a solid into a liquid at its melting point. Energy must be supplied to break the bonds in the **crystal lattice*** of the solid.

- **Molar enthalpy change of vaporization** or **molar heat of vaporization**. The heat energy needed to change one **mole*** of a liquid into a vapour at its boiling point.

- **Enthalpy change of formation** or **heat of formation**. The heat energy given out or taken in when one **mole*** of a compound is formed from elements.

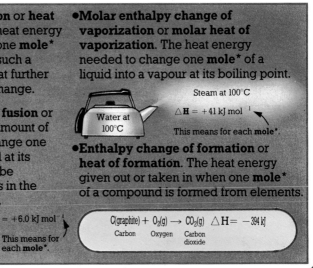

Oxidation and reduction

The terms **oxidation** and **reduction** originally referred to the gain and loss of oxygen by a substance. They have now been extended to include the gain and loss of hydrogen and electrons. There is always a transfer of electrons in reactions involving oxidation and reduction, that is, the **oxidation state** of one or more of the elements is always changed.

●**Oxidation**. A chemical reaction in which one of the following occurs:

1. An element or compound gains oxygen

$$2CuO(s) + C(s) \rightarrow CO_2(g) + 2Cu(s)$$

Oxidizing agent — Element oxidized — Carbon gains oxygen

2. A compound loses hydrogen

$$Cl_2(g) + H_2S(g) \rightarrow 2HCl(g) + S(s)$$

Oxidizing agent — Compound oxidized — Hydrogen sulphide loses hydrogen

3. An atom or ion loses electrons

$$Cl_2(g) + 2Na(s) \rightarrow 2Na^+Cl^-(s)$$

Oxidizing agent — Atom oxidized — Sodium loses electrons

A substance that undergoes oxidation is said to be **oxidized**, and its **oxidation state** is increased. Oxidation is the opposite of **reduction**.

●**Oxidizing agent**. A substance which accepts electrons, and so causes the **oxidation** of another substance. The oxidizing agent is always **reduced** in a reaction.

●**Reduction**. A chemical reaction in which one of the following occurs:

1. A compound loses oxygen

$$2CuO(s) + C(s) \rightarrow CO_2(g) + 2Cu(s)$$

Compound reduced — Reducing agent — Copper(II) oxide loses oxygen

2. A compound or element gains hydrogen

$$Cl_2(g) + H_2S(g) \rightarrow 2HCl(g) + S(s)$$

Element reduced — Reducing agent — Chlorine gains hydrogen

3. An atom or ion gains electrons.

$$Cl_2(g) + 2Na(s) \rightarrow 2Na^+Cl^-(s)$$

Atom reduced — Reducing agent — Chlorine gains electron

A substance that undergoes reduction is said to be **reduced**, and its **oxidation state** is decreased. Reduction is the opposite of **oxidation**.

●**Reducing agent**. A substance which donates electrons, and so causes the **reduction** of another substance. The reducing agent is always **oxidized** in a reaction.

●**Redox**. Describes a chemical reaction involving **oxidation** and **reduction**. The two processes always occur together because an **oxidizing agent** is always reduced during oxidation and a **reducing agent** is always oxidized during reduction. The simultaneous oxidation and reduction of the same element in a reaction is called **disproportionation**.

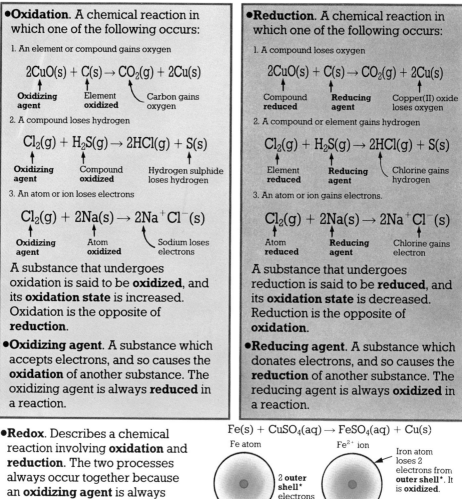

$$Fe(s) + CuSO_4(aq) \rightarrow FeSO_4(aq) + Cu(s)$$

Fe atom

Fe²⁺ ion

Iron atom loses 2 electrons from **outer shell***. It is **oxidized**.

2 **outer shell*** electrons

Cu²⁺ ion

Electrons transfer.

Cu atom

Copper ion gains 2 electrons. It is **reduced**.

Full outer shell

- **Oxidation state.** The number of electrons which have been removed from, or added to, an atom when it forms a compound. The oxidation state of an element is usually equal to the charge on its ion. An element's oxidation state increases when it is **oxidized** and decreases when it is **reduced**.

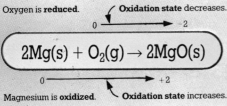

Oxygen is reduced. — Oxidation state decreases.

$$0 \longrightarrow -2$$

$$2Mg(s) + O_2(g) \rightarrow 2MgO(s)$$

$$0 \longrightarrow +2$$

Magnesium is **oxidized**. — Oxidation state increases.

These rules help to work out the oxidation state of an element:

1. The **oxidation state** of a free element (one that is not part of a compound) is zero.

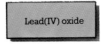

O_2

The **oxidation state** of oxygen is 0. No electrons have been lost or gained.

2. The **oxidation state** of an element in an **ionic compound*** is equal to the electrical charge on its ion.

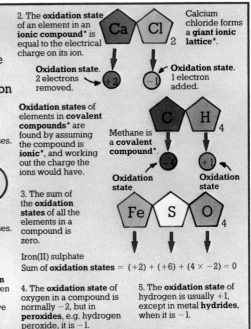

Calcium chloride forms a **giant ionic lattice***.

Oxidation state. 2 electrons removed. (+2)

Oxidation state. 1 electron added. (−1)

Oxidation states of elements in **covalent compounds*** are found by assuming the compound is **ionic***, and working out the charge the ions would have.

Methane is a **covalent compound***.

C   H 4

Oxidation state (−4)   **Oxidation state** (+1)

3. The sum of the **oxidation states** of all the elements in a compound is zero.

Fe   S   O 4

Iron(II) sulphate
Sum of **oxidation states** = $(+2) + (+6) + (4 \times -2) = 0$

4. The **oxidation state** of oxygen in a compound is normally −2, but in **peroxides**, e.g. hydrogen peroxide, it is −1.

5. The **oxidation state** of hydrogen is usually +1, except in metal **hydrides**, when it is −1.

- **Oxidation number.** A number that shows the **oxidation state** of an element in a compound. It is written in Roman numerals and placed in brackets after the name of the element. It is only included in the name of a compound when the element has more than one oxidation state.

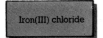
Iron(III) chloride   Lead(IV) oxide

Oxidation number of 3 and **oxidation state** of +3

Oxidation number of 4 and **oxidation state** of +4

- **Redox series.** A list of substances arranged in order of their **redox potentials**, the substance with the most negative redox potential being placed at the top. A substance usually **oxidizes** any substance above it in the series and **reduces** any substance below it. The further apart substances are in the series, the more easily they oxidize or reduce each other. The redox series is an extended version of the **electrochemical series***.

- **Redox potential.** A measurement of the power of a substance to gain electrons in solution. A strong **reducing agent**, which readily loses electrons (which it can give to another substance), will have a high negative redox potential. A strong **oxidizing agent**, which easily gains electrons, will have a high positive redox potential. Redox potential is the same as **electrode potential***.

Reducing agents		Oxidizing agents	
Lithium			
Potassium		Iodine	
Calcium		Bromine	
Sodium	Increase in power. **Redox potential** becomes more negative.	Dichromate ion	Increase in power. **Redox potential** becomes more positive.
Magnesium		Chlorine	
Aluminium		Manganate ion	
Zinc		Hydrogen peroxide	
Lead			
Iron		Fluorine	
Hydrogen			
Copper			
Silver			

* Covalent compounds, 18; Electrochemical series, 45; Electrode potential, 44; Giant ionic lattice, 23; Ionic compound, 17.

Acids and bases

All chemicals are either **acidic**, **basic** or **neutral**. In pure water, a small number of molecules **ionize***, each one forming a hydrogen ion (a single **proton***) and a hydroxide ion. The number of hydrogen and hydroxide ions is equal, and the water is described as **neutral**. Some compounds dissolve in, or react with, water to produce hydrogen ions or hydroxide ions, which upset the balance. These compounds are either **acids** or **bases**.

●**Acid**. A compound containing hydrogen which dissolves in water to produce hydrogen ions (H^+ – **protons***) in the solution. Hydrogen ions do not exist on their own in the solution, but join with water molecules to produce **hydroxonium ions**. These ions can only exist in solution, so an acid will only display its properties when it dissolves.

Some **acids** are corrosive and may have warning labels.

●**Acidic**. Describes any compound with the properties of an **acid**.

●**Hydroxonium ion (H_3O^+)** or **oxonium ion** . An ion formed when a hydrogen ion attaches itself to a water molecule (see **acid**). When a reaction takes place in a solution containing hydroxonium ions, only the hydrogen ion takes part. Hence usually the hydroxonium ion can be considered to be a hydrogen ion.

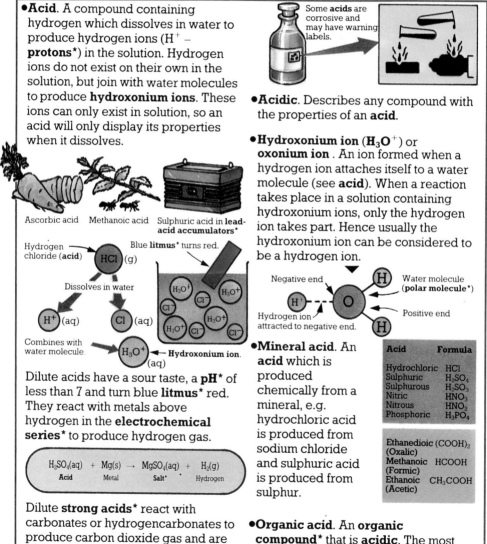

Ascorbic acid   Methanoic acid   Sulphuric acid in **lead-acid accumulators***

Hydrogen chloride (**acid**) — HCl (g)

Blue **litmus*** turns red.

Dissolves in water

H^+ (aq)   Cl (aq)

Combines with water molecule H_3O^+ (aq) ← **Hydroxonium ion**.

Negative end   Water molecule (**polar molecule***)

H^+ O   Positive end

Hydrogen ion attracted to negative end.

Dilute acids have a sour taste, a **pH*** of less than 7 and turn blue **litmus*** red. They react with metals above hydrogen in the **electrochemical series*** to produce hydrogen gas.

$$H_2SO_4(aq) + Mg(s) \rightarrow MgSO_4(aq) + H_2(g)$$
Acid   Metal   **Salt***   Hydrogen

Dilute **strong acids*** react with carbonates or hydrogencarbonates to produce carbon dioxide gas and are **neutralized** by bases.

●**Mineral acid**. An **acid** which is produced chemically from a mineral, e.g. hydrochloric acid is produced from sodium chloride and sulphuric acid is produced from sulphur.

Acid	Formula
Hydrochloric	HCl
Sulphuric	H_2SO_4
Sulphurous	H_2SO_3
Nitric	HNO_3
Nitrous	HNO_2
Phosphoric	H_3PO_4

Ethanedioic (COOH)$_2$ (Oxalic)	
Methanoic (Formic)	HCOOH
Ethanoic (Acetic)	CH_3COOH

●**Organic acid**. An **organic compound*** that is **acidic**. The most common ones are **carboxylic acids***.

* Carboxylic acids, 81; Electrochemical series, 45; Ionization, 16; Lead-acid accumulator, 45; Litmus, 38; Organic compounds, 76; pH, 38; Polar molecule, 19; Proton, 12; Salts, 39; Strong acid, 38.

- **Base**. A substance that will **neutralize** an **acid** by accepting hydrogen ions. It is the chemical opposite of an acid. Bases are usually metal oxides and hydroxides, although ammonia is also a base. A substance with the properties of a base is described as **basic**. A base which dissolves in water is an **alkali**. Ammonia is produced when a base is heated with an ammonium **salt***.

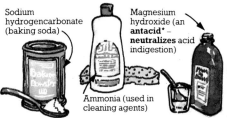

Sodium hydrogencarbonate (baking soda)

Magnesium hydroxide (an **antacid*** – **neutralizes** acid indigestion)

Ammonia (used in cleaning agents)

- **Alkali**. A **base**, normally a hydroxide of a Group 1 or Group 2 metal, which is soluble in water and produces hydroxide ions (OH^-) in solution. These make a solution **alkaline**.

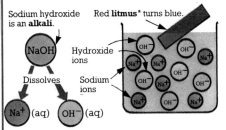

Sodium hydroxide is an **alkali**.

Red **litmus*** turns blue.

NaOH — Hydroxide ions

Dissolves — Sodium ions

Na^+ (aq) OH^- (aq)

- **Alkaline**. Describes a solution formed when a **base** dissolves in water to form a solution which contains more hydroxide ions than hydrogen ions.

Alkaline solutions have a **pH*** of more than 7, turn red **litmus*** blue, and feel soapy because they react with the skin. Alkaline solutions produced from **strong bases*** react with a few metals, e.g. zinc and aluminium, to give off hydrogen gas.

$$2Al(s) + 2NaOH(aq) + 6H_2O(l) \rightarrow 2NaAl(OH)_4(aq) + 3H_2(g)$$

Aluminium — Sodium hydroxide — Water — Sodium aluminate — Hydrogen

- **Amphoteric**. Describes a substance that acts as an **acid** in one reaction, but as a **base** in another, e.g. zinc hydroxide.

ACID   BASE

- **Anhydride**. A substance that reacts with water to form either an **acidic** or an **alkaline** solution (see **hydrolysis**, page 41). It is usually an oxide.

$$SO_2(g) + H_2O(l) \rightarrow H_2SO_3(aq)$$

Sulphur dioxide (**anhydride**) — Water — Sulphurous acid

- **Neutral**. Describes a substance that does not have the properties of an **acid** or **base**. A neutral solution has an equal number of hydrogen and hydroxide ions. It has a **pH*** of 7 and does not change the colour of **litmus***.

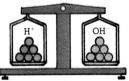

H^+ OH^-

A **neutral** solution contains an equal number of hydrogen and hydroxide ions.

- **Neutralization**. The reaction between an **acid** and a **base** to produce a **salt*** and water only. An equal number of hydrogen and hydroxide ions react together to form a **neutral** solution. The **acid radical*** from the acid and **cation*** from the base form a salt.

Neutralization is:

ACID + BASE → SALT* + WATER

- **Bronsted-Lowry theory**. Another way of describing **acids** and **bases**. It defines an acid as a substance which donates **protons***, and a base as one which accepts them.

Ethanoic acid donates a **proton*** – it is an **acid**.
Water accepts a **proton*** – it is a **base**.

$$CH_3COOH(aq) + H_2O(l) \rightleftharpoons H_3O^+(aq) + CH_3COO^-(aq)$$

Hydroxonium ion donates **proton*** – it is an **acid**.
Ethanoate ion accepts **proton*** – it is a **base**.

* **Acid radical**, 39; **Antacid**, 114; **Cation**, 16; **Litmus, pH**, 38; **Proton**, 12; **Salts**, 39; **Strong base**, 38.

37

Acids and bases continued – strength and concentration.

The **concentration*** of **acids** and **bases** (see previous two pages) depends on how many **moles*** of the acid or base are in a solution, but the strength depends on the proportion of their molecules which **ionize*** to produce **hydroxonium ions*** or hydroxide ions. A dilute **strong acid** can produce more hydrogen ions than a concentrated **weak acid**.

●**Strong acid.** An acid that completely **ionizes*** in water, producing a large number of hydrogen ions in solution.

Hydrochloric acid (**strong acid**). All hydrogen chloride molecules split up.

Acid radical (Cl^-)

H^+

●**Weak acid.** An acid that only partially **ionizes*** in water, i.e. only a small percentage of its molecules split into hydrogen ions and **acid radicals**.

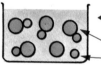

Ethanoic acid (**weak acid**). Only some molecules split up.

Acid radical (CH_3COO^-)

H^+

●**Strong base.** A base that is completely **ionized*** in water. A large number of hydroxide ions are released to give a strongly alkaline solution.

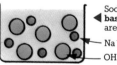

Sodium hydroxide (**strong base**). All the molecules are **ionized***.

Na^+

OH^-

●**Weak base.** A base that is only partially **ionized*** in water. Only some of the molecules of the base split up to produce hydroxide ions, giving a weakly alkaline solution.

Ammonia reacts slightly with water to give a low concentration of hydroxide ions:

$$NH_3(aq) + H_2O(l) \rightleftharpoons NH_4^+(aq) + OH^-(aq)$$
Ammonium ion   Hydroxide ion

●**pH.** Stands for **power of hydrogen**, a measure of hydrogen ion **concentration*** in a solution.

The **pH** scale

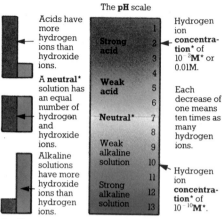

Acids have more hydrogen ions than hydroxide ions.		1	Hydrogen ion concentration* of $10^{-2}M^*$ or 0.01M.
	Strong acid	2	
		3	
A **neutral*** solution has an equal number of hydrogen and hydroxide ions.		4	Each decrease of one means ten times as many hydrogen ions.
	Weak acid	5	
		6	
	Neutral*	7	
		8	
	Weak alkaline solution	9	
Alkaline solutions have more hydroxide ions than hydrogen ions.		10	Hydrogen ion concentration* of $10^{-10}M^*$.
	Strong alkaline solution	11	
		12	
		13	

●**Indicator.** A substance whose colour depends on the **pH** of the solution it is in. Indicators can be used in solid or liquid form. Some common ones are shown at the bottom of this column.

●**Litmus.** An **indicator** which shows whether a solution is acidic or alkaline. Acids turn blue litmus paper red, and alkaline solutions turn red litmus paper blue.

Acidic solution

Alkaline solution

●**Universal indicator.** An **indicator**, either in the form of paper or in solution, which shows the **pH** of a solution with a range of colours.

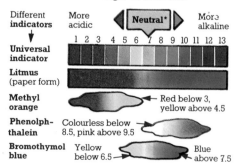

Different indicators	More acidic	Neutral*	More alkaline

1 2 3 4 5 6 7 8 9 10 11 12 13

Universal indicator

Litmus (paper form)

Methyl orange — Red below 3, yellow above 4.5

Phenolph-thalein Colourless below 8.5, pink above 9.5

Bromothymol blue Yellow below 6.5 — Blue above 7.5

Salts

All **salts** are **ionic compounds*** which contain at least one **cation*** and one **anion*** (called the **acid radical**). Theoretically, they can all be formed by replacing one or more of the hydrogen ions in an acid by other cations (one or more) e.g. metal ions (see below) or ammonium ions. Salts have many industrial and domestic uses.

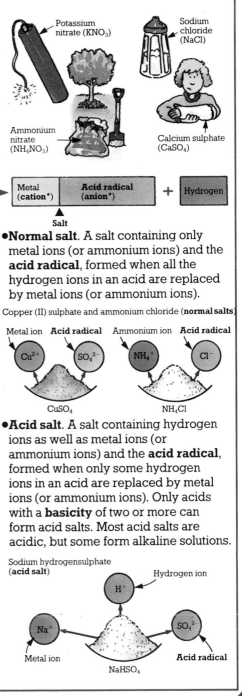

Potassium nitrate (KNO_3)

Sodium chloride ($NaCl$)

Ammonium nitrate (NH_4NO_3)

Calcium sulphate ($CaSO_4$)

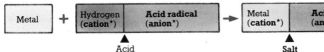

| Metal | + | Hydrogen (**cation***) | Acid radical (**anion***) | → | Metal (**cation***) | Acid radical (**anion***) | + | Hydrogen |

▲ Acid ▲ Salt

- **Acid radical**. The **anion*** left after the hydrogen ions have been removed from an acid. See table below.

Acid	Radical	Radical name
Hydrochloric	Cl^-	Chloride
Sulphuric	SO_4^{2-}	Sulphate
Sulphurous	SO_3^{2-}	Sulphite
Nitric	NO_3^-	Nitrate
Nitrous	NO_2^-	Nitrite
Carbonic	CO_3^{2-}	Carbonate
Ethanoic	CH_3COO^-	Ethanoate
Phosphoric	PO_4^{3-}	Phosphate

The radical name identifies the salt.

Copper (II) sulphate

| Cu^{2+} | SO_4^{2-} |

Cation* Acid radical

Sodium chloride

| Na^+ | Cl^- |

Cation* Acid radical

- **Basicity**. The number of hydrogen ions in an acid that can be replaced to form a salt. Not all the hydrogen ions are necessarily replaced.

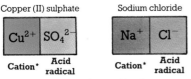

| H | Cl   Hydrochloric acid is **monobasic**.

CH_3COO | H | Ethanoic acid is **monobasic**.

| H_2 | SO_4 Sulphuric acid is **dibasic**.

| H_3 | PO_4 Phosphoric acid is **tribasic**.

- **Normal salt**. A salt containing only metal ions (or ammonium ions) and the **acid radical**, formed when all the hydrogen ions in an acid are replaced by metal ions (or ammonium ions).

Copper (II) sulphate and ammonium chloride (**normal salts**)

Metal ion **Acid radical**   Ammonium ion **Acid radical**

Cu^{2+} SO_4^{2-} NH_4^+ Cl^-

$CuSO_4$ NH_4Cl

- **Acid salt**. A salt containing hydrogen ions as well as metal ions (or ammonium ions) and the **acid radical**, formed when only some hydrogen ions in an acid are replaced by metal ions (or ammonium ions). Only acids with a **basicity** of two or more can form acid salts. Most acid salts are acidic, but some form alkaline solutions.

Sodium hydrogensulphate (**acid salt**)

Hydrogen ion

H^+

Na^+ SO_4^{2-}

Metal ion   **Acid radical**

$NaHSO_4$

Salts (continued)

•**Basic salt**. A salt containing a metal oxide or hydroxide, metal ions and an **acid radical***. It is formed when a **base*** is not completely **neutralized*** by an acid.

•**Double salt**. A salt formed when solutions of two **normal salts*** react together. It contains two different **cations*** (either two different metal ions or a metal ion and an ammonium ion) and one or more acid **radicals***.

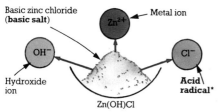

Basic zinc chloride (**basic salt**) — Metal ion — Zn^{2+}
OH^- — Hydroxide ion
Cl^- — Acid radical*
Zn(OH)Cl

•**Complex salt**. A salt in which one of the ions is a **complex ion**. This is made up of a central **cation*** linked (frequently by **dative covalent bonds***) to several small molecules (usually **polar molecules***) or ions.

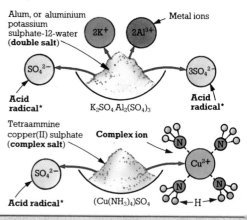

Alum, or aluminium potassium sulphate-12-water (**double salt**) — Metal ions — $2K^+$ $2Al^{3+}$
SO_4^{2-} — Acid radical*
$3SO_4^{2-}$ — Acid radical*
$K_2SO_4\,Al_2(SO_4)_3$

Tetraammine copper(II) sulphate (**complex salt**) — **Complex ion**
SO_4^{2-} — Acid radical*
Cu^{2+} — N — H
$(Cu(NH_3)_4)SO_4$

Preparation of salts.

Salts can be made in a number of ways, the method depending on whether a salt is soluble or insoluble in water (see table below). Soluble salts are **crystallized*** from solutions of the salts (obtained in various ways – see right) and insoluble salts are obtained in the form of **precipitates***.

Soluble salts can be made by the following methods, which all produce a solution of the salt. This is partly evaporated and left to **crystallize***.

1. **Neutralization***, in which an acid is neutralized by an alkali.

$$2NaOH(aq) + H_2SO_4(aq) \rightarrow Na_2SO_4(aq) + 2H_2O(l)$$

Sodium hydroxide — Sulphuric acid — Sodium sulphate — Water

Alkali — Acid — Salt — Water

2. The action of an acid on an insoluble carbonate.

$$MgCO_3(s) + 2HCl(aq) \rightarrow MgCl_2(aq) + H_2O(l) + CO_2(g)$$

Magnesium carbonate — Hydrochloric acid — Magnesium chloride — Water — Carbon dioxide

Insoluble carbonate — Acid — Salt — Water — Carbon dioxide

3. The action of an acid on an insoluble **base***.

$$CuO(s) + H_2SO_4(aq) \rightarrow CuSO_4(aq) + H_2O(l)$$

Copper (II) oxide — Sulphuric acid — Copper (II) sulphate — Water

Insoluble base* — Acid — Salt — Water

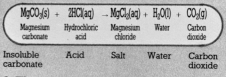

Solubility* of salts.	
Soluble salt	Insoluble salt
All ammonium salts sodium salts potassium salts	
All nitrates	
Chlorides —— EXCEPT ➜	Silver Lead
Sulphates —— EXCEPT ➜	Barium Lead (slightly soluble) Calcium
Ammonium Sodium ⟵ EXCEPT —— Most carbonates Potassium	

*Acid radical, 39; Base, 37; Cation, 16; Crystallization, 21; Dative covalent bond, 18; Neutralization, 37; Normal salt, 39; Polar molecule, 19; Precipitate, 31; Solubility, 31.

- **Hydrate**. A salt that contains **water of crystallization***, (it is **hydrated**). The salt becomes an **anhydrate** if the water is removed.

- **Anhydrate**. A salt that does not contain **water of crystallization*** (it is **anhydrous**). The salt becomes a **hydrate** if it absorbs water.

- **Hydrolysis**. The reaction of a salt with water. The ions of the salt react with water molecules, upsetting the balance of hydrogen and hydroxide ions, and so giving an acidic or alkaline solution. A salt which has been made from the reaction between a **weak acid*** and a **strong base*** dissolves to give an alkaline solution. One which has been made from the reaction between a **strong acid*** and a **weak base*** dissolves to give an acidic solution.

Copper(II) sulphate can be a

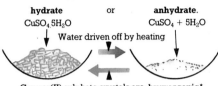

hydrate or anhydrate.
$CuSO_4 \cdot 5H_2O$ $CuSO_4 + 5H_2O$
Water driven off by heating

Copper(II) sulphate crystals are **hygroscopic*** (absorb water from the air).

- **Dehydration**. The removal of water from a substance. It is either removal of hydrogen and oxygen in the correct ratio to give water, or removal of water from a **hydrate** to give an **anhydrate**.

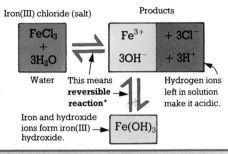

Iron(III) chloride (salt) Products
$FeCl_3 + 3H_2O$ $Fe^{3+} + 3Cl^-$
$3OH^- + 3H^+$

Water This means **reversible reaction*** Hydrogen ions left in solution make it acidic.

Iron and hydroxide ions form iron(III) hydroxide. $Fe(OH)_3$

- **Double decomposition**. A chemical reaction between the solutions of two or more **ionic compounds*** in which ions are exchanged. One of the new compounds formed is an insoluble salt, which forms a **precipitate***. Most insoluble salts and hydroxides are made by this method - the precipitate is filtered out and washed.

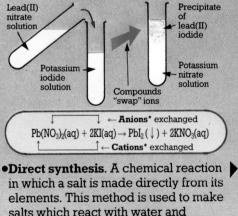

Lead(II) nitrate solution

Precipitate of lead(II) iodide

Potassium iodide solution

Potassium nitrate solution

Compounds "swap" ions

← **Anions*** exchanged
$Pb(NO_3)_2(aq) + 2KI(aq) \rightarrow PbI_2(\downarrow) + 2KNO_3(aq)$
← **Cations*** exchanged

- **Direct synthesis**. A chemical reaction in which a salt is made directly from its elements. This method is used to make salts which react with water and therefore cannot be made by using solutions.

- **Direct replacement**. A reaction in which all or some of the hydrogen in an acid is replaced by another element, usually a metal. It is used to prepare soluble salts, except salts of sodium or potassium, both of which react too violently with the acid.

$Zn(s) + H_2SO_4(aq) \rightarrow ZnSO_4(aq) + H_2(g)$

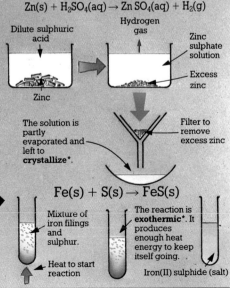

Dilute sulphuric acid Hydrogen gas Zinc sulphate solution

Excess zinc

Zinc

The solution is partly evaporated and left to **crystallize***.

Filter to remove excess zinc

$Fe(s) + S(s) \rightarrow FeS(s)$

Mixture of iron filings and sulphur.

The reaction is **exothermic***. It produces enough heat energy to keep itself going.

Heat to start reaction

Iron(II) sulphide (salt)

Electrolysis

Electrolysis is a term describing the chemical reactions which occur when an electric **current*** is passed through a liquid containing ions. Metals and graphite conduct electric current because some electrons are free to move through the **crystal lattice***, but **molten* ionic compounds*** or compounds which **ionize*** in solution conduct electric current by the movement of ions.

●**Electrolyte.** A compound which conducts electricity when **molten*** or in **aqueous solution*** and decomposes during electrolysis. All **ionic compounds*** are electrolytes. They conduct electricity because when molten or in solution their ions are free to move. **Cations*** carry a positive charge and **anions*** a negative one. The number of ions in an electrolyte determines how well it conducts electricity.

●**Electrode.** A piece of metal or graphite placed in an **electrolyte** via which **current*** enters or leaves. There are two electrodes, the **anode** and **cathode.**

●**Inert electrode.** An **electrode** that does not change during electrolysis, e.g. platinum. Some inert electrodes do react with the substances liberated.

●**Active electrode.** An **electrode**, usually a metal, which undergoes chemical change during electrolysis.

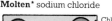

Molten* sodium chloride   Copper(II) sulphate solution

Chloride **anion***
Sodium **cation***
Water molecule
Copper **cation***
Sulphate **anion***

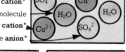

Non-electrolyte. A compound which does not **ionize***.

Weak electrolyte. An **electrolyte** which is only partially **ionized***.

Strong electrolyte. An **electrolyte** which is **ionized*** completely.

●**Electrolytic cell.** A vessel containing the **electrolyte** (either **molten*** or in **aqueous solution***) and the **electrodes.**

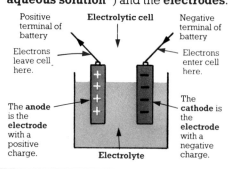

Positive terminal of battery

Electrolytic cell

Negative terminal of battery

Electrons leave cell here.

Electrons enter cell here.

The **anode** is the electrode with a positive charge.

The **cathode** is the electrode with a negative charge.

Electrolyte

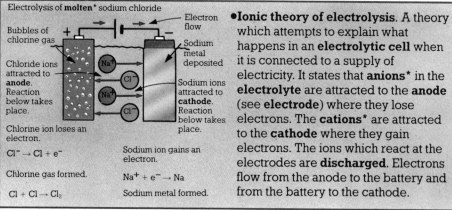

Electrolysis of **molten*** sodium chloride

Bubbles of chlorine gas

Chloride ions attracted to **anode**. Reaction below takes place.

Chlorine ion loses an electron.

$Cl^- \rightarrow Cl + e^-$

Chlorine gas formed.

$Cl + Cl \rightarrow Cl_2$

Electron flow

Sodium metal deposited

Sodium ions attracted to **cathode**. Reaction below takes place.

Sodium ion gains an electron.

$Na^+ + e^- \rightarrow Na$

Sodium metal formed.

●**Ionic theory of electrolysis.** A theory which attempts to explain what happens in an **electrolytic cell** when it is connected to a supply of electricity. It states that **anions*** in the **electrolyte** are attracted to the **anode** (see **electrode**) where they lose electrons. The **cations*** are attracted to the **cathode** where they gain electrons. The ions which react at the electrodes are **discharged**. Electrons flow from the anode to the battery and from the battery to the cathode.

* **Anion**, 16; **Aqueous solution**, 30; **Cation**, 16; **Crystal lattice**, 22; **Current**, 45; **Ionic compound**, 17; **Ionization**, 16; **Molten**, 6.

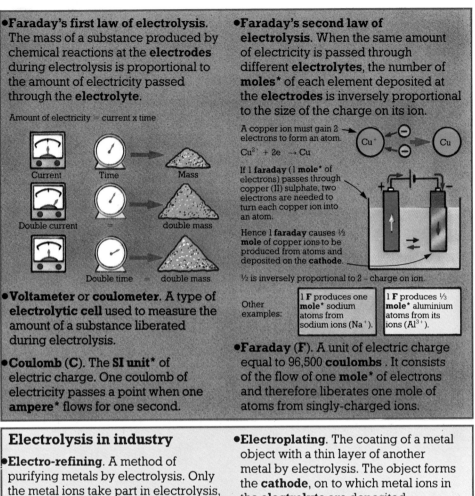

- **Faraday's first law of electrolysis.** The mass of a substance produced by chemical reactions at the **electrodes** during electrolysis is proportional to the amount of electricity passed through the **electrolyte**.

Amount of electricity = current x time

Current   Time   Mass

Double current   =   double mass

Double time   =   double mass

- **Voltameter** or **coulometer.** A type of **electrolytic cell** used to measure the amount of a substance liberated during electrolysis.

- **Coulomb (C).** The **SI unit*** of electric charge. One coulomb of electricity passes a point when one **ampere*** flows for one second.

- **Faraday's second law of electrolysis.** When the same amount of electricity is passed through different **electrolytes**, the number of **moles*** of each element deposited at the **electrodes** is inversely proportional to the size of the charge on its ion.

A copper ion must gain 2 electrons to form an atom.
$$Cu^{2+} + 2e \rightarrow Cu$$

If 1 **faraday** (1 **mole*** of electrons) passes through copper (II) sulphate, two electrons are needed to turn each copper ion into an atom.

Hence 1 **faraday** causes ½ **mole** of copper ions to be produced from atoms and deposited on the **cathode**.

½ is inversely proportional to 2 – charge on ion.

Other examples:

1 **F** produces one **mole*** sodium atoms from sodium ions (Na$^+$).	1 **F** produces ⅓ **mole*** aluminium atoms from its ions (Al^{3+}).

- **Faraday (F).** A unit of electric charge equal to 96,500 **coulombs**. It consists of the flow of one **mole*** of electrons and therefore liberates one mole of atoms from singly-charged ions.

Electrolysis in industry

- **Electro-refining.** A method of purifying metals by electrolysis. Only the metal ions take part in electrolysis, the impurities are lost.

Impure copper **anode** — Pure copper **cathode**

Copper atoms give up electrons to form copper ions in the solution. These are attracted to the **cathode**.

Cu^{2+}

Copper(II) sulphate solution

Impurities form a sludge.

- **Metal extraction.** A process which produces metals from their **molten*** ores by electrolysis. Metals at the top of the **reactivity series*** are obtained in this way (see **aluminium**, page 62 and **sodium**, page 54).

- **Electroplating.** The coating of a metal object with a thin layer of another metal by electrolysis. The object forms the **cathode**, on to which metal ions in the **electrolyte** are deposited.

Zinc plating stops **corrosion*** (see **sacrificial protection**, page 45).

Ornamental plating

Aluminium oxide protects aluminium from **corrosion***. Dyes can be added during **anodizing** to colour surfaces.

- **Anodizing.** The coating of a metal object with a thin layer of its oxide. Hydroxide ions are **oxidized*** at the metal **anode** in the electrolysis of dilute sulphuric acid, forming water and oxygen, which oxidizes the metal.

---

* **Ampere**, 112; **Corrosion**, 95; **Mole**, 25; **Molten**, 6; **Oxidation**, 34; **Reactivity series**, 44; **SI units**, 112.

Reactivity

The **reactivity** of an element depends on its ability to gain or lose the electrons which are used for **bonding** (see pages 16-20). The more reactive an element, the more easily it will combine with others. Some elements are very reactive, others very unreactive. This difference can be used to produce electricity and protect metals from **corrosion***.

●**Reactivity series** or **activity series**. A list of elements (usually metals), placed in order of their reactivity. The series is constructed by comparing the reactions of the metals with other substances, e.g. acids and oxygen (for a summary of reactions, see page 97).

●**Displacement**. A reaction in which one element replaces another in a compound. An element will only displace another lower than itself in the **reactivity series**.

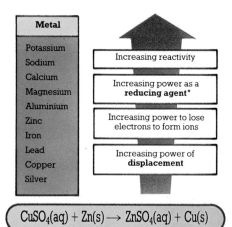

Metal
Potassium
Sodium
Calcium
Magnesium
Aluminium
Zinc
Iron
Lead
Copper
Silver

Increasing reactivity

Increasing power as a **reducing agent***

Increasing power to lose electrons to form ions

Increasing power of **displacement**

Zinc **displaces** copper from copper(II) sulphate solution. ▶

$$CuSO_4(aq) + Zn(s) \longrightarrow ZnSO_4(aq) + Cu(s)$$

●**Half cell**. An element in contact with water or an **aqueous solution*** of one of its compounds. Atoms on the surface form **cations***, which are released into the solution, leaving electrons behind. The solution has a positive charge and the metal a negative charge, so there is a **potential difference** between them.

●**Electrode potential (E)**. The **potential difference** in a **half cell**. It is impossible to measure directly, so is measured relative to that of another half cell, normally a **hydrogen electrode** (see diagram). Electrode potentials show the ability to **ionize*** in **aqueous solution*** and are used to construct the **electrochemical series**.

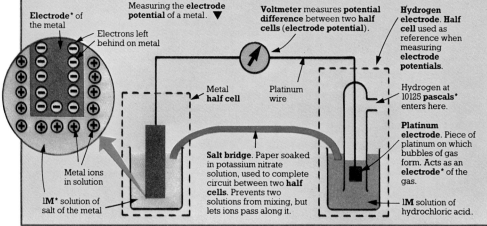

Electrode* of the metal

Electrons left behind on metal

Measuring the **electrode potential** of a metal. ▼

Voltmeter measures **potential difference** between two **half cells (electrode potential)**.

Metal **half cell**

Platinum wire

Metal ions in solution

1M* solution of salt of the metal

Salt bridge. Paper soaked in potassium nitrate solution, used to complete circuit between two **half cells**. Prevents two solutions from mixing, but lets ions pass along it.

Hydrogen electrode. Half cell used as reference when measuring electrode potentials.

Hydrogen at 10125 **pascals*** enters here.

Platinum electrode. Piece of platinum on which bubbles of gas form. Acts as an **electrode*** of the gas.

1M solution of hydrochloric acid.

* **Aqueous solution**, 30; **Cation**, 16; **Corrosion**, 95; **Electrode**, 42; **Ionization**, 16; **M-value**, 25 (**Molarity**); **Pascal**, 112; **Reducing agent**, 34.

- **Electrochemical series**. A list of the elements in order of their **electrode potentials**. The element with the most negative electrode potential is placed at the top. The position of an element in the series shows how readily it forms ions in **aqueous solution***, and is thus an indication of how reactive it is likely to be.

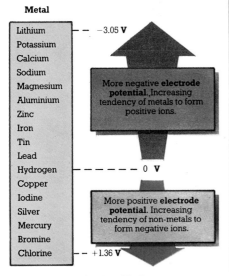

Metal

Lithium	− −3.05 **V**
Potassium	
Calcium	
Sodium	
Magnesium	
Aluminium	
Zinc	
Iron	
Tin	
Lead	
Hydrogen	− − − − 0 **V**
Copper	
Iodine	
Silver	
Mercury	
Bromine	
Chlorine	− − +1.36 **V**

More negative **electrode potential**. Increasing tendency of metals to form positive ions.

More positive **electrode potential**. Increasing tendency of non-metals to form negative ions.

- **Potential difference (pd)** or **voltage**. A difference in electric charge between two points, measured in **volts** (**V**) by an instrument called a **voltmeter**. If two points with a potential difference are joined, an electric **current**, proportional to the potential difference, flows between them.

- **Current**. A flow of charged particles, either electrons or ions (negative or positive). Its size is measured in **amperes***(**A**), using an instrument called an **ammeter**. A current will flow in a loop, or **circuit**, between two points if there is a **potential difference** between them.

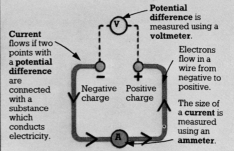

Current flows if two points with a **potential difference** are connected with a substance which conducts electricity.

Potential difference is measured using a **voltmeter**.

Electrons flow in a wire from negative to positive.

The size of a **current** is measured using an **ammeter**.

Negative charge   Positive charge

- **Electrochemical cell**. An arrangement of two **half cells** of different elements. The half cell with the most negative **electrode potential** forms the **negative terminal** and the other forms the **positive terminal**. When these are connected, a **current** flows between them. There are two types of cell – **primary cells**, which cannot be recharged and **secondary cells**, which can be recharged. A **battery** is a number of linked cells.

- **Electromotive force (emf)**. The name given to the difference between the **electrode potentials** in an **electrochemical cell**. It is the **potential difference** between the two terminals of the cell.

- **Sacrificial protection**. Also known as **cathodic protection** or **electrical protection**. A method of preventing iron from **rusting*** by attaching a metal higher in the **electrochemical series** to it, which rusts instead.

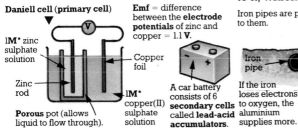

Daniell cell (primary cell)

Emf = difference between the **electrode potentials** of zinc and copper = 1.1 **V**.

1M* zinc sulphate solution

Copper foil

Zinc rod

1M* copper(II) sulphate solution

Porous pot (allows liquid to flow through).

A car battery consists of 6 **secondary cells** called **lead-acid accumulators**.

Iron pipes are protected by attaching scrap aluminium to them.

Iron pipe   Bag of aluminium

If the iron loses electrons to oxygen, the aluminium supplies more.

Aluminium loses electrons more easily (higher in the **electrochemical series**).

Galvanizing is a type of **sacrificial protection**. See page 60.

Rates of reaction

The time it takes for a chemical reaction to finish varies from less than a millionth of a second to weeks or even years. It is possible to predict how long a particular reaction will take and how to speed it up or slow it down by altering the conditions under which it takes place. The efficiency of many industrial processes is improved by increasing the **rate of reaction**, e.g. by using high temperature and pressure, or a **catalyst**.

●**Rate of reaction.** A measurement of the speed of a reaction. It is calculated by measuring how quickly reactants are used up or products are formed. The experimental method used to measure the rate of reaction depends on the **physical states*** of the reactants and products, and the data from such an experiment is plotted on a **rate curve**. The speed of a reaction varies as it proceeds. The rate at any time during the reaction is the **instantaneous rate**. The instantaneous rate at the start of the reaction is the **initial rate**. The **average rate** is calculated by dividing the total change in the amount of products or reactants by the time the reaction took to finish.

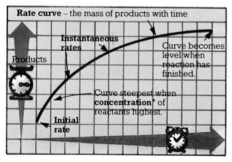

Rate curve – the mass of products with time

Instantaneous rates
Products
Curve becomes level when reaction has finished.
Curve steepest when **concentration*** of reactants highest.
Initial rate

●**Collision theory.** Explains why altering the conditions under which a reaction takes place affects its rate. For a reaction to take place between two particles, they must collide, so if more collisions occur, the **rate of reaction** increases. However, only some collisions cause a reaction, since not all particles have enough energy to react (see **activation energy**).

●**Photochemical reaction.** A reaction whose speed is affected by the intensity of light, e.g. **photosynthesis***. Light gives reacting particles more energy and so increases the **rate of reaction**.

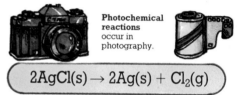

Photochemical reactions occur in photography.

$$2AgCl(s) \rightarrow 2Ag(s) + Cl_2(g)$$

Silver crystals form where light falls on the film, recording the picture.

●**Activation energy (E).** The minimum energy that the particles of reactants must have for them to react when they collide (see **collision theory**). The **rate of reaction** depends on how many reacting particles have this minimum energy. In many reactions, the particles already have this energy and react straight away. In others, energy has to be supplied for the particles to reach the activation energy.

Friction produces heat, giving particles in match **activation energy**.

Hydrogen molecule
Chlorine molecule
HCl molecules formed after collision.

Molecules do not collide with enough energy to react. They do not have the **activation energy**.

Molecules collide with enough energy to react. They have the **activation energy**.

Changing rates of reaction

The **rate of reaction** will increase if the temperature is increased. The heat energy gives more particles an energy greater than the **activation energy**.

 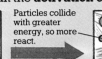

Particles collide with greater energy, so more react.

For reactions involving gases, the **rate of reaction** will increase if the pressure is increased. An increase in the pressure of a gas increases the temperature and decreases the volume (i.e. increases the **concentration*** – see also **gas laws**, page 28). The particles collide more often and with greater energy.

The **rate of reaction** will increase if the **concentration*** of one or more of the reactants is increased.

More molecules in the same space means more collisions.

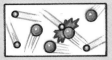

Low **concentration***   High **concentration***

The **rate of reaction** will increase if the surface area of a solid reactant is increased. Reactions in which one reactant is a solid can only take place at the surface of the solid.

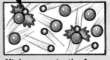

Extra surface area after breaking up.

- **Catalyst**. A substance that increases the rate of a chemical reaction, but is chemically unchanged itself at the end of the reaction. This process is known as **catalysis**. Catalysts work by lowering the **activation energy** of a reaction. The catalyst used in a reaction is written over the arrow in the equation (see page 68). A catalyst which increases the rate of one reaction may have no effect on another.

Catalysts provide an alternative chemical route for a reaction to take.

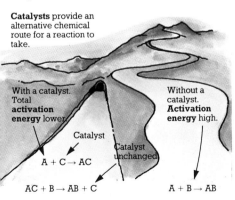

With a catalyst. Total **activation energy** lower.

Without a catalyst. **Activation energy** high.

Catalyst

Catalyst unchanged

A + C → AC

AC + B → AB + C   A + B → AB

- **Autocatalysis**. A process in which one of the products of a reaction acts as a **catalyst** for the reaction.

- **Surface catalyst**. A **catalyst** which attracts the reactants to itself. It holds them close to each other on its surface, so they react easily.

- **Promoter**. A substance which increases the power of a **catalyst**, so speeding up the reaction.

- **Inhibitor**. A substance that slows a reaction. Some work by reducing the power of a **catalyst**.

- **Enzyme**. A **catalyst** found in living things which increases the **rate of reaction** in a natural chemical process.

- **Homogeneous catalyst**. A **catalyst** that is in the same **physical state*** as the reactants.

- **Heterogeneous catalyst**. A **catalyst** that is in a different **physical state*** to the reactants.

Reversible reactions

Many chemical reactions continue until one or all of the reactants are used up, and their products do not react together. This is known as **completion**. Other reactions, however, never reach this stage. They are called **reversible reactions**.

●**Reversible reaction.** A chemical reaction in which the products react together to reform the original reactants. These react again to form the products and so on. The two reactions are simultaneous, and the process will not come to **completion** (see introduction) if it takes place in a **closed system**. At some stage during a reversible reaction, **chemical equilibrium** is reached.

●**Dissociation.** A type of **reversible reaction** in which a compound is divided into other compounds or elements. **Thermal dissociation** is dissociation caused by heating (the products formed recombine when cooled). Dissociation should not be confused with **decomposition**, in which a compound is irreversibly split up.

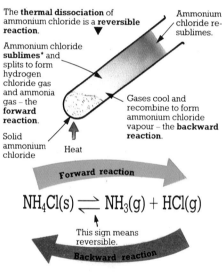

The **thermal dissociation** of ammonium chloride is a **reversible reaction**.

Ammonium chloride **sublimes*** and splits to form hydrogen chloride gas and ammonia gas – the **forward reaction**.

Solid ammonium chloride

Heat

Ammonium chloride re-sublimes.

Gases cool and recombine to form ammonium chloride vapour – the **backward reaction**.

Forward reaction

$$NH_4Cl(s) \rightleftharpoons NH_3(g) + HCl(g)$$

This sign means reversible.

Backward reaction

Nitrogen dioxide undergoes **thermal dissociation** into nitrogen monoxide and oxygen.

Brown nitrogen dioxide gas.

Increase temperature – colour fades.

Heat

Cool

Decrease temperature – gases recombine.

Nitrogen monoxide and oxygen are colourless.

$$2NO_2(g) \rightleftharpoons 2NO(g) + O_2(g)$$

●**Closed system.** A **system*** in which no chemicals can escape or enter. If a product of a **reversible reaction** escapes, for example into the atmosphere, the reaction can no longer move back the other way. A system from which chemicals can escape is an **open system**.

●**Equilibrium.** The cancelling out of two equal but opposite movements. **Chemical equilibrium** is an example of this – it occurs when the **forward** and **backward reactions** are taking place, but are cancelling each other out.

●**Forward reaction.** The reaction in which products are formed from the original reactants in a **reversible reaction**. It goes from left to right in the equation.

●**Backward reaction** or **reverse reaction.** The reaction in which the original reactants are reformed from their products in a **reversible reaction**. It goes from right to left in the equation.

A person walking up an escalator at the same speed as the escalator is moving down is in **equilibrium**.

* Sublimation, 7; System, 115.

- **Chemical equilibrium.** A stage reached in a **reversible reaction** in a **closed system** when the **forward** and **backward reactions** take place at the same rate. Their effects cancel each other out, and the **concentrations*** of the reactants and products no longer change. Chemical equilibrium is a form of **equilibrium**.

Start of reaction

Fast **forward reaction**

Reactants → Products

Slow **backward reaction**

Higher **concentration*** of reactants than products

At **chemical equilibrium**

Reactants ⇌ Products

Products and reactants formed at same rate.

The position of chemical equilibrium

Any change of conditions (temperature, **concentration*** or pressure) during a **reversible reaction** alters the rate of either the **forward** or **backward reaction**, destroying the **chemical equilibrium**. This is eventually restored, but with a different proportion of reactants and products. The **equilibrium position** is said to have changed.

First **equilibrium position** ▶

Reactants ⇌ Products

Alter conditions to favour **forward reaction** – **equilibrium position** said to move right.

More products formed.

Alter conditions to favour **backward reaction** – **equilibrium position** is said to move left.

More reactants formed.

- **Le Chatelier's principle.** A law stating that if changes are made to a **system*** in equilibrium, the system adjusts itself to reduce the effects of the change.

Changing the pressure in **reversible reactions** involving gases may alter the equilibrium position.

In the reaction $A(g) + B(g) \rightleftharpoons AB(g)$:

Molecule of A
Molecule of B
Molecule of AB

Raise pressure – position moves right – more AB formed – i.e. number of molecules decreases to lower pressure again.

Lower pressure – position moves left – more A and B formed – i.e. number of molecules increases to raise pressure again.

Changing the temperature in a **reversible reaction** also alters the equilibrium position. This depends on whether the reaction is **exothermic*** or **endothermic***. A reversible reaction which is exothermic in one direction is endothermic in the other.

Ammonia is made by the **Haber process***.

$$N_2(g) + 3H_2(g) \underset{\text{Endothermic*}}{\overset{\text{Exothermic*}}{\rightleftharpoons}} 2NH_3(g)$$

Nitrogen   Hydrogen   Ammonia

Temperature rises – rate of **endothermic*** **backward reaction** increases to absorb heat. Less ammonia formed – position moves left.

Temperature falls – rate of **exothermic*** **forward reaction** increases giving out more heat energy. More ammonia produced – position moves right.

Changing the **concentration*** of the reactants or products in a **reversible reaction** also changes the equilibrium position.

Raise **concentration*** of reactants – increases rate of **forward reaction**.   OR   Lower **concentration** of products – decreases rate of **backward reaction**.

Equilibrium position moves right.

Lower **concentration** of reactants – decreases rate of **forward reaction**.   OR   Raise **concentration** of products – increases rate of **backward reaction**.

Equilibrium position moves left.

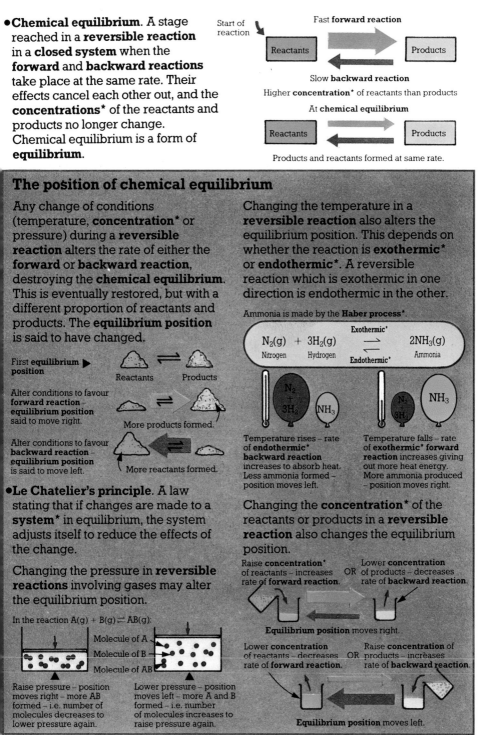

The periodic table

During the 19th century, many chemists tried to arrange the elements in an order which related to the size of their atoms and also showed regular repeating patterns in their behaviour or properties. The most successful attempt was published by the Russian, Dimitri Mendeléev, in 1869, and still forms the basis of the modern **periodic table**.

•**Periodic table**. An arrangement of the elements in order of their **atomic numbers***. Both the physical properties and chemical properties of an element and its compounds are related to the position of the element in the periodic table. This relationship has led to the table being divided into **groups** and **periods**. The arrangement of elements starts on the left of period 1 with hydrogen and moves in order of increasing atomic number from left to right across each period in turn (see picture on the right).

•**Period**. A horizontal row of elements in the **periodic table**. There are seven periods in all. Period 1 has only two elements – hydrogen and helium. Periods 2 and 3 each contain eight elements and are called the **short periods**. Periods 4, 5, 6 and 7 each contain between 18 and 32 elements. They are called the **long periods**. Moving from left to right across a period, the **atomic number*** increases

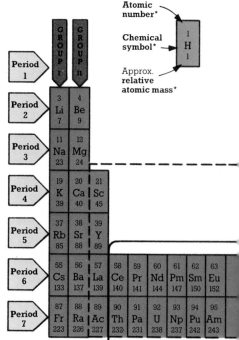

Periodic table

by one from one element to the next. Each successive element has one more electron in the **outer shell*** of its atoms. All elements in the same period have the same number of shells, and the regular change in the number of electrons from one element to the next leads to a fairly regular pattern of change in the chemical properties of the elements across a period. For an example of such a gradual change in property, see below.

Electron configuration* of elements across **Period 2**

All elements have the same **outer shell***, but each successive element, going from left to right, has one more electron added to that shell.

Strong **reducing agents*** ────▶ Weak **reducing agents** ────▶ Strong **oxidizing agents***

This shows a regular pattern of change across **Period 2** in the ability of elements to **reduce*** or **oxidize*** other elements and compounds (see also page 52). Neon is the exception – it is unreactive.

*Atomic number, 13; Chemical symbol, 8; Electron configuration, Outer shell, 13; Oxidation, Oxidizing agent, Reducing agent, Reduction, 34; Relative atomic mass, 24.

- **Group**. A vertical column of elements in the **periodic table**. All groups are numbered (except for **transition metal*** groups) using roman numerals and some have names. Elements in the same group have the same number of electrons in their **outer shell***, and so have similar chemical properties.

Groups with alternative names:

Group number	Group name
Group I	The **alkali metals** (see pages 54-55)
Group II	The **alkaline-earth metals** (see pages 56-57)
Group VII	The **halogens** (see pages 72-74)
Group VIII (or **Group 0**)	The **noble gases** (see page 75)

Colour-coding used in table.

■ Metals ■ Metalloids □ Non-metals

Transition metals (see pages 58-61)

Inner transition series

Metals and non-metals

- **Metal**. An element with characteristic physical properties that distinguish it from a **non-metal**. Elements on the left of a **period** have metallic properties. Moving to the right, the elements gradually become less metallic. Elements that are not distinctly metal or non-metal, but have a mixture of properties, are called **metalloids**. Elements to the right of metalloids are non-metals.

Property	Metal	Non-metal
Physical state*	Solids (except mercury)	Solid, liquid or gas (bromine is the only liquid).
Appearance	Shiny	Mainly non-shiny (iodine is one of the exceptions).
Conductivity*	Good	Poor (except graphite)
Malleability*	Good	Poor
Ductility*	Good	Poor
Melting point	Generally high	Generally low
Boiling point	Generally high	Generally low

Inorganic chemistry

Inorganic chemistry is the study of all the elements and their compounds, except those compounds made of chains of carbon atoms (see **organic chemistry**, pages 76-91). The properties and reactions of inorganic elements and compounds follow certain patterns, or **trends**, in the periodic table. By looking up and down **groups*** and across **periods*** of the table, it is possible to predict the reactions of elements.

Major periodic table trends

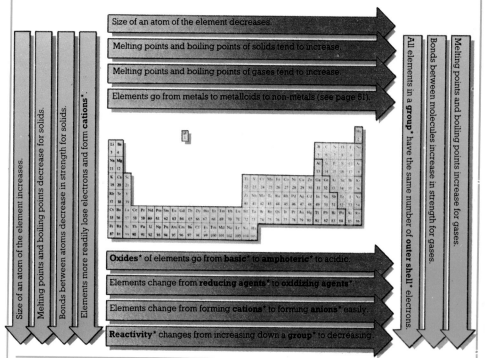

Size of an atom of the element decreases.

Melting points and boiling points of solids tend to increase.

Melting points and boiling points of gases tend to increase.

Elements go from metals to metalloids to non-metals (see page 51).

All elements in a **group*** have the same number of **outer shell*** electrons.

Bonds between molecules increase in strength for gases.

Melting points and boiling points increase for gases.

Size of an atom of the element increases.

Melting points and boiling points decrease for solids.

Bonds between atoms decrease in strength for solids.

Elements more readily lose electrons and form **cations***.

Oxides* of elements go from **basic*** to **amphoteric*** to acidic.

Elements change from forming **reducing agents*** to **oxidizing agents***.

Elements change from forming **cations*** to forming **anions*** easily.

Reactivity* changes from increasing down a **group*** to decreasing.

Predicting reactions

Throughout the inorganic section of this book, each **group*** of elements has an introduction and chart which summarizes some of the properties of the group's elements. Below the charts are blue boxes which highlight trends going down the group. After the introduction more common group members are defined. Information on the other members of the group can often be worked out from trends in **reactivity*** going down the group.

The following two steps show how to predict the **reactivity*** of caesium with cold water. Caesium is in Group I (see pages 54-55).

1. The chart introducing Group I shows that the reactivity of the elements increases going down the group.

2. From the definitions of lithium, sodium and potassium it is found that all three elements react with water with increasing violence going down the group – lithium reacts gently, sodium reacts violently and potassium reacts very violently.

It is predicted that caesium, as it comes after potassium going down the group, will react extremely violently with water.

* **Amphoteric**, 37; **Anion**, 16; **Basic**, 37 (**Base**); **Cation**, 16; **Group**, 51; **Outer shell**, 13; **Oxides**, 69; **Oxidizing agent**, 34; **Period**, 50; **Reactivity**, 44; **Reducing agent**, 34.

Hydrogen

Hydrogen (H₂), with an **atomic number*** of one, is the first and lightest element in the periodic table, and the commonest in the universe. It is a **diatomic***, odourless, inflammable gas which only occurs naturally on Earth in compounds. It is made by the reaction of natural gas and steam at high temperatures, or the reaction of **water gas*** and steam over a **catalyst***. It is a **reducing agent***, burns in air with a light blue flame and, when heated, reacts with many substances, e.g. with sodium to form sodium hydride (all compounds of hydrogen and one other element are **hydrides**). Hydrogen is used, for example, to make margarines (see **hydrogenation**, page 79) and ammonia (see **Haber process**, page 66), and as a rocket fuel. See also pages 103 and 105.

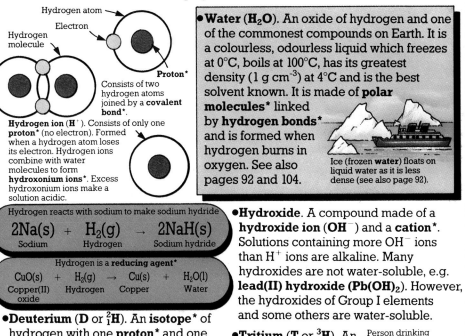

Hydrogen atom

Electron

Hydrogen molecule

Proton*

Consists of two hydrogen atoms joined by a **covalent bond***.

Hydrogen ion (H⁺). Consists of only one **proton*** (no electron). Formed when a hydrogen atom loses its electron. Hydrogen ions combine with water molecules to form **hydroxonium ions***. Excess hydroxonium ions make a solution acidic.

●**Water (H₂O)**. An oxide of hydrogen and one of the commonest compounds on Earth. It is a colourless, odourless liquid which freezes at 0°C, boils at 100°C, has its greatest density (1 g cm⁻³) at 4°C and is the best solvent known. It is made of **polar molecules*** linked by **hydrogen bonds*** and is formed when hydrogen burns in oxygen. See also pages 92 and 104.

Ice (frozen **water**) floats on liquid water as it is less dense (see also page 92).

Hydrogen reacts with sodium to make sodium hydride

$$2Na(s) + H_2(g) \rightarrow 2NaH(s)$$
Sodium   Hydrogen   Sodium hydride

Hydrogen is a **reducing agent***

$$CuO(s) + H_2(g) \rightarrow Cu(s) + H_2O(l)$$
Copper(II) oxide   Hydrogen   Copper   Water

●**Deuterium (D or ²₁H)**. An **isotope*** of hydrogen with one **proton*** and one **neutron***. It makes up 0.0156% of natural hydrogen. Water molecules containing deuterium are called **deuterium oxide (D₂O)** or **heavy water** molecules. Heavy water is used in nuclear reactors to slow the fast moving neutrons.

●**Hydrogen peroxide (H₂O₂)**. A syrupy liquid. It is an oxide of hydrogen and a strong **oxidizing agent***. It is sold in solution as disinfectant and bleach.

●**Hydroxide**. A compound made of a hydroxide ion (OH⁻) and a **cation***. Solutions containing more OH⁻ ions than H⁺ ions are alkaline. Many hydroxides are not water-soluble, e.g. **lead(II) hydroxide (Pb(OH)₂)**. However, the hydroxides of Group I elements and some others are water-soluble.

●**Tritium (T or ³₁H)**. An **isotope*** of hydrogen with one **proton*** and two **neutrons***. It is rare in hydrogen but is produced by nuclear reactors. It is **radioactive**, emitting **beta particles** (see pages 14-15).

Person drinking **tritiated water**.

Tritiated molecule

Tritiated water contains some water molecules in which a hydrogen atom has been replaced by a **tritium** atom. It is used by doctors to help find out how much fluid a patient passes.

* **Atomic number**, 13; **Catalyst**, 47; **Cation**, 16; **Covalent bond**, 18; **Diatomic**, 10; **Hydrogen bond**, 20; **Hydroxonium ion**, 36; **Isotope**, 13; **Neutron**, 12; **Oxidizing agent**, 34; **Polar molecule**, 19; **Proton**, 12; **Reducing agent**, 34; **Water gas**, 65 (**Carbon monoxide**).

53

Group I, the alkali metals

The elements in **Group I** of the periodic table are called **alkali metals** as they are all metals which react with water to form alkaline solutions. They all have similar chemical properties and their physical properties follow certain patterns. The chart below shows some of their properties.

Some properties of Group I elements

Name of element	Chemical symbol	Relative atomic mass*	Electron configuration*	Reactivity	Appearance	Uses
Lithium	Li	6.94	2,1	I N C R E A S I N G	Silver-white metal	See below.
Sodium	Na	22.99	2,8,1		Soft silver-white metal	See below.
Potassium	K	39.10	2,8,8,1		Soft silver-white metal	See page 55.
Rubidium	Rb	85.47	Complex configuration, but still one outer electron		Soft silver-white metal	To make special glass.
Caesium	Cs	132.90			Soft metal with gold sheen	In **photocells*** and as a **catalyst***.
Francium	Fr	No known stable isotope*				

The atoms of all Group I elements have one electron in their **outer shell***, hence the elements are powerful **reducing agents*** because this electron is easily lost in reactions. The resulting ion has a charge of $+1$ and is more stable because its new outer shell is complete (see **octet**, page 13). All Group I elements react in this way to form **ionic compounds***.

Going down the group, the reaction of the elements with water gets more violent. The first three tarnish in air and **rubidium** and **caesium** catch fire. All members are stored under oil because of their reactivity.

These two pages contain more information on **lithium**, **sodium**, **potassium** and their compounds. They are typical Group I elements.

●**Lithium (Li)**. The least reactive element in Group I of the periodic table and the lightest solid element. Lithium is rare and is only found in a few compounds, from which it is extracted by **electrolysis***. It burns in air with a pinkish flame. A piece of lithium placed on water glides across the surface, fizzing gently.

$$2Li(s) + 2H_2O(l) \rightarrow 2LiOH(aq) + H_2(g)$$
Lithium   Water   Lithium hydroxide   Hydrogen

After the reaction, the solution is strongly alkaline, due to the **lithium hydroxide** formed.

Lithium reacts vigorously with chlorine to form **lithium chloride (LiCl)** which is used in welding flux and air conditioners.

●**Sodium (Na)**. A member of Group I of the periodic table, found in many compounds. Its main ore is **rock salt** (containing **sodium chloride** – see also **potassium**). It is extracted from molten sodium chloride by **electrolysis***, using a **Downs' cell**. Sodium burns in air with an orange flame and reacts violently with non-metals and water (see equation for **lithium**, and substitute Na for Li). It is used in sodium vapour lamps and as a coolant in nuclear power stations.

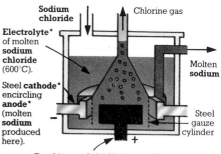

Downs' cell. Used to extract **sodium** from molten **sodium chloride** by **electrolysis***.

Sodium chloride

Chlorine gas

Electrolyte* of molten **sodium chloride** (600°C).

Molten **sodium**

Steel **cathode*** encircling **anode*** (molten **sodium** produced here).

Steel gauze cylinder

Graphite **anode*** (chlorine produced here).

* **Anode**, 42 (**Electrode**); **Catalyst**, 47; **Cathode**, 42 (**Electrode**); **Electrolysis, Electrolyte**, 42; **Electron configuration**, 13; **Ionic compound**, 17; **Isotope, Outer shell**, 13; **Photocell**, 115; **Reducing agent**, 34; **Relative atomic mass**, 24.

- **Sodium hydroxide (NaOH)** or **caustic soda**. A white, **deliquescent*** solid, produced by **electrolysis*** of brine. A **strong base***, it reacts with acids to form a sodium **salt*** and water. It is used to make soaps and paper.

- **Sodium carbonate (Na₂CO₃)**. A white solid that dissolves in water to form an alkaline solution. Its **hydrate***, called **washing soda (Na₂CO₃.10H₂O** – see also page 93), has white, **efflorescent*** crystals and is made when ammonia, water and **sodium chloride** react with carbon dioxide in the **Solvay process**.

Washing soda is used in the making of glass, as a **water softener*** and in bath crystals.

- **Sodium hydrogencarbonate (NaHCO₃)**. Also called **sodium bicarbonate** or **bicarbonate of soda**. A white solid made by the **Solvay process** (see **sodium carbonate**). In water it forms a weak alkaline solution.

Sodium hydrogencarbonate is used in baking. The carbon dioxide gas it gives off when heated makes dough rise. It is also used as an **antacid*** to relieve indigestion.

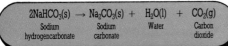
$$2NaHCO_3(s) \rightarrow Na_2CO_3(s) + H_2O(l) + CO_2(g)$$
Sodium hydrogencarbonate   Sodium carbonate   Water   Carbon dioxide

- **Sodium chloride (NaCl)** or **salt**. A white solid which occurs in sea water and **rock salt** (see **sodium**). It forms **brine** when dissolved in water and is used to make **sodium hydroxide** and **sodium carbonate**.

Sodium chloride is used to preserve and flavour food.

- **Sodium nitrate (NaNO₃)** or **Chile saltpetre**. A white solid used as a fertilizer and also to preserve meat.

- **Potassium (K)**. A member of Group I of the periodic table. Potassium compounds are found in sea water and **rock salt** (containing **potassium chloride** – see also **sodium**). Potassium is extracted from molten potassium chloride by **electrolysis***. It is very reactive, reacting violently with chlorine and also with water (see equation for **lithium**, and substitute K for Li). It has few uses, but some of its compounds are important.

Potassium reacting with water. It whizzes across the water giving off so much heat that the hydrogen produced bursts into flames. ▼

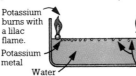
Potassium burns with a lilac flame.

A very small piece of **potassium** was put in here, using tweezers.

Potassium metal

Water   Hydrogen bubbles

- **Potassium hydroxide (KOH)** or **caustic potash**. A white, **deliquescent*** solid. It is a **strong base*** which reacts with acids to form a potassium **salt*** and water. It is used to make toilet soap, see page 88.

- **Potassium carbonate (K₂CO₃)**. A white solid which is very water-soluble, forming an alkaline solution. It is used to make glass, dyes and soap.

- **Potassium chloride (KCl)**. A white, water-soluble solid. Large amounts are found in sea water and **rock salt** (see **potassium**). It is used in fertilizer and to produce **potassium hydroxide**.

- **Potassium nitrate (KNO₃)**, or **saltpetre**. A white solid which dissolves in water to form a **neutral*** solution.

Potassium nitrate is used:
To preserve meats.
In fertilizers
In explosives

- **Potassium sulphate (K₂SO₄)**. A white solid, forming a **neutral*** solution in water. It is an important fertilizer.

Group II, the alkaline-earth metals

The elements in **Group II** of the periodic table are called the **alkaline-earth metals**. The physical properties of the members of Group II follow certain trends, and, except **beryllium**, they all have similar chemical properties. They are very reactive, though less reactive than Group I elements. The chart below shows some of their properties.

Some properties of Group II elements						
Name of element	Chemical symbol	Relative atomic mass*	Electron configuration*	Reactivity	Appearance	Uses
Beryllium	Be	9.01	2,2	I N C R E A S I N G	Hard, white metal	In light, corrosion-resistant alloys*
Magnesium	Mg	24.31	2,8,2		Silver-white metal	See below
Calcium	Ca	40.31	2,8,8,2		Soft, silver-white metal	See below
Strontium	Sr	87.62	Complex configuration, but still 2 outer electrons		Soft, silver-white metal	In fireworks
Barium	Ba	137.34			Soft, silver-white metal	In fireworks and medicine
Radium	Ra	Rare radioactive* metal			Soft, silver-white metal	An isotope* is used to treat cancer.

The atoms of all Group II elements have two electrons in their **outer shell***, hence the elements are good **reducing agents*** because these electrons are fairly easily lost in reactions. Each resulting ion has a charge of $+2$ and is more stable because its new outer shell is complete (see **octet**, page 13). All Group II elements react this way to form **ionic compounds***, though some **beryllium** compounds have **covalent*** properties.

Going down the group, elements react more readily with both water and oxygen (see **magnesium** and **calcium**). They all **tarnish*** in air but **barium** reacts so violently with both water and oxygen that it is stored under oil.

These two pages contain more information on **magnesium**, **calcium** and their compounds. These metals are typical Group II elements.

●**Magnesium (Mg)**. A member of Group II of the periodic table. It only occurs naturally in compounds, mainly in either **dolomite** ($CaCO_3.MgCO_3$ – a rock made of magnesium and **calcium carbonate**) or in **magnesium chloride** ($MgCl_2$), found in sea water. Magnesium is produced by the **electrolysis*** of molten magnesium chloride. It burns in air with a bright white flame.

$$Mg(s) + Cl_2(g) \rightarrow MgCl_2(s)$$
Magnesium   Chlorine   Magnesium chloride

Magnesium burns vigorously in chlorine (see above), reacts slowly with cold water and rapidly with steam (see below).

$$Mg(s) + H_2O(g) \rightarrow MgO(s) + H_2(g)$$
Magnesium   Steam   Magnesium oxide   Hydrogen

$$2Mg(s) + O_2(g) \rightarrow 2MgO(s)$$
Magnesium   Oxygen   Magnesium oxide

Magnesium reacts rapidly with dilute acids:

$$Mg(s) + 2HCl(aq) \rightarrow MgCl_2(aq) + H_2(g)$$
Magnesium   Hydrochloric   Magnesium   Hydrogen
            acid   chloride

Magnesium is used to make **alloys***, e.g. for building aircraft. It is also needed for plant **photosynthesis*** (it is found in **chlorophyll** – the leaf pigment which absorbs light energy).

* Alloy, 114; Covalent compounds, 18; Electrolysis, 42; Electron configuration, 13; Ionic compound, 17; Isotope, Outer shell, 13; Photosynthesis, 95; Radioactivity, 14; Reducing agent, 34; Relative atomic mass, 24; Tarnish, 115.

- **Magnesium hydroxide (Mg(OH)$_2$).** A white solid that is only slightly soluble in water. It is a **base*** and therefore **neutralizes*** acids.

Magnesium hydroxide is used in **antacids*** for treating stomach upsets, particularly indigestion.

- **Magnesium sulphate (MgSO$_4$).** A white solid used in medicines for treating constipation, in leather processing and in fire-proofing.

- **Magnesium oxide (MgO).** A white solid which is slightly water-soluble. It is a **base***, forming magnesium **salts*** when it reacts with acids. It has a very high melting point and is used to line some furnaces.

Magnesium oxide is added to cocoa powder to stop the particles sticking together.

$$MgO(s) + 2HCl(aq) \rightarrow MgCl_2(aq) + H_2O(l)$$

Magnesium oxide   Hydrochloric acid   Magnesium chloride   Water

---

- **Calcium (Ca).** A member of Group II of the periodic table. It occurs naturally in many compounds, e.g. those found in the Earth's crust, milk and bones. Calcium is extracted from its compounds by **electrolysis***. It burns in oxygen with a red flame and reacts readily with cold water and very rapidly with dilute acids (for equations see **magnesium** and substitute Ca for Mg). Calcium is used to make high-grade steel and in the production of uranium.

- **Calcium hydroxide (Ca(OH)$_2$)** or **slaked lime.** A white solid which dissolves slightly in water to form **limewater.** This is weakly alkaline and is used to test for carbon dioxide (see page 105). Calcium hydroxide is used in mortars and to remove excess acidity in soils.

- **Calcium sulphate.** A white solid that occurs both as **anhydrite calcium sulphate (CaSO$_4$)** and **gypsum (CaSO$_4$.2H$_2$O).** When heated, gypsum forms plaster of Paris.

Calcium sulphate is used in:

Plaster casts

Plaster moulds

- **Calcium oxide (CaO)** or **quicklime.** A white solid. It is a **base*** which is made by heating **calcium carbonate** in a lime kiln.

$$CaCO_3(s) \rightleftharpoons CaO(s) + CO_2(g)$$

Calcium carbonate   Calcium oxide   Carbon dioxide

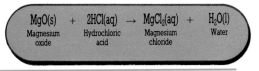

Calcium oxide, calcium carbonate and calcium hydroxide are used to remove excess soil acidity.

- **Calcium carbonate (CaCO$_3$).** A white insoluble solid that occurs naturally as **limestone, chalk, marble** and **calcite.** It dissolves in dilute acids.

Limestone rock is corroded because rain water containing dissolved carbon dioxide reacts with the limestone to form **calcium hydrogencarbonate** which dissolves slightly in water.

$$CaCO_3(s) + H_2O(l) + CO_2(g) \rightarrow Ca(HCO_3)_2(aq)$$

Calcium carbonate   Water   Carbon dioxide   Calcium hydrogencarbonate

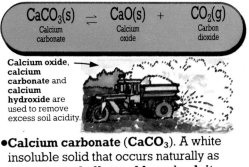

Calcium hydrogen-carbonate formed when **limestone** dissolves in water causes **temporary hardness*.**

Calcium carbonate is used to obtain **calcium oxide,** make cement and as building stone.

- **Calcium chloride (CaCl$_2$).** A white, **deliquescent*,** water-soluble solid which is used as a **drying agent*.**

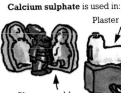

---

* Antacid, 114; Base, 37; Deliquescent, 92; Drying agent, 114; Electrolysis, 42; Neutralization, 37; Salts, 39; Temporary hardness, 93.

Transition metals

Transition metals have certain properties in common – they are hard, tough, shiny, **malleable*** and **ductile***. They **conduct*** heat and electricity, and have high melting points, boiling points and densities. Transition metals form **complex ions*** which are coloured in solution. They also have more than one possible charge, e.g. Fe^{2+} and Fe^{3+}.

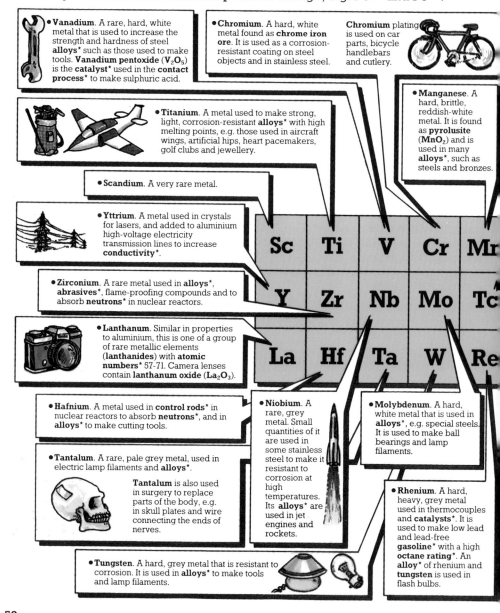

- **Vanadium**. A rare, hard, white metal that is used to increase the strength and hardness of steel **alloys*** such as those used to make tools. **Vanadium pentoxide** (V_2O_5) is the **catalyst*** used in the **contact process*** to make sulphuric acid.

- **Chromium**. A hard, white metal found as **chrome iron ore**. It is used as a corrosion-resistant coating on steel objects and in stainless steel.

Chromium plating is used on car parts, bicycle handlebars and cutlery.

- **Manganese**. A hard, brittle, reddish-white metal. It is found as **pyrolusite** (MnO_2) and is used in many **alloys***, such as steels and bronzes.

- **Titanium**. A metal used to make strong, light, corrosion-resistant **alloys*** with high melting points, e.g. those used in aircraft wings, artificial hips, heart pacemakers, golf clubs and jewellery.

- **Scandium**. A very rare metal.

- **Yttrium**. A metal used in crystals for lasers, and added to aluminium high-voltage electricity transmission lines to increase **conductivity***.

- **Zirconium**. A rare metal used in **alloys***, **abrasives***, flame-proofing compounds and to absorb **neutrons*** in nuclear reactors.

- **Lanthanum**. Similar in properties to aluminium, this is one of a group of rare metallic elements (**lanthanides**) with **atomic numbers*** 57-71. Camera lenses contain **lanthanum oxide** (La_2O_3).

Sc	Ti	V	Cr	Mr
Y	Zr	Nb	Mo	Tc
La	Hf	Ta	W	Re

- **Hafnium**. A metal used in **control rods*** in nuclear reactors to absorb **neutrons***, and in **alloys*** to make cutting tools.

- **Tantalum**. A rare, pale grey metal, used in electric lamp filaments and **alloys***.

Tantalum is also used in surgery to replace parts of the body, e.g. in skull plates and wire connecting the ends of nerves.

- **Niobium**. A rare, grey metal. Small quantities of it are used in some stainless steel to make it resistant to corrosion at high temperatures. Its **alloys*** are used in jet engines and rockets.

- **Molybdenum**. A hard, white metal that is used in **alloys***, e.g. special steels. It is used to make ball bearings and lamp filaments.

- **Rhenium**. A hard, heavy, grey metal used in thermocouples and **catalysts***. It is used to make low lead and lead-free **gasoline*** with a high **octane rating***. An **alloy*** of rhenium and **tungsten** is used in flash bulbs.

- **Tungsten**. A hard, grey metal that is resistant to corrosion. It is used in **alloys*** to make tools and lamp filaments.

* **Abrasive, Alloy**, 114; **Atomic number**, 13; **Catalyst**, 47; **Complex ion**, 40 (**Complex salt**); **Conductivity**, 114; **Contact process**, 71; **Control rods, Ductile**, 114; **Gasoline**, 85; **Malleable**, 115; **Neutron**, 12; **Octane rating**, 85.

Transition metals have many uses, some of which are shown below. There is more information on iron, copper and zinc on pages 60-61. The members of the **inner transition series** (see page 51) are not shown below, as they are very rare and often unstable.

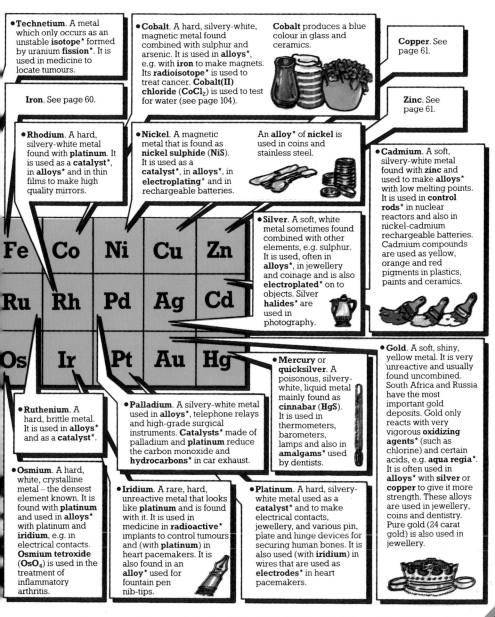

- **Technetium**. A metal which only occurs as an unstable **isotope** * formed by uranium **fission** *. It is used in medicine to locate tumours.

Iron. See page 60.

- **Cobalt**. A hard, silvery-white, magnetic metal found combined with sulphur and arsenic. It is used in **alloys** *, e.g. with **iron** to make magnets. Its **radioisotope** * is used to treat cancer. **Cobalt(II) chloride ($CoCl_2$)** is used to test for water (see page 104).

Cobalt produces a blue colour in glass and ceramics.

Copper. See page 61.

Zinc. See page 61.

- **Rhodium**. A hard, silvery-white metal found with **platinum**. It is used as a **catalyst** *, in **alloys** * and in thin films to make high quality mirrors.

- **Nickel**. A magnetic metal that is found as **nickel sulphide (NiS)**. It is used as a **catalyst** *, in **alloys** *, in **electroplating** * and in rechargeable batteries.

An **alloy** * of **nickel** is used in coins and stainless steel.

- **Cadmium**. A soft, silvery-white metal found with **zinc** and used to make **alloys** * with low melting points. It is used in **control rods** * in nuclear reactors and also in nickel-cadmium rechargeable batteries. Cadmium compounds are used as yellow, orange and red pigments in plastics, paints and ceramics.

- **Silver**. A soft, white metal sometimes found combined with other elements, e.g. sulphur. It is used, often in **alloys** *, in jewellery and coinage and is also **electroplated** * on to objects. Silver **halides** * are used in photography.

Fe Co Ni Cu Zn

Ru Rh Pd Ag Cd

Os Ir Pt Au Hg

- **Gold**. A soft, shiny, yellow metal. It is very unreactive and usually found uncombined. South Africa and Russia have the most important gold deposits. Gold only reacts with very vigorous **oxidizing agents** * (such as chlorine) and certain acids, e.g. **aqua regia** *. It is often used in **alloys** * with **silver** or **copper** to give it more strength. These alloys are used in jewellery, coins and dentistry. Pure gold (24 carat gold) is also used in jewellery.

- **Mercury** or **quicksilver**. A poisonous, silvery-white, liquid metal mainly found as **cinnabar (HgS)**. It is used in thermometers, barometers, lamps and also in **amalgams** * used by dentists.

- **Ruthenium**. A hard, brittle metal. It is used in **alloys** * and as a **catalyst** *.

- **Palladium**. A silvery-white metal used in **alloys** *, telephone relays and high-grade surgical instruments. **Catalysts** * made of palladium and **platinum** reduce the carbon monoxide and **hydrocarbons** * in car exhaust.

- **Osmium**. A hard, white, crystalline metal – the densest element known. It is found with **platinum** and used in **alloys** * with platinum and **iridium**, e.g. in electrical contacts. **Osmium tetroxide (OsO_4)** is used in the treatment of inflammatory arthritis.

- **Iridium**. A rare, hard, unreactive metal that looks like **platinum** and is found with it. It is used in medicine in **radioactive** * implants to control tumours and (with **platinum**) in heart pacemakers. It is also found in an **alloy** * used for fountain pen nib-tips.

- **Platinum**. A hard, silvery-white metal used as a **catalyst** * and to make electrical contacts, jewellery, and various pin, plate and hinge devices for securing human bones. It is also used (with **iridium**) in wires that are used as **electrodes** * in heart pacemakers.

* **Alloy, Amalgam**, 114; **Aqua regia**, 68 (**Nitric acid**); **Catalyst**, 47; **Control rods**, 114; **Electrode**, 42; **Electroplating**, 43; **Halides**, 72; **Hydrocarbons**, 77; **Isotope**, 13; **Neutron**, 12; **Nuclear fission**, 15; **Oxidizing agent**, 34; **Radioactivity, Radioisotope**, 14.

Iron, copper and zinc

●**Iron (Fe)**. A **transition metal*** in Period 4 of the periodic table. It is a fairly soft, white, magnetic metal which only occurs naturally in compounds. One of its main ores is **haematite (Fe_2O_3)**, or **iron(III) oxide**, from which it is extracted in a **blast furnace**. Iron reacts to form both **ionic** and **covalent compounds*** and reacts with moist air to form **rust**. It burns in air when cut very finely into iron filings and also reacts with dilute acids. It is above hydrogen in the **electrochemical series***.

Extracting **iron** using a **blast furnace**.

Raw materials fed in here are iron ore (Fe_2O_3), coke (C) and limestone ($CaCO_3$).

Skip

Gas outlet

Heat-resistant brick lining

Blast furnace

Melting zone

Blast of hot air

Molten iron tapped off here.

Reactions in the furnace

Heated limestone forms calcium oxide and gives off carbon dioxide. Oxygen from hot air reacts with coke and also forms carbon dioxide.

Carbon dioxide reacts with coke to form carbon monoxide.

$$CO_2 + C \rightarrow 2CO$$

Iron ore is **reduced*** to iron by carbon monoxide.

$$Fe_2O_3 + 3CO \rightleftharpoons 2Fe + 3CO_2$$

Slag removed (impurities plus calcium oxide).

Iron made in the blast furnace is called **pig iron**. It contains about 5% carbon and 4% other impurities, such as sulphur. Most pig iron is converted to **steel**, although some is converted to **wrought iron** (by **oxidizing*** impurities) and some is melted down again along with scrap steel to make **cast iron**.

Wrought iron is used to make crane hooks and anchor chains.

Cast iron is used to make drain covers.

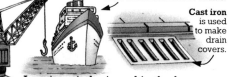

Iron is a vital mineral in the human diet, as it is needed for respiration.

●**Steel**. An **alloy*** of **iron** and carbon which usually contains below 1.5% carbon. The carbon gives the alloy strength and hardness but reduces **malleability*** and **ductility***. Measured amounts of one or more **transition metals*** are often added to steel to give it specific properties, such as corrosion-resistance in the case of **stainless steel** (which contains 11-14% chromium). Steel is often made by the **basic oxygen process**. Scrap steel, molten iron and lime are put into a furnace, and oxygen is blasted on to the metal to **oxidize*** impurities.

Steel is used to make many objects, e.g:

Fridges Cookers Cars

●**Iron(II)** or **ferrous compounds**. Iron compounds containing Fe^{2+} ions, e.g. **iron(II) chloride ($FeCl_2$)**. Their solutions are green.

●**Iron(III)** or **ferric compounds**. Iron compounds containing Fe^{3+} ions, e.g. **iron(III) chloride ($FeCl_3$)**. Their solutions are yellow or orange.

Rust

Rust ($Fe_2O_3.xH_2O$) or **hydrated iron(III) oxide**. A brown solid formed when **iron**, water and air react together (see **corrosion**, page 95). The "x" in the formula shows that the number of water molecules varies.

Iron objects are given a protective coating to prevent rust, e.g. cars are painted and grease is put on engine parts. If a car rusts, **phosphoric acid*** can be put on to stop the rust spreading.

Iron and **steel** can be protected from **rust** by **galvanizing** – coating with a layer of zinc (see also **sacrificial protection**, page 45). The surface zinc **oxidizes*** in air, stopping the zinc and iron below being oxidized.

Even when the zinc coating is scratched, exposing iron, it is zinc that reacts with oxygen and water. Galvanized cars remain rust-free longer than others.

• **Copper (Cu)**. A **transition metal*** in Period 4 of the periodic table. It is a red-brown, soft but tough metal found naturally in certain rocks. Its compounds are found in several ores, e.g. **copper pyrites ((CuFe)S$_2$)** and **malachite (CuCO$_3$.Cu(OH)$_2$)**. Copper is extracted from the former by crushing and removing sand and then roasting in a limited supply of air and with silica. The iron combines with silica and forms **slag**. The sulphur is removed by burning to form sulphur dioxide. The copper produced is purified further by **electro-refining***. It is an unreactive metal and only **tarnishes*** very slowly in air to form a thin, green surface film of **basic copper sulphate (CuSO$_4$.3Cu(OH)$_2$)**. Copper is below hydrogen in the **electrochemical series***. It does not react with water, dilute acids or alkalis. However, it does react with concentrated nitric or concentrated sulphuric acid. (See also page 104).

Copper is a very good conductor of electricity (although silver is better), so it is used to make wires for electric circuits.

It is used in **alloys*** such as **brass** (copper plus zinc) and **bronze** (copper plus tin) to make "copper" coins, and in an alloy with nickel to make "silver" coins.

Because it is soft but tough, it is used to make pipes for plumbing and central-heating systems.

An **alloy*** of copper and gold is used in jewellery. The greater the amount of copper, the less the number of carats (i.e. less than 24 carats (pure gold).

Copper(II) sulphate (CuSO$_4$) has many uses, e.g. in dyeing and **electroplating***. It is also used in **Bordeaux mixture**, which kills moulds growing on fruit and vegetables. (See also test for water, page 104.)

Copper(II) chloride (CuCl$_2$) is used in fireworks to give a green colour. It is also used to remove sulphur from **petroleum***.

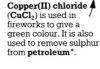

Copper(I) oxide (Cu$_2$O) is used to make glass and paint.

• **Copper(I)** or **cuprous compounds**. Compounds containing Cu$^+$ ions, e.g. **copper(I) oxide** (see left) and **copper(I) chloride (CuCl)**. Copper(I) compounds do not dissolve in water.

• **Copper(II)** or **cupric compounds**. Compounds that contain Cu^{2+} ions, e.g. **copper(II) sulphate** and **copper(II) chloride** (see left). Copper(II) compounds dissolve in water to form light blue solutions, and are much more common than **copper(I) compounds**.

• **Zinc (Zn)**. An element in Period 4 of the periodic table. It is a silvery, soft metal which **tarnishes*** in air. It is too reactive to occur naturally, and its main ores are **zinc blende (ZnS)**, **calamine (ZnCO$_3$)** and **zincite (ZnO)**. The zinc is extracted by roasting the ore to form **zinc oxide (ZnO)** and then **reducing*** it by heating it with coke. Zinc is above hydrogen in the **electrochemical series***. It reacts with oxygen, with steam when red-hot, and with acids. It is used to coat iron and steel to prevent rust (**galvanizing** – see also page 60 and **sacrificial protection**, page 45). It is also used in **alloys***, particularly **brass** (copper and zinc).

Zinc oxide is used in a cream as a protection against skin irritation, e.g. nappy rash.

Zinc is used in batteries.

* **Alloy**, 114; **Electrochemical series**, 45; **Electroplating, Electro-refining**, 43; **Petroleum**, 84; **Reduction**, 34; **Tarnish**, 115; **Transition metals**, 58.

Group III elements

The elements in **Group III** of the periodic table are generally not as reactive as the elements in Groups I and II. Unlike those elements they show no overall trend in reactivity and the first member of the group is a non-metal. The chart below shows some of their properties.

Some properties of Group III elements

Name of element	Chemical symbol	Relative atomic mass*	Electron configuration*	Reactivity	Appearance	Uses
Boron	B	10.81	2,3	N O T R E N D	Brown powder or yellow crystals	In **control rods***, glass and to harden steel
Aluminium	Al	26.98	2,8,3		White metal	See below
Gallium	Ga	69.72	Complex configuration but still 3 outer electrons		Silver-white metal	In **semiconductors***
Indium	In	114.82			Soft silver-white metal	In **control rods*** and transparent electrodes
Thallium	Tl	204.37			Soft silver-white metal	In rat poison

Although all atoms of Group III elements have three outer electrons they react to form different types of compound. Those of **boron**, and some of **aluminium**, are **covalent***. Other members of the group form mostly **ionic compounds***.

Boron oxide (B$_2$O$_3$) is added to glass to make special glassware which can be heated or cooled rapidly without cracking.

More information on **aluminium** and its compounds can be found below. Aluminium is the most widely used member of this group.

- **Aluminium (Al)**. A member of Group III of the periodic table. It is the commonest metal found on earth, and occurs naturally in many compounds, e.g. **bauxite** (see **aluminium oxide**) from which it is extracted by **electrolysis***. It is hard, light, **ductile***, **malleable*** and a good conductor of heat and electricity. It reacts with the oxygen in air to form a surface layer of **aluminium oxide** which stops further corrosion. It also reacts with chlorine, dilute acids and alkalis.

Some uses of **aluminium** and its **alloys***:

Powerlines are aluminium as aluminium conducts electricity better for its weight than copper.

Thin sheets of aluminium are used to wrap food, e.g. chocolate bars. It is also used to make fizzy drink cans.

Its light weight makes it ideal for making many things, from aircraft to ladders.

- **Aluminium oxide (Al$_2$O$_3$)** or **alumina**. An **amphoteric***, white solid that is almost insoluble in water. It occurs naturally as **bauxite (Al$_2$O$_3$.2H$_2$O** – see also **aluminium**) and as **corundum (Al$_2$O$_3$)** – an extremely hard crystalline solid. It is used in some cements, and to line furnaces.

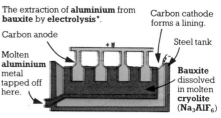

The extraction of **aluminium** from **bauxite** by **electrolysis***.

Carbon anode

Molten **aluminium** metal tapped off here.

Carbon cathode forms a lining.

Steel tank

Bauxite dissolved in molten **cryolite (Na$_3$AlF$_6$)**

- **Aluminium hydroxide (Al(OH)$_3$)**. A white, slightly water-soluble, **amphoteric*** solid, which is used in dyeing cloth, to make ceramics and as an **antacid***.

- **Aluminium sulphate (Al$_2$(SO$_4$)$_3$)**. A white, water-soluble, crystalline solid used to purify water and make paper.

* Alloy, 114; Amphoteric, 37; Antacid, 114; Control rods, 114; Covalent compounds, 18; Ductile, 114; Electrolysis, 42; Electron configuration, 13; Ionic compound, 17; Malleable, 115; Relative atomic mass, 24; Semiconductor, 115.

Group IV elements

The elements in **Group IV** of the periodic table are generally not very reactive and the members show increasing metallic properties going down the group. For more about the properties of these elements, see the chart below, **silicon** and **lead** (this page) and **carbon**, pages 64-65.

Some properties of Group IV elements						
Name of element	Chemical symbol	Relative atomic mass*	Electron configuration*	Reactivity	Appearance	Uses
Carbon	C	12.01	2,4		Solid non-metal (see pages 64-65)	See page 64
Silicon	Si	20.09	2,8,4	NO TREND	Shiny, grey metalloid* solid	See below
Germanium	Ge	72.59	Complex configuration but still 4 outer electrons		Greyish-white metalloid* solid	In transistors
Tin	Sn	118.69			Soft silver-white metal	Tin plating, e.g. food containers
Lead	Pb	207.19			Soft silver-grey metal	See below

•**Silicon (Si).** A member of Group IV of the periodic table. It is a hard, shiny, grey **metalloid*** with a high melting point. Silicon is the second most common element in the Earth's crust - it is found in sand and rocks as **silicon dioxide** and **silicates**. When it is ground into a powder it reacts with some alkalis and elements, otherwise it is generally unreactive.

> Although all atoms of Group IV elements have four outer electrons they react to form different compound types. They all form **covalent compounds***, but **tin** and **lead** form **ionic compounds*** as well.

Silicon is a **semiconductor*** and is used to make silicon chips – complete microelectronic circuits.

•**Silicon dioxide (SiO₂).** Also called **silicon(IV) oxide**, or **silica**. An insoluble, white, crystalline solid. It occurs in many forms, such as **flint** and **quartz**. It is acidic and reacts with concentrated alkalis.

Silicon dioxide has many uses, e.g. in the making of glass and ceramics.

Quartz crystals are used in watches.

Sand is impure quartz.

•**Silicates. Silicon** compounds that also contain a metal and oxygen, e.g. **calcium metasilicate (CaSiO₃)**, and make up most of the earth's crust. They are used to make glass and ceramics.

•**Silicones.** Complex, man-made compounds contaning very long chains of **silicon** and oxygen atoms.

Silicones are used in high-performance oils and greases and for non-stick surfaces. They are also used in waxes, polishes and varnishes as they are water-repellant.

•**Lead (Pb).** A member of Group IV of the periodic table. A soft, **malleable*** metal extracted from **galena (lead(II) sulphide)**. It is not very reactive, though it **tarnishes*** in air, reacts slightly with **soft water*** and slowly with chlorine and nitric acid. It forms **ionic compounds*** called **lead(II)** or **plumbous compounds**, e.g. **lead(II) oxide (PbO)**, and **covalent compounds*** called **lead(IV)** or **plumbic compounds**, e.g. **lead(IV) oxide (PbO₂)**.

X-ray machine

Lead has many uses, e.g. in car batteries and roofing. It is used in hospitals to protect people from the harmful effects of X-rays.

The lead inside this rubber apron protects the radiologist.

---

* Covalent compounds, 18; Electron configuration, 13; Ionic compounds, 17; Malleable, 115; Metalloids, 51 (Metal); Relative atomic mass, 24; Semiconductor, 115; Soft water, 93 (Hard water); Tarnish, 115.

Carbon

Carbon (C) is a member of Group IV of the periodic table (see also chart, page 62). It is a non-metal and has two **allotropes*** – **diamond** and **graphite** – and an **amorphous*** (unstructured) form – **charcoal**. Carbon is not very reactive. It only reacts with steam when heated, and with hot, **concentrated*** sulphuric or nitric acids (see equation below).

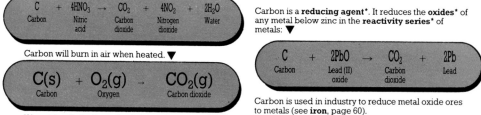

$$C + 4HNO_3 \rightarrow CO_2 + 4NO_2 + 2H_2O$$

Carbon · Nitric acid · Carbon dioxide · Nitrogen dioxide · Water

Carbon is a **reducing agent***. It reduces the **oxides*** of any metal below zinc in the **reactivity series*** of metals: ▼

Carbon will burn in air when heated. ▼

$$C(s) + O_2(g) \rightarrow CO_2(g)$$

Carbon · Oxygen · Carbon dioxide

$$C + 2PbO \rightarrow CO_2 + 2Pb$$

Carbon · Lead (II) oxide · Carbon dioxide · Lead

Carbon is used in industry to reduce metal oxide ores to metals (see **iron**, page 60).

If burnt in a limited supply of air, **carbon monoxide** forms.

Carbon atoms can bond with up to four other atoms, including other carbon atoms. As a result there are a vast number of carbon-based compounds (**organic compounds** – see page 76). Living tissue is made of carbon compounds and animals break down these carbon compounds to liberate energy (see **carbon cycle**, page 95).

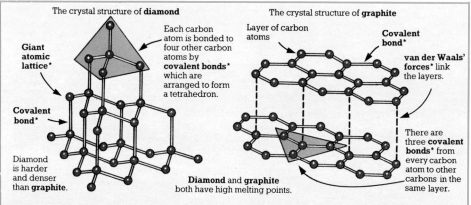

The crystal structure of **diamond**

Giant atomic lattice*

Covalent bond*

Diamond is harder and denser than **graphite**.

Each carbon atom is bonded to four other carbon atoms by **covalent bonds*** which are arranged to form a tetrahedron.

Diamond and **graphite** both have high melting points.

The crystal structure of **graphite**

Layer of carbon atoms

Covalent bond*

van der Waals' forces* link the layers.

There are three **covalent bonds*** from every carbon atom to other carbons in the same layer.

- **Diamond.** A crystalline, transparent form of carbon. It is the hardest naturally-occurring substance. All the carbon atoms are joined by strong **covalent bonds*** – accounting for its hardness and high melting point (3750°C). Diamonds are used as record player styli, **abrasives***, glass cutters, jewellery and on drill bits. **Synthetic diamonds** are made by subjecting **graphite** to high pressure and temperature, a very costly process.

- **Graphite.** A grey, crystalline form of carbon. The atoms in each layer are joined by strong **covalent bonds***, but the layers are only linked by weak **van der Waals' forces*** which allow them to slide over each other, making graphite soft and flaky. Graphite is the only non-metal to conduct electricity well. It also conducts heat. It is used as a lubricant, in **electrolysis*** (as **inert electrodes***), as contacts in electric motors, and in pencil leads.

* **Abrasive**, 114; **Allotropes**, 22 (**Allotropy**); **Amorphous**, 21; **Concentrated**, 30; **Covalent bond**, 18; **Electrolysis**, 42; **Giant atomic lattice**, 23; **Inert electrode**, 42; **Oxides**, 69; **Reactivity series**, 44; **Reducing agent**, 34; **van der Waals' forces**, 20.

- **Coal**. A hard, black solid formed over millions of years from the fossilized remains of plant material. It is mainly carbon, but contains hydrogen, oxygen, nitrogen and sulphur as well. Three types of coal exist – **lignite**, **anthracite** and **bituminous coal**. Coal is used as a fuel in power stations, industry and homes. It also used to be an important source of chemicals (produced by **destructive distillation of coal** – see below) but these are now mostly produced from **petroleum***

This picture shows the products of the **destructive distillation of coal**, achieved by heating coal in the absence of air.

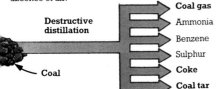

Destructive distillation

Coal

Coal gas
Ammonia
Benzene
Sulphur
Coke
Coal tar

- **Carbon fibres**. Black silky threads of pure carbon made from organic textile fibres. They are stronger and stiffer than other materials of the same weight and are used to make light boats.

- **Coke**. A greyish, porous, brittle solid containing over 80% carbon. It is made by heating **coal** in the absence of air in coke ovens, or as a by-product of making **coal gas** (see **carbon monoxide**). It is a smokeless fuel.

- **Charcoal**. A porous, black, **amorphous***, impure form of carbon. It is made by heating organic material in the absence of air.

Some uses of **charcoal**

Charcoal is used by artists for drawing.

Activated charcoal absorbs small molecules onto its surface. It is used in shoe lining pads to absorb odours.

Charcoal is used as a smokeless fuel, e.g. at barbecues.

- **Carbon dioxide** (CO_2). A colourless, odourless gas found in the atmosphere (see **carbon cycle**, page 95). It is made industrially by heating calcium carbonate in a lime kiln (see also page 102 for preparation). It dissolves in water to form **carbonic acid** (H_2CO_3).

$$CO_2(aq) + H_2O(l) \rightleftharpoons 2H^+(aq) + CO_3^{2-}(aq)$$
Carbon dioxide   Water   Carbonic acid

Carbon dioxide is not very reactive, though it reacts with both sodium and calcium hydroxide solutions (see page 104) and magnesium ribbon burns in it.

Carbon dioxide has many uses.

It is used to make drinks fizzy. Carbon dioxide escapes when the can is opened, as the pressure is released.

It is used in fire extinguishers. It forms a blanket over the flames and does not allow air to reach the fire.

- **Carbon monoxide** (**CO**). A poisonous, colourless, odourless gas, made by passing **carbon dioxide** over hot carbon, and also by burning carbon fuels in a limited supply of air. It is not water-soluble, burns with a blue flame and is a **reducing agent*** (used to reduce metal oxide ores to metal, see **iron**, page 60). It is also used, mixed with other gases, in fuels, e.g. mixed with hydrogen in **water gas**, with nitrogen in **producer gas**, and with hydrogen (50%), methane and other gases in **coal gas**.

If there is not enough oxygen, the **carbon monoxide** produced when fuel is burnt is not changed to **carbon dioxide**. When a car engine runs in a closed garage carbon monoxide accumulates.

- **Carbonates**. Compounds made of a metal **cation*** and a **carbonate anion*** (CO_3^{2-}), e.g. **calcium carbonate** ($CaCO_3$). Except Group I carbonates, they are insoluble in water and decompose on heating. They all react with acids to give off **carbon dioxide**.

Group V elements

The elements in **Group V** of the periodic table become increasingly metallic going down the group, see chart below.

Some properties of Group V elements						
Name of element	Chemical symbol	Relative atomic mass*	Electron configuration*	Reactivity	Appearance	Uses
Nitrogen	N	14.00	2,5	I N C R E A S I N G ↓	Colourless gas	See below.
Phosphorus	P	30.97	2,8,5		Non-metallic solid, see page 69.	See page 68.
Arsenic	As	74.92	Complex configuration but still 5 outer electrons		3 **allotropes***, one of which is metallic.	In **semiconductors*** and **alloys**
Antimony	Sb	121.75			Silver-white metal	In type metal and other **alloys**
Bismuth	Bi	208.98			White metal with reddish tinge	In low melting point **alloys** and medicines

More information on **nitrogen**, **phosphorus** and their compounds can be found below and on pages 67-68. They are the two most abundant members of the group.

All the atoms of Group V elements have five electrons in their **outer shell***. They all react to form **covalent compounds*** in which they share three of these electrons with three from another atom, or atoms (see **octet**, page 13). **Antimony**, **bismuth** and **nitrogen** also form **ionic compounds***.

- **Nitrogen (N₂)**. A member of Group V of the periodic table. A colourless, odourless, **diatomic*** gas that makes up 78% of the atmosphere. It can be produced by **fractional distillation of liquid air*** (but see also page 103). Its **oxidation state*** in compounds varies from -3 to +5. It reacts with a few reactive metals to form **nitrides**.

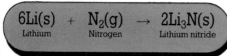

$$6\text{Li(s)} + \text{N}_2\text{(g)} \rightarrow 2\text{Li}_3\text{N(s)}$$
Lithium   Nitrogen   Lithium nitride

Nitrogen is essential for all organisms as it is found in molecules in living cells, e.g. proteins (see also **nitrogen cycle**, page 95). It is used in the manufacture of **ammonia** (see **Haber process**) and nitric acid. **Liquid nitrogen**, which exists below $-196°C$, has many uses including freezing food.

Packets of crisps are filled with **nitrogen** gas to keep them fresh longer (when air is left in the packet the crisps go stale). The gas in the packet also cushions the crisps against damage in transport.

- **Haber process**. This process is used to make **ammonia** from **nitrogen** and hydrogen which are reacted in a ratio of 1:3. Ammonia is produced as fast and economically as possible by using a suitable temperature, pressure and **catalyst*** (see below). The reaction is **exothermic*** and **reversible***.

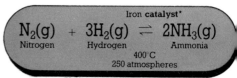

$$\text{N}_2\text{(g)} + 3\text{H}_2\text{(g)} \rightleftharpoons 2\text{NH}_3\text{(g)}$$
Nitrogen   Hydrogen   Ammonia
Iron **catalyst***
400°C
250 atmospheres

(Under these conditions 15% of the reactants combine to form **ammonia**.)

Haber process

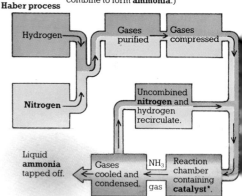

* **Allotropes**, 22 (**Allotropy**); **Alloy**, 114; **Catalyst**, 47; **Covalent compounds**, 18; **Diatomic**, 10; **Electron configuration**, 13; **Exothermic reaction**, 33; **Fractional distillation of liquid air**, 69; **Ionic compound**, 17; **Outer shell**, 13; **Oxidation state**, 35; **Relative atomic mass**, 24; **Reversible reaction**, 48; **Semiconductor**, 115.

- **Ammonia (NH$_3$).** A colourless, strong-smelling gas that is less dense than air and is a **covalent compound*** made by the **Haber process**. It is a **reducing agent*** and the only common gas to form an alkaline solution in water – this solution is known as **ammonia solution (NH$_4$OH)** or **ammonium hydroxide**. Ammonia burns in pure oxygen to give nitrogen and water, and reacts with chlorine to give **ammonium chloride**.

Ammonia is used to make nitric acid, fertilizers, plastics, explosives and household cleaners.

- **Ammonium chloride (NH$_4$Cl)** or **sal ammoniac**. A white, water-soluble, crystalline solid made when **ammonia solution** (see **ammonia**) reacts with dilute hydrochloric acid. When heated it **sublimes*** and **dissociates*** (see equation below and page 48). It is used in the dry batteries which run many electrical appliances.

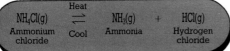

$$NH_4Cl(g) \underset{Cool}{\overset{Heat}{\rightleftharpoons}} NH_3(g) + HCl(g)$$

Ammonium chloride — Ammonia — Hydrogen chloride

- **Ammonium sulphate ((NH$_4$)$_2$SO$_4$).** A white, water-soluble, crystalline solid produced by the reaction of **ammonia** and sulphuric acid. It is a fertilizer.

- **Ammonium nitrate (NH$_4$NO$_3$).** A white, water-soluble, crystalline solid formed when **ammonia solution** (see **ammonia**) reacts with dilute nitric acid. It gives off dinitrogen oxide when heated.

Ammonium nitrate is used in explosives and fertilizers. It is also found in mixtures used to feed pot plants.

- **Dinitrogen oxide (N$_2$O).** Also called **nitrous oxide** or **laughing gas**. A colourless, slightly sweet-smelling, water-soluble gas. It is a **covalent compound*** formed by gently heating **ammonium nitrate**. It supports the combustion of some reactive substances and relights a glowing splint.

Dinitrogen oxide is used as an anaesthetic by both dentists (see **halothane***) and hospital anaesthetists.

- **Nitrogen monoxide (NO).** Also called **nitric oxide** or **nitrogen oxide**. A colourless gas that is insoluble in water. It is a **covalent compound*** made when copper reacts with 50% concentrated nitric acid. It reacts with oxygen to form **nitrogen dioxide** and also supports the combustion of reactive elements.

- **Nitrogen dioxide (NO$_2$).** A very dark brown gas with a choking smell. It is a **covalent compound***.

$$Cu + 4HNO_3 \rightarrow Cu(NO_3)_2 + 2H_2O + 2NO_2$$

Copper — Concentrated nitric acid — Copper(II) nitrate — Water — Nitrogen dioxide

Nitrogen dioxide is made when copper reacts with concentrated nitric acid and when some **nitrates*** are heated. It supports combustion and dissolves in water to give a mixture of nitric acid and **nitrous acid (HNO$_2$)**. It is used as an **oxidizing agent***.

Nitrogen dioxide dimerizes (two molecules of the same substance bond together) below 21.5°C to form **dinitrogen tetraoxide (N$_2$O$_4$)**, a colourless gas.

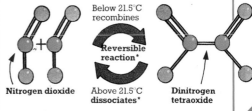

Below 21.5°C recombines

Reversible reaction*

Nitrogen dioxide — Above 21.5°C dissociates* — Dinitrogen tetraoxide

* Covalent compounds, 18; Dissociation, 48; Halothane, 81; Nitrates, 68; Oxidizing agent, Reducing agent, 34; Reversible reaction, 48; Sublimation, 7.

67

Group V continued

●**Nitric acid (HNO$_3$)** or **nitric(V) acid**. A light yellow, oily, water-soluble liquid. It is a **covalent compound*** containing nitrogen in **oxidation state*** +5. It is a very strong and corrosive acid which is made industrially by the three-stage **Ostwald process**. This process is shown below:

Stage 1: Ammonia reacts with oxygen.

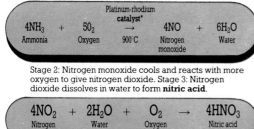

$$4NH_3 + 5O_2 \xrightarrow[900°C]{\text{Platinum-rhodium catalyst*}} 4NO + 6H_2O$$

Ammonia — Oxygen — Nitrogen monoxide — Water

Stage 2: Nitrogen monoxide cools and reacts with more oxygen to give nitrogen dioxide. Stage 3: Nitrogen dioxide dissolves in water to form **nitric acid**.

$$4NO_2 + 2H_2O + O_2 \rightarrow 4HNO_3$$

Nitrogen dioxide — Water — Oxygen — Nitric acid

Concentrated nitric acid is a mixture of 70% nitric acid and 30% water. It is a powerful **oxidizing agent***. **Dilute nitric acid** is a solution of 10% nitric acid in water. It reacts with **bases*** to give **nitrate salts*** and water. Nitric acid is used to make fertilizers and explosives.

A mixture of concentrated hydrochloric acid and **concentrated nitric acid**, called **aqua regia** (Latin for King's water), will dissolve gold.

●**Nitrates** or **nitrate(V) compounds**. Solid **ionic compounds*** containing the **nitrate anion*** (NO$_3^-$) and a metal **cation*** (see test for nitrate ion, page 104). Nitrogen in a nitrate ion has an **oxidation state*** of +5. Nitrates are **salts*** of **nitric acid** and are made by adding a metal oxide, hydroxide or carbonate to **dilute nitric acid**. All nitrates are water-soluble and most give off nitrogen dioxide and oxygen on heating (some exceptions are sodium, potassium and ammonium nitrates).

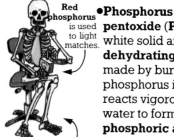

Sodium nitrate (**NaNO$_3$**) is used to make gunpowder.

Sodium and ammonium nitrates are used as fertilizers.

●**Nitrites** or **nitrite(III) compounds**. Solid ionic compounds* that contain the **nitrite anion*** (NO$_2^-$) and metal **cation***. They are usually **reducing agents***.

Sodium nitrite (**NaNO$_2$**) is used to preserve meat products.

●**Phosphorus (P)**. A non-metallic member of Group V (see chart, page 66). Phosphorus only occurs naturally in compounds. Its main ore is **apatite** (**3Ca$_3$(PO$_4$)$_2$.CaF$_2$**). It has two common forms. **White phosphorus**, the most reactive form, is a poisonous, waxy, white solid that bursts into flames in air. **Red phosphorus** is a dark red powder that is not poisonous and not very flammable.

Red phosphorus is used to light matches.

Living organisms contain **phosphorus compounds**, e.g. bones are mainly **calcium phosphate**.

●**Phosphorus pentoxide (P$_2$O$_5$)**. A white solid and **dehydrating agent***, made by burning phosphorus in air. It reacts vigorously with water to form **phosphoric acid** (**H$_3$PO$_4$**) and is used to protect against **rust***.

* Anion, 16; Base, 37; Catalyst, 47; Cation, 16; Covalent compounds, 18; Dehydrating agent, 114; Ionic compound, 17; Oxidation state, 35; Oxidizing agent, Reducing agent, 34; Rust, 60; Salts, 39.

Group VI elements

The elements in **Group VI** of the periodic table show increasing metallic properties and decreasing chemical reactivity going down the group. The chart below shows some of the properties of these elements.

Name of element	Chemical symbol	Relative atomic mass*	Electron configuration*	Reactivity	Appearance	Uses
Oxygen	O	15.99	2,6	D E C R E A S I N G	Colourless gas, see below	See below
Sulphur	S	32.06	2,8,6		Yellow, non-metallic solid, see page 70	See page 70
Selenium	Se	78.96	Complex configuration but still 6 outer electrons		Several forms, metallic and non-metallic	In photocells*
Tellurium	Te	127.60			Silver-white metalloid* solid	In alloys*, coloured glass, semiconductors*
Polonium	Po	Radioactive* element			Metal	

Some properties of Group VI elements

More information on **oxygen**, **sulphur** and their compounds can be found below and on pages 70-71. They are found widely and have many uses.

> The atoms of all the elements in Group VI have six electrons in their **outer shell***. They need two electrons to fill their outer shell (see **octet**, page 13) and react with other substances to form both **ionic*** and **covalent compounds***. The elements with the smallest atoms are most reactive, as the atoms produce the most powerful attraction for the two electrons.

- **Oxygen (O_2).** A colourless, odourless, **diatomic*** gas that makes up 21% of the atmosphere. It is the most abundant element in the Earth's crust and is vital for life (see **respiration**, page 95). It supports combustion, dissolves in water to form a **neutral*** solution and is a very reactive **oxidizing agent***, e.g. it oxidizes iron to iron(III) oxide. Plants produce oxygen by photosynthesis and it is obtained industrially by **fractional distillation of liquid air**. It has many uses, e.g. in hospitals and to break down sewage. See test for, and preparation of, oxygen, pages 103 and 105.

- **Ozone (O_3).** A poisonous, bluish gas whose molecules contain three **oxygen** atoms. It is an **allotrope*** of oxygen, found in the upper atmosphere where it absorbs most of the sun's harmful ultra-violet radiation. It is produced when electrical sparks pass through air, e.g. when lightning occurs. Ozone is a powerful **oxidizing agent*** and is sometimes used to sterilize water.

Fractional distillation of liquid air (see also page 106).

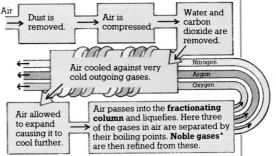

Air → Dust is removed. → Air is compressed. → Water and carbon dioxide are removed.

Air cooled against very cold outgoing gases.

Air allowed to expand causing it to cool further.

Air passes into the **fractionating column** and liquefies. Here three of the gases in air are separated by their boiling points. **Noble gases*** are then refined from these.

Nitrogen / Argon / Oxygen

- **Oxides.** Compounds of oxygen and one other element. Metal oxides are mostly **ionic compounds*** and **bases***, e.g. **calcium oxide (CaO)**. Some metal and **metalloid*** oxides are **amphoteric***, e.g. **aluminium oxide (Al_2O_3)**. Non-metal oxides are **covalent*** and often **acidic***, e.g. **carbon dioxide (CO_2)**.

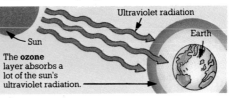

Ultraviolet radiation

Sun

Earth

The **ozone** layer absorbs a lot of the sun's ultraviolet radiation.

* Acidic, 36; Allotropes, 22 (Allotropy); Alloy, 114; Amphoteric, Base, 37; Covalent compounds, 18; Diatomic, 10; Electron configuration, 13; Ionic compound, 17; Metalloids, 51 (Metal); Neutral, 37; Noble gases, 75; Outer shell, 13; Oxidizing agent, 34; Photocell, 115; Radioactivity, 14; Relative atomic mass, 24; Semiconductor, 115.

Sulphur

Sulphur (S) is a member of **Group VI** of the periodic table (see chart, page 69). It is a yellow non-metallic solid that is insoluble in water. It is **polymorphic*** and has two **allotropes*** – **rhombic** and **monoclinic sulphur**. Sulphur is found uncombined in underground deposits (see **Frasch process**) and is also extracted from **petroleum*** and metal **sulphides** (compounds of sulphur and another element), e.g. **iron(II) sulphide (FeS)**. It burns in air with a blue flame to form **sulphur dioxide** and reacts with many metals to form sulphides. It is used to **vulcanize*** rubber, and to make **sulphuric acid**, medicines and **fungicides***.

●**Rhombic sulphur.** Also called **alpha sulphur (α-sulphur)** or **orthorhombic sulphur**. A pale yellow, crystalline **allotrope*** of sulphur, the most stable form at room temperature.

●**Monoclinic sulphur** or **beta sulphur (β-sulphur)**. A yellow, crystalline, **allotrope*** of sulphur. It is more stable than **rhombic sulphur** at temperatures over 96°C.

Crystal of **rhombic sulphur** (see also page 22).

Molecular lattice* of sulphur rings (arranged differently to **monoclinic sulphur**).

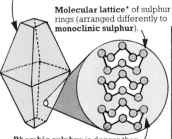

Both **rhombic** and **monoclinic sulphur** are made of puckered rings of eight sulphur atoms.

Sulphur atom

Covalent bond*

At temperatures above 96°C

At temperatures below 96°C

Rhombic sulphur is denser than **monoclinic sulphur** as the sulphur rings are more tightly packed together.

Crystal of **monoclinic sulphur** (long, thin and angular)

The sulphur rings are arranged in a **molecular lattice***, but in a different way to **rhombic sulphur**.

●**Plastic sulphur.** A form of sulphur made when hot liquid sulphur is poured into water to cool it quickly. It can be kneaded and stretched into long fibres. It is not stable and hardens when rings of eight sulphur atoms reform (see above).

●**Flowers of sulphur.** A fine yellow powder formed when sulphur vapour is cooled quickly. The molecules are in rings of eight atoms.

●**Frasch process.** The method used to extract sulphur from underground deposits by melting it. Sulphur produced this way is 99.5% pure.

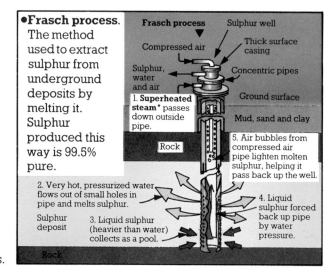

Frasch process

Sulphur well

Compressed air

Thick surface casing

Sulphur, water and air

Concentric pipes

1. **Superheated steam*** passes down outside pipe.

Ground surface

Mud, sand and clay

Rock

5. Air bubbles from compressed air pipe lighten molten sulphur, helping it pass back up the well.

2. Very hot, pressurized water flows out of small holes in pipe and melts sulphur.

Sulphur deposit

3. Liquid sulphur (heavier than water) collects as a pool.

4. Liquid sulphur forced back up pipe by water pressure.

Rock

*Allotropes, 22 (Allotropy); Covalent bond, 18; Fungicides, 114; Molecular lattice, 23; Petroleum, 84; Polymorphism, 22; Superheated steam, Vulcanization, 115.

- **Sulphur dioxide (SO_2)** or **sulphur(IV) oxide**. A poisonous, choking gas which forms **sulphurous acid** when dissolved in water. It is a **covalent compound*** made by burning sulphur in air or adding dilute acid to a **sulphite**. It usually acts as a **reducing agent***. It is used to make **sulphuric acid**, in **fumigation*** and as a **bleach***.

Sulphur dioxide is used to preserve many food products containing fruit.

- **Sulphur trioxide (SO_3)** or **sulphur(VI) oxide**. A white **volatile*** solid that is formed by the **contact process**. Sulphur trioxide reacts very vigorously with water to form **sulphuric acid**.

- **Sulphurous acid (H_2SO_3)** or **sulphuric(IV) acid**. A colourless, **weak acid***, formed when **sulphur dioxide** dissolves in water.

- **Hydrogen sulphide (H_2S)**. A colourless, poisonous gas, smelling of bad eggs. It dissolves in water to form a **weak acid***. It is given off when organic matter rots and when a dilute acid is added to a metal sulphide.

- **Sulphates** or **sulphate(VI) compounds**. Solid **ionic compounds*** that contain a **sulphate ion (SO_4^{2-})** and a **cation***. Many occur naturally, e.g. **calcium sulphate ($CaSO_4$)**. They are **salts*** of **sulphuric acid**, made by adding **bases*** to dilute sulphuric acid.

Sodium sulphate solution is used to "fix" photographs. This process stops prints going completely black when exposed to light.

- **Sulphites** or **sulphate(IV) compounds**. Ionic compounds* containing a **sulphite ion (SO_3^{2-})** and a metal **cation*** e.g. **sodium sulphite (Na_2SO_3)**. They are **salts*** of **sulphurous acid**, and react with dilute **strong acids*** giving off **sulphur dioxide**.

- **Sulphuric acid (H_2SO_4)** or **sulphuric(VI) acid**. An oily, colourless, corrosive liquid. It is a **dibasic*** acid, made by the **contact process**. **Concentrated sulphuric acid** contains about 2% water, is **hygroscopic*** and a powerful **oxidizing** and **dehydrating agent***. **Dilute sulphuric acid**, a **strong acid***, contains about 90% water. It reacts with metals above hydrogen in the **electrochemical series*** to give the metal **sulphate** and hydrogen.

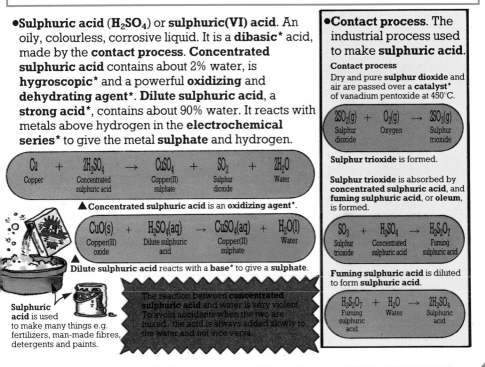

$$Cu + 2H_2SO_4 \rightarrow CuSO_4 + SO_2 + 2H_2O$$

Copper + Concentrated sulphuric acid → Copper(II) sulphate + Sulphur dioxide + Water

▲ Concentrated sulphuric acid is an **oxidizing agent***.

$$CuO(s) + H_2SO_4(aq) \rightarrow CuSO_4(aq) + H_2O(l)$$

Copper(II) oxide + Dilute sulphuric acid → Copper(II) sulphate + Water

Dilute sulphuric acid reacts with a **base*** to give a **sulphate**.

Sulphuric acid is used to make many things e.g. fertilizers, man-made fibres, detergents and paints.

The reaction between concentrated sulphuric acid and water is very violent. To avoid accidents when the two are mixed, the acid is always added slowly to the water and not vice versa.

- **Contact process**. The industrial process used to make **sulphuric acid**.

Contact process

Dry and pure **sulphur dioxide** and air are passed over a **catalyst*** of vanadium pentoxide at 450°C.

$$2SO_2(g) + O_2(g) \rightarrow 2SO_3(g)$$

Sulphur dioxide + Oxygen → Sulphur trioxide

Sulphur trioxide is formed.

Sulphur trioxide is absorbed by **concentrated sulphuric acid**, and **fuming sulphuric acid**, or **oleum**, is formed.

$$SO_3 + H_2SO_4 \rightarrow H_2S_2O_7$$

Sulphur trioxide + Concentrated sulphuric acid → Fuming sulphuric acid

Fuming sulphuric acid is diluted to form **sulphuric acid**.

$$H_2S_2O_7 + H_2O \rightarrow 2H_2SO_4$$

Fuming sulphuric acid + Water → Sulphuric acid

Group VII, the halogens

The elements in **Group VII** of the periodic table are called the **halogens**, and their compounds and ions are generally known as **halides**. Group VII members are all non-metals and their reactivity decreases going down the group – the chart below shows some of their properties. For further information on members of the group see below and pages 73-74.

Some properties of Group VII elements						
Name of element	Chemical symbol	Relative atomic mass*	Electron configuration*	Oxidizing* power	Reactivity	Appearance
Fluorine	F	18.99	2,7	D E C R E A S I N G	D E C R E A S I N G	Pale yellow -green gas
Chlorine	Cl	35.45	2,8,7			Pale green -yellow gas
Bromine	Br	79.91	2,8,18,7			Dark-red fuming liquid
Iodine	I	126.90	2,8,18,18,7			Non-metallic, black-grey solid
Astatine	At	No stable **isotope***				

The atoms of all the elements in Group VII contain seven electrons in their **outer shell*** and they all react to form both **ionic** and **covalent compounds***. The elements at the top of the group form more ionic compounds than those further down the group.

Fluorine is never used in school laboratories as it is very poisonous and attacks glass containers. **Chlorine**, **bromine** and **iodine** do not react with glass, but chlorine is very poisonous, and so are the gases given off by the other two.

The power of Group VII elements as **oxidizing agents*** decreases down the group. They can all oxidize the ions of any members below them in the group. For example, **chlorine** displaces both **bromide** and **iodide anions*** from solution by oxidizing them to **bromine** and **iodine** molecules respectively. Bromine only displaces iodide anions from solution and iodine cannot displace any halide anions from solution.

$$2KI(aq) + Br_2(l) \rightarrow 2KBr(aq) + I_2(s)$$

◄ **Bromine** displaces **iodide anions*** from potassium iodide. Each iodide anion loses an electron (is **oxidized***) when it is displaced by a **bromide anion***.

• **Fluorine (F$_2$).** A member of Group VII of the periodic table. It is a **diatomic*** gas, extracted from **fluorospar (CaF$_2$)** and **cryolite (Na$_3$AlF$_6$)**. It is the most reactive member of the group and is a very powerful **oxidizing agent***. It reacts with almost all elements. See pictures for some examples of its uses.

Fluorine reacts to form useful, stable **organic compounds***, called **fluorocarbons**, e.g. **poly(tetrafluoroethene)**, or **PTFE** (see also page 81). Pans are coated with PTFE because it stops food sticking, and skis are coated with PTFE to reduce friction.

Some **fluorides** (inorganic compounds of fluorine) are added to toothpastes, and in some countries to drinking water, to reduce tooth decay.

*Bromide anion, 74 (Bromides); Covalent compounds, 18; Diatomic, 10; Electron configuration, 13; Iodide anion, 74 (Iodides); Ionic compound, 17; Isotope, 13; Organic compounds, 76; Outer shell, 13; Oxidation, Oxidizing agent, 34; Relative atomic mass, 24.

●**Chlorine (Cl$_2$).** A member of Group VII of the periodic table. A poisonous, choking **diatomic*** gas which is very reactive and only occurs naturally in compounds. **Sodium chloride (NaCl)**, its most important compound, is found in rock salt and brine. Chlorine is extracted from brine by **electrolysis***, using the **Downs' cell** (see **sodium**, page 54 and also **chlorine**, page 102). It is a very strong **oxidizing agent***. Many elements react with chlorine to form **chlorides** (see equation below).

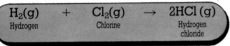

$$H_2(g) \quad + \quad Cl_2(g) \quad \rightarrow \quad 2HCl\,(g)$$

Hydrogen   Chlorine   Hydrogen chloride

▲ In sunlight this reaction is explosive.

Chlorine has many uses. It is used to make **hydrochloric acid** (see **hydrogen chloride**), some organic solvents and also as a **germicide*** in swimming pools.

It is also used as a germicide in drinking water and disinfectants.

●**Chlorides.** Compounds formed when **chlorine** combines with another element. Chlorides of non-metals (see **hydrogen chloride**) are **covalent compounds***, usually liquids or gases. Chlorides of metals, e.g. **sodium chloride (NaCl)**, are usually solid, water-soluble, **ionic compounds*** made of a **chloride anion*** (Cl⁻) and metal **cation***. See also page 104.

●**Hydrogen chloride (HCl).** A colourless, **covalent*** gas that forms ions when dissolved in a **polar solvent***. It is made by burning hydrogen in **chlorine**. It reacts with ammonia and dissolves in water to form **hydrochloric acid**, a **strong acid***. **Concentrated hydrochloric acid**, 35% hydrogen chloride and 65% water, is a fuming, corrosive and colourless solution. **Dilute hydrochloric acid**, about 7% hydrogen chloride and 93% water, is a colourless solution that reacts with **bases***, and with metals above hydrogen in the **electrochemical series***. Concentrated hydrochloric acid is used industrially to remove rust from steel sheets before they are **galvanized***.

Concentrated hydrochloric acid is used to etch metals.

Resin* covering metal.

Bath of **concentrated hydrochloric acid**

Line of metal exposed to acid.

The metal exposed to the acid is eaten away leaving a groove in the surface. When printing a picture the groove is filled with ink.

●**Sodium hypochlorite (NaOCl)** or **sodium chlorate(I).** A crystalline, white solid, stored dissolved in water, and formed when **chlorine** is added to a cold, dilute sodium hydroxide solution. It is used in domestic **bleach*** and also to bleach paper pulp white for writing.

●**Sodium chlorate (NaClO$_3$)** or **sodium chlorate(V).** A white, crystalline solid, formed when **chlorine** is added to warm concentrated sodium hydroxide, and also when **sodium hypochlorite** is warmed.

Sodium chlorate kills weeds.

---

* **Anion**, 16; **Base**, 37; **Bleach**, 114; **Cation**, 16; **Covalent compounds**, 18; **Diatomic**, 10; **Electrochemical series**, 45; **Electrolysis**, 42; **Galvanizing**, 60; **Ionic compound**, 17; **Oxidizing agent**, 34; **Polar solvent**, 30; **Resin**, 115; **Strong acid**, 38.

Halogens continued

●**Bromine (Br$_2$)**. A member of **Group VII** of the periodic table (the **halogens** – see chart, page 72). It is a **volatile***, **diatomic*** liquid that gives off a poisonous, choking vapour. It is very reactive and only occurs naturally in compounds e.g. those found in marine organisms, rocks, sea water and some inland lakes. It is extracted from **sodium bromide (NaBr)** in sea water by adding chlorine. Bromine is a strong **oxidizing agent***. It reacts with most elements to form **bromides**, and dissolves slightly in water to give an orange solution of **bromine water**. Bromine compounds are used in medicine, photography, and disinfectants. It is used to make **1,2-dibromoethane (CH$_2$BrCH$_2$Br)** which is added to petrol to stop lead accumulating in engines.

Silver bromide crystal

Silver bromide is used in photographic film. When exposed to light it decomposes to form silver.

Film — Lens — Sun

Before exposure to light

After exposure to light

In areas of film exposed to light the silver bromide decomposes to form silver which appears black.

In areas of the film not exposed to light the silver bromide is unaffected.

●**Bromides**. Compounds of bromine and one other element. Bromides of non-metals are **covalent compounds*** (see **hydrogen bromide**). Bromides of metals are usually **ionic compounds*** made of **bromide anions*** (Br$^-$) and metal **cations***. Excepting **silver bromide (AgBr)**, they are all water-soluble. See also page 104.

●**Hydrogen bromide (HBr)**. A colourless, pungent-smelling gas, made by the reaction of **bromine** with hydrogen. Its chemical properties are similar to those of hydrochloric acid.

●**Iodine (I$_2$)**. A member of **Group VII** of the periodic table (the **halogens** – see chart, page 72). A reactive, **diatomic***, crystalline solid. It is extracted from **sodium iodate (NaIO$_3$)** and seaweed. It is an **oxidizing agent*** and reacts with many elements to form **iodides**. When heated it **sublimes***, giving off a purple vapour. Iodine is only slightly soluble in pure water, however, it dissolves well in **potassium iodide (KI)** solution and also in some organic solvents.

Lack of **iodine** in the diet means that the thyroid gland cannot produce enough **thyroxin** hormone. Thyroxin is needed to regulate body metabolism. People with a thyroxin deficiency suffer from goitre.

The main food sources of **iodine** are sea food, cod liver oil, fruit and vegetables. Some table salt has iodine added to it.

Seaweed contains up to 0.5% **iodine** (by weight).

Tincture of iodine (**iodine** dissolved in ethanol) is used as an antiseptic for cuts.

●**Iodides**. Compounds of **iodine** and one other element. Iodides of non-metals are **covalent compounds*** (see **hydrogen iodide**). Iodides of metals are usually **ionic***, made of **iodide anions*** (I$^-$) and metal **cations***. Except **silver iodide (AgI)**, ionic iodides are water-soluble. See page 104.

●**Hydrogen iodide (HI)**. A colourless gas with a pungent smell. It is a **covalent compound***, formed when hydrogen and **iodine** react. It dissolves in water to give a strongly **acidic*** solution called **hydroiodic acid** (its chemical properties are similar to those of hydrochloric acid).

* Acidic, 36; Anion, Cation, 16; Covalent compounds, 18; Diatomic, 10; Ionic compound, 17; Oxidizing agent, 34; Sublimation, 7; Volatile, 115.

Group VIII, the noble gases

The **noble gases**, also called **inert** or **rare gases**, make up **Group VIII** of the periodic table, also called **Group 0**. They are all **monatomic*** gases, obtained by the **fractional distillation of liquid air***. Argon forms 0.9% of the air and the other gases occur in even smaller amounts. They are all unreactive because their atoms' **electron configuration*** is very stable (they all have a full **outer shell***). The lighter members do not form any compounds, but the heavier members form a few.

● **Helium (He).** The first member of Group VIII of the periodic table. It is a colourless, odourless, **monatomic*** gas found in the atmosphere (one part in 200,000) and in some natural gases in the USA. It is obtained by the **fractional distillation of liquid air*** and is completely unreactive, having no known compounds. It is used in airships and balloons, as it is eight times less dense than air and not inflammable, and also by deep-sea divers to avoid "the bends".

Helium-filled airship

● **Neon (Ne).** A member of Group VIII of the periodic table. A colourless, odourless **monatomic*** gas found in the atmosphere (one part in 55,000). It is obtained by the **fractional distillation of liquid air*** and is totally unreactive, having no known compounds. It is used in neon signs and fluorescent lighting as it emits an orange-red glow when an electric discharge passes through it at low pressure.

Neon sign

● **Radon (Rn).** The last member of Group VIII of the periodic table. It is **radioactive***, occurring as a result of the **radioactive decay*** of radium.

● **Argon (Ar).** The most abundant member of Group VIII of the periodic table. It is a colourless, odourless, **monatomic*** gas that makes up 0.9% of the air. Obtained by the **fractional distillation of liquid air***, it is totally unreactive, having no known compounds. It is used in electric light bulbs and fluorescent tubes.

Electric light bulb

● **Krypton (Kr).** A member of Group VIII of the periodic table. It is a colourless, odourless, **monatomic*** gas found in the atmosphere (one part in 670,000). It is obtained by the **fractional distillation of liquid air*** and is unreactive, only forming one known compound, **krypton fluoride (KrF$_2$).** Krypton is used in some lasers and in fluorescent tubes.

Krypton is used in the light bulbs on miners helmets.

● **Xenon (Xe).** A member of Group VIII of the periodic table. A colourless, odourless, **monatomic*** gas found in the atmosphere (0.006 parts per million). Obtained from the **fractional distillation of liquid air***, it is unreactive, forming only a very few compounds, e.g. **xenon tetrafluoride (XeF$_4$).** It is used to fill fluorescent tubes and light bulbs.

Xenon is used in some lighthouse light bulbs.

* **Electron configuration**, 13; **Fractional distillation of liquid air**, 69; **Monatomic**, 10; **Outer shell**, 13; **Radioactive decay**, **Radioactivity**, 14.

Organic chemistry

Originally **organic chemistry** was the study of chemicals found in living organisms. However, it now refers to the study of all carbon-containing compounds, except the **carbonates*** and the **oxides*** of carbon. There are well over two million such compounds (**organic compounds**), more than all the other chemical compounds added together. This vast number of **covalent compounds*** is possible because carbon atoms can bond with each other to make a huge variety of **chains** and **rings**.

●**Aliphatic compounds.** Organic compounds whose molecules contain a **main chain** of carbon atoms. The chain may be **straight**, **branched** or even in **ring** form (though never a benzene ring – see aromatic compounds).

Straight **chain** of carbon atoms in a butan-1-ol molecule. No carbon atom is bonded to more than two other carbons.

Main chain – the longest continuous chain of carbon atoms in the molecule.

Side chain – a shorter chain of carbon atoms coming off the main chain.

Branched chain of carbon atoms in a 3-methyl pentane molecule. In a branched chain a carbon atom may be bonded to more than two other carbon atoms.

Cyclohexane molecule. An example of a molecule containing a ring of carbon atoms.

●**Aromatic compounds.** Organic compounds whose molecules contain a **benzene ring**. A benzene ring has six carbon atoms but differs from an **aliphatic** ring because bonds between carbon atoms are neither **single** nor **double bonds*** but midway between both in length and reactivity.

There are two possible ways of representing a **benzene ring**.

or

The bonds linking the carbon atoms are midway between **single** and **double bonds*** because some electrons are free to move around the molecule.

●**Stereochemistry.** The study of the 3-dimensional (3-D) structure of molecules. Comparing the 3-D structure of very similar organic molecules, e.g. **stereoisomers**, helps distinguish between them. The 3-D structure of a molecule is often shown by a **stereochemical formula*** – a diagram that shows how atoms are arranged in space.

Structural formula* of methane. This simplified version of the molecule does not show the 3-D arrangement of the atoms.

Stereochemical formula* of methane.

Symbol for bond going into page.

Symbol for bond along plane of page.

Symbol for bond coming out of the page.

The carbon-hydrogen bonds are arranged to form a tetrahedron.

●**Isomers.** Two or more compounds with the same **molecular formula***, but different arrangements of atoms in their molecules. As a result the compounds have different properties. There are two main types of isomer, **structural isomers** and **stereoisomers**.

* Carbonates, 65; Covalent compounds, Double bond, 18; Molecular formula, 26; Oxides, 69; Single bond, 18; Stereochemical formula, Structural formula (shortened), 26.

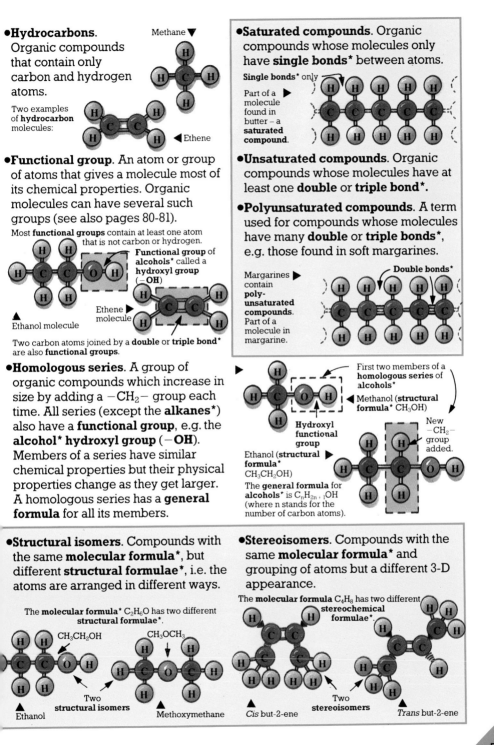

- **Hydrocarbons.** Organic compounds that contain only carbon and hydrogen atoms.

Methane ▼

Two examples of **hydrocarbon** molecules:

◄ Ethene

- **Functional group.** An atom or group of atoms that gives a molecule most of its chemical properties. Organic molecules can have several such groups (see also pages 80-81).

Most **functional groups** contain at least one atom that is not carbon or hydrogen.

Functional group of alcohols* called a hydroxyl group ($-OH$)

Ethene molecule ►

▲ Ethanol molecule

Two carbon atoms joined by a **double** or **triple bond*** are also **functional groups**.

- **Homologous series.** A group of organic compounds which increase in size by adding a $-CH_2-$ group each time. All series (except the **alkanes***) also have a **functional group**, e.g. the **alcohol* hydroxyl group** ($-OH$). Members of a series have similar chemical properties but their physical properties change as they get larger. A homologous series has a **general formula** for all its members.

- **Saturated compounds.** Organic compounds whose molecules only have **single bonds*** between atoms.

Single bonds* only

Part of a ► molecule found in butter – a **saturated compound.**

- **Unsaturated compounds.** Organic compounds whose molecules have at least one **double** or **triple bond***.

- **Polyunsaturated compounds.** A term used for compounds whose molecules have many **double** or **triple bonds***, e.g. those found in soft margarines.

Margarines ► contain **poly-unsaturated compounds.** Part of a molecule in margarine.

Double bonds*

First two members of a **homologous series** of alcohols*

◄ Methanol (**structural formula*** CH_3OH)

Hydroxyl functional group

Ethanol (**structural formula*** ► CH_3CH_2OH)

The **general formula** for alcohols* is $C_nH_{2n+1}OH$ (where n stands for the number of carbon atoms).

New $-CH_2-$ group added.

- **Structural isomers.** Compounds with the same **molecular formula***, but different **structural formulae***, i.e. the atoms are arranged in different ways.

The **molecular formula*** C_2H_6O has two different **structural formulae***.

CH_3CH_2OH

CH_3OCH_3

Two **structural isomers**

▲ Ethanol

▲ Methoxymethane

- **Stereoisomers.** Compounds with the same **molecular formula*** and grouping of atoms but a different 3-D appearance.

The **molecular formula** C_4H_8 has two different stereochemical formulae*.

Two **stereoisomers**

Cis but-2-ene

Trans but-2-ene

---

* **Alcohols**, 82; **Alkanes**, 78; **Double bond**, 18; **Molecular formula**, 26; **Single bond**, 18; **Stereochemical formula**, 26; **Structural formula (shortened)**, 26; **Triple bond**, 18.

Alkanes

Alkanes, or **paraffins,** are all **saturated* hydrocarbons*** and **aliphatic compounds***. They form a **homologous series*** which has a **general formula*** of C_nH_{2n+2}. As the molecules in the series increase in size, so the physical properties of the compounds change (see below).

Some properties of alkanes				
Name of compound	Molecular formula*	Structural formula*	Physical state at 25°C	Boiling point(°C)
Methane	CH_4	CH_4	Gas	−161.5
Ethane	C_2H_6	CH_3CH_3	Gas	−88.0
Propane	C_3H_8	$CH_3CH_2CH_3$	Gas	−42.2
Butane	C_4H_{10}	$CH_3CH_2CH_2CH_3$	Gas	−0.5
Pentane	C_5H_{12}	$CH_3CH_2CH_2CH_2CH_3$	Liquid	36.0
Hexane	C_6H_{14}	$CH_3CH_2CH_2CH_2CH_2CH_3$	Liquid	69.0

The first part of the name indicates the number of carbon atoms in the molecule. The -ane ending means the molecule is an alkane (see page 100).

The next molecule in the series is always a $-CH_2-$ group longer.

Gradual change of state as molecules get longer.

The boiling points of the alkanes increase regularly as the molecules get longer. Melting points and densities follow the same trend, getting higher as the molecules increase in size.

Alkanes are **non-polar molecules***. They burn in air to form carbon dioxide and water, and react with **halogens***, otherwise they are unreactive. Excepting **methane**, they are obtained from **petroleum***. They are used as fuels and to make other organic substances, e.g. plastics.

●**Methane (CH_4).** The simplest alkane. It is a colourless, odourless, inflammable gas, which reacts with **halogens*** (see picture below) and is a source of hydrogen. **Natural gas** is composed of 99% methane.

●**Ethane (C_2H_6).** A member of the alkanes. A gas found in small amounts in **natural gas** (see **methane**), but mostly obtained from **petroleum***. Its properties are similar to methane. It is used to make other organic chemicals.

●**Propane (C_3H_8).** A member of the alkanes. A gas that is usually obtained from **petroleum***. Its properties are similar to **ethane**. It is bottled and sold as fuel for cooking and heating.

●**Cycloalkanes.** Alkane molecules whose carbon atoms are joined in a ring, e.g. **cyclohexane** (see picture, page 76). Their properties are similar to other alkanes.

●**Substitution reaction.** A reaction in which an atom or **functional group*** of a molecule is replaced by a different atom or functional group. The molecules of **saturated compounds***, e.g. alkanes, can undergo substitution reactions, but not **addition reactions**.

Alkanes react with **halogens*** by undergoing a **substitution reaction**. Here is an example:

A chlorine atom is substituted for the hydrogen atom.

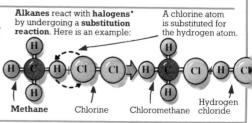

Methane   Chlorine   Chloromethane   Hydrogen chloride

* Aliphatic compounds, 76; Functional group, General formula, 77 (Homologous series); Halogens, 72; Hydrocarbons, 77; Molecular formula, 26; Non-polar molecule, 19; Petroleum, 84; Saturated compounds, 77; Structural formula (shortened), 26.

Alkenes

Alkenes, or **olefins**, are **unsaturated* hydrocarbons*** and **aliphatic compounds***. Alkene molecules contain one or more **double bonds*** between carbon atoms. Those with only one form a **homologous series*** with the **general formula* C_nH_{2n}**. As the molecules increase in size their physical properties change gradually (see below).

Some properties of alkenes				
Name of compound	Molecular formula*	Structural formula*	Physical state at 25°C	Boiling point(°C)
Ethene	C_2H_4	$CH_2=CH_2$	Gas	− 104.0
Propene	C_3H_6	$CH_3CH=CH_2$	Gas	− 47.0
But-1-ene	C_4H_8	$CH_3CH_2CH=CH_2$	Gas	− 6.0
Pent-1-ene	C_5H_{10}	$CH_3CH_2CH_2CH=CH_2$	Liquid	30.0

The number denotes the position of the **double bond*** in the molecule. Alkenes are named in the same way as **alkanes**, but end in -ene, not -ane (see page 100).

Each molecule is a -CH_2- group longer. The position of the **double bond*** is shown.

Gradual change from gases to liquids to solids as the molecules get longer.

As the molecules get longer, the boiling points of the alkenes increase regularly. Melting points and densities follow the same trend.

Alkenes are **non-polar molecules***. They burn with a smoky flame and in excess oxygen are completely **oxidized*** to carbon dioxide and water. Alkenes are more reactive than **alkanes**, because of their double bond – they undergo **addition reactions**, and some form **polymers***. Alkenes are made by **cracking*** alkanes and are used to make many products including plastics and antifreeze.

●**Ethene (C_2H_4)** or **ethylene**. The simplest alkene (see chart above) – it is a colourless, sweet-smelling gas which undergoes **addition reactions** to form polymers of **polythene**. It is used to make plastics, ethanol, and many other organic chemicals.

●**Propene (C_3H_6)** or **propylene**. A member of the alkenes. It is a colourless gas used to make propanone and **poly(propene)**, also called **polypropylene**.

Some kitchen tools are made from **poly(propene)**, the **polymer*** of propene.

●**Addition reaction.** A reaction in which two molecules react together to produce a single larger molecule. One of the molecules must be **unsaturated*** (have a **double** or **triple bond***).

●**Hydrogenation.** An **addition reaction** in which hydrogen atoms are added to an **unsaturated compound*** molecule.

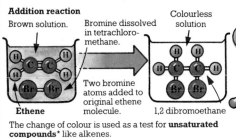

Addition reaction

Brown solution. Bromine dissolved in tetrachloro-methane. Colourless solution.

Two bromine atoms added to original ethene molecule.

Ethene 1,2 dibromoethane

The change of colour is used as a test for **unsaturated compounds*** like alkenes.

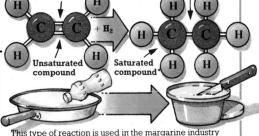

Ethene + H_2 → Ethane

Unsaturated compound → Saturated compound*

This type of reaction is used in the margarine industry to harden animal and vegetable oils. (These oils are **unsaturated compounds***, but not alkenes.)

* Aliphatic compounds, 76; Cracking, 84; Double bond, 18; General formula, 77 (Homologous series); Hydrocarbons, 77; Molecular formula, 26; Non-polar molecule, 19 (Polar molecule); Oxidation, 34; Polymers, 86; Saturated compounds, 77; Structural formula (shortened), 26; Triple bond, 18; Unsaturated compounds, 77.

79

Alkynes

Alkynes, or **acetylenes**, are **unsaturated*** (each molecule has a carbon-carbon **triple bond***) and **aliphatic compounds***. They are **hydrocarbons*** and form a **homologous series*** with a **general formula*** C_nH_{2n-2}. Alkynes are named in the same way as **alkanes***, but end in -yne, not -ane (see page 100). They are **non-polar molecules*** with chemical properties similar to **alkenes***. They burn with a sooty flame in air and a very hot flame in pure oxygen. Alkynes are produced by **cracking***. They are used to make plastics and solvents.

Structural formulae* of some alkynes	
Name of compound	Structural formula*
Ethyne	$CH \equiv CH$
Propyne	$CH_3C \equiv CH$
	$CH_3CH_2C \equiv CH$

●**Ethyne (C_2H_2)** or **acetylene**. The simplest member of the alkynes. A colourless gas, less dense than air and with a slightly sweet smell. It is the only common alkyne. Ethyne undergoes the same reactions as the other alkynes but more vigorously, e.g. it reacts explosively with chlorine. It is made by **cracking*** and is used to make polyvinyl chloride (PVC) and other vinyl compounds.

Molecule of ethyne.

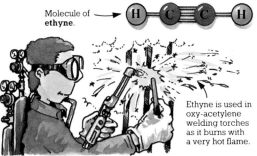

Ethyne is used in oxy-acetylene welding torches as it burns with a very hot flame.

More homologous series

The following groups of organic compounds each form a **homologous series*** of **aliphatic compounds***. Each series has a particular **functional group*** and its members have similar chemical properties.

●**Aldehydes**. Compounds that contain a −**CHO functional group***. They form a **homologous series*** with a **general formula*** $C_nH_{2n+1}CHO$ and are named like **alkanes*** but end in -anal, not -ane (see page 101). They are colourless liquids (except **methanal**) and **reducing agents***, and undergo **addition***, **condensation*** and **polymerization reactions***. When **oxidized***, they form **carboxylic acids**.

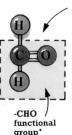

Molecule of **methanal** (**HCHO**) or **formaldehyde**, the simplest **aldehyde**. It is a colourless, poisonous gas with a strong smell. It dissolves in water to make **formalin** – used to preserve biological specimens. It is also used to make **polymers*** and adhesives.

-CHO functional group*

●**Ketones**. Compounds that contain a **carbonyl group** (a **-CO- functional group***). Ketones form a **homologous series*** with a complex **general formula***. They are named like **alkanes*** but end in -anone, not -ane. Most are colourless liquids. They have chemical properties similar to **aldehydes** but are not **reducing agents***

Carbonyl group (-CO-)

Molecule of **propanone** (CH_3COCH_3) or **acetone**, the simplest **ketone**

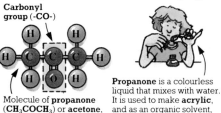

Propanone is a colourless liquid that mixes with water. It is used to make **acrylic**, and as an organic solvent, e.g. to remove nail varnish.

*Addition reaction, 79; Aliphatic compounds, 76; Alkanes, 78; Alkenes, 79; Condensation reaction, 83; Cracking, 84; Functional group, 77; General formula, 77 (Homologous series); Hydrocarbons, 77; Non-polar molecule, 19 (Polar molecule); Oxidation, 34; Polymerization reaction, Polymers, 86; Reducing agent, 34; Structural formula (shortened), 26; Triple bond, 18; Unsaturated compounds.

- **Carboxylic acids**. Compounds that contain a **carboxyl group** (a **-COOH functional group***) and form a **homologous series*** of **general formula*** $C_nH_{2n+1}COOH$. Their names end in -anoic acid (see page 101). Pungent, colourless **weak acids***, they react with **alcohols*** to give **esters** (see **condensation reaction**, page 83).

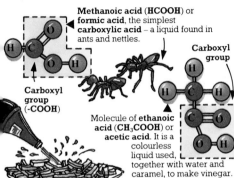

Methanoic acid (**HCOOH**) or formic acid, the simplest carboxylic acid – a liquid found in ants and nettles.

Carboxyl group (-COOH)

Carboxyl group

Molecule of **ethanoic acid** (**CH₃COOH**) or acetic acid. It is a colourless liquid used, together with water and caramel, to make vinegar.

- **Dicarboxylic acids**. Compounds that contain two **carboxyl groups** (see **carboxylic acids**) in each molecule.

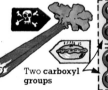

Molecule of **ethanedioic acid** (**(COOH)₂**) or **oxalic acid** – a poisonous, **dicarboxylic acid** found in rhubarb leaves but not stalks.

Two **carboxyl groups**

- **Esters**. A **homologous series*** of compounds containing a **-COO- functional group*** in every molecule. They are unreactive, colourless liquids made by reacting a **carboxylic acid** and **alcohol*** (see **condensation reaction**, page 83). Found in vegetable oils and animal fats, they give fruit and flowers their flavours and smells. They are used in perfumes and flavourings.

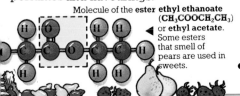

Molecule of the ester **ethyl ethanoate** (**CH₃COOCH₂CH₃**) or **ethyl acetate**. Some esters that smell of pears are used in sweets.

- **Halogenoalkanes** or **alkyl halides**. A **homologous series*** that contains one or more **halogen*** atoms (see also page 101). Most halogenoalkanes are colourless, **volatile*** liquids which do not mix with water. They will undergo **substitution reactions***. The most reactive contain iodine, and the least reactive contain fluorine.

Molecule of **chloroethane** (**CH₃CH₂Cl**), a halogenoalkane. Used to keep fridges cold (see **refrigerant**, page 115).

The chlorine atom is the **halogen* functional group***. It is called a **chloro group** (**-Cl**) (see page 101).

Some important organic compounds have more than one **halogen*** atom in their molecules.

Chloro group (**-Cl functional group***)

Bromo group (**-Br functional group***)

Fluoro groups (**-F functional groups***)

Molecule of **halothane** or **1-bromo, 1-chloro, 2,2,2-trifluoroethane**. Used with dinitrogen oxide as an anaesthetic.

Molecule of **poly(tetrafluoroethene)** (**PTFE**) (see also page 72).

PTFE is used as a non-stick coating on saucepans.

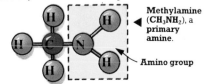

- **Primary amines**. Compounds that contain an **amino group** (**-NH₂ functional group***). They are **weak bases***, and have a fishy smell.

Methylamine (**CH₃NH₂**), a primary amine.

Amino group

- **Diamines**. Compounds with two **amino groups** in each molecule.

---

* Alcohols, 82; Functional group, 77; General formula, 77 (Homologous series); Halogens, 72; Substitution reaction, 78; Volatile, 115; Weak acid, Weak base, 38.

Alcohols

Alcohols are organic compounds that contain one or more **hydroxyl groups (-OH functional groups*)** in each molecule. The alcohols shown below in the chart are all members of a **homologous series*** of alcohols which are **aliphatic compounds*** with the **general formula*** $C_nH_{2n+1}OH$. As the molecules in the series increase in size, their physical properties change steadily. Some of the trends are shown here:

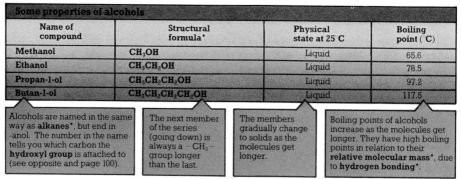

Some properties of alcohols			
Name of compound	Structural formula*	Physical state at 25°C	Boiling point (°C)
Methanol	CH_3OH	Liquid	65.6
Ethanol	CH_3CH_2OH	Liquid	78.5
Propan-1-ol	$CH_3CH_2CH_2OH$	Liquid	97.2
Butan-1-ol	$CH_3CH_2CH_2CH_2OH$	Liquid	117.5

Alcohols are named in the same way as **alkanes***, but end in -anol. The number in the name tells you which carbon the **hydroxyl group** is attached to (see opposite and page 100).

The next member of the series (going down) is always a $-CH_2-$ group longer than the last.

The members gradually change to solids as the molecules get longer.

Boiling points of alcohols increase as the molecules get longer. They have high boiling points in relation to their **relative molecular mass***, due to **hydrogen bonding***.

As a result of their **hydroxyl groups**, alcohol molecules are **polar***, and have **hydrogen bonds***. Short chain alcohols mix completely with water, but long chain alcohols do not as their molecules have more $-CH_2-$ groups, making them less polar. Alcohols do not **ionize*** in water and are **neutral***. They burn, giving off carbon dioxide and water.

Alcohols react with sodium:

$$2CH_3CH_2OH + 2Na \rightarrow 2CH_3CH_2ONa + H_2$$
Ethanol   Sodium   Sodium ethoxide   Hydrogen

Alcohols react with phosphorus halides to give **halogenoalkanes** (see page 81), and with **carboxylic acids** to give **esters** (see **condensation reaction** and page 81).

Primary alcohols are **oxidized*** first to aldehydes* and then to **carboxylic acids***

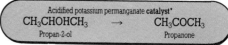

Acidified potassium permanganate **catalyst***
$$CH_3CH_2CH_2OH \rightarrow CH_3CH_2CHO \rightarrow CH_3CH_2COOH$$
Propan-1-ol   Propanal   Propanoic acid

Secondary alcohols are **oxidized*** to **ketones** (see page 80).

Acidified potassium permanganate **catalyst***
$$CH_3CHOHCH_3 \rightarrow CH_3COCH_3$$
Propan-2-ol   Propanone

●**Ethanol (**CH_3CH_2OH**,** often written C_2H_5OH**).** Also called **ethyl alcohol**, or **alcohol**. An alcohol which is a slightly sweet smelling water-soluble liquid with a relatively high boiling point. It burns with an almost colourless flame and is made by ethene reacting with steam. It is also produced by **alcoholic fermentation**.

Ethanol is used as a solvent and in methylated spirits. It has many more uses some are shown below:

Toiletries

Alcoholic drinks

A **breathalyser** is used to see if a person has drunk too much alcohol to drive safely. It contains an electronic device that measures the alcohol concentration in the breath.

* Aldehydes, 80; Aliphatic compounds, 76; Alkanes, 78; Carboxylic acids, 81; Catalyst, 47; Functional group, 77; General formula, 77 (Homologous series); Hydrogen bond, 20; Ionization, 16; Neutral, 37; Oxidation, 34; Polar molecule, 19; Relative molecular mass, 24; Structural formula (shortened), 26.

- **Alcoholic fermentation**. The name of the process used to produce **ethanol** (the potent chemical in alcoholic drinks) from fruits or grain. **Glucose*** from fruit or grain is converted into ethanol by **enzymes* (catalysts*)** of the reactions in living cells). **Yeast** is used in alcoholic fermentation because it has the enzyme **zymase** which catalyses the change of glucose to ethanol.

Wine making

Airlock stops air entering (it would **oxidize*** the **ethanol** to ethanoic acid).

Water

Grape juice and yeast. Yeast **enzyme*** **zymase** ferments **glucose*** from the juice, making carbon dioxide gas and ethanol.

Demi-john (special container)

Whisky distillery

Yeast dies if **ethanol** concentration gets too high. Stronger alcoholic drinks, e.g. whisky, are made by **distilling*** the ethanol solution – this removes water and concentrates the ethanol, making the drink very potent.

$$C_6H_{12}O_6 \quad \xrightarrow{\text{Enzyme*}} \quad 2CH_3CH_2OH \quad + \quad 2CO_2$$

Glucose solution from fruit or barley

Ethanol

Carbon dioxide

Primary, secondary and tertiary alcohols

Molecule of **butan-1-ol, a primary alcohol**. The carbon atom attached to the hydroxyl group (see introduction) has two hydrogen atoms attached to it.

Molecule of **butan-2-ol, a secondary alcohol**. The carbon atom attached to the hydroxyl group (see introduction) has one hydrogen atom attached to it.

Molecule of **2-methyl propan-2-ol**, a **tertiary alcohol**. The carbon atom attached to the **hydroxyl group** (see introduction) has no hydrogen atoms attached to it.

The numbers in the names of the alcohols give the position of the carbon atom that the **hydroxyl group** is bonded to (see page 100 for more information on naming alcohols).

- **Polyhydric alcohols**. Alcohols whose molecules contain more than one **hydroxyl group** (see introduction).

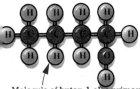

Ethane-1,2-diol, or ethylene glycol is a diol (contains two hydroxyl groups). Used as antifreeze.

Propane-1,2,3-triol, glycerine, or glycerol, is a **triol** (contains three hydroxyl groups). Used to make explosives.

- **Condensation reaction**. A type of reaction in which two molecules react together to form one, with the loss of a small molecule, e.g. water. (See also **condensation polymerization**, page 86.)

Example of a **condensation reaction**:

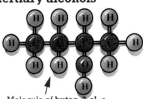

$$CH_3CH_2OH \rightarrow CH_3COOH \rightarrow CH_3COOCH_2CH_3 + H_2O$$

Ethanol

Ethanoic acid

Ethyl ethanoate

Water molecule is lost

This reaction is also an **esterification reaction** as the product ethyl ethanoate is an **ester***. An alcohol and an organic acid always react to form an ester.

* Catalyst, 47; Distillation, 106; Enzyme, 47; Esters, 81; Glucose, 90; Oxidation, 34.

Petroleum

Petroleum, or **crude oil**, is a dark, viscous liquid, usually found at great depths beneath the earth or sea-bed. It is often found with **natural gas***, which consists mainly of **methane***. Petroleum is formed over millions of years by the decomposition of animals and plants under pressure. It is a mixture of **alkanes*** which vary greatly in size and structure. Many useful products are produced by **refining** petroleum.

- **Refining**. A set of processes which convert petroleum to more useful products. Refining consists of three main processes – **primary distillation**, **cracking** and **reforming**.

- **Primary distillation** or **fractional distillation of petroleum**. A process used to separate petroleum into **fractions**, according to their boiling points (see also page 106). A **fractionating column** (see diagram) is kept very hot at the bottom but it gets cooler towards the top. Boiled petroleum passes into the column as vapour, losing heat as it rises. When a fraction reaches a tray at a temperature just below its own boiling point, it condenses onto the tray. It is then drawn off along pipes. Fractions are distilled again to give better separations.

- **Fraction**. A mixture of liquids with similar boiling points, obtained from **primary distillation**. **Light fractions** have low boiling points and short **hydrocarbon*** chains. **Heavy fractions** have higher boiling points and longer chains.

- **Cracking**. A reaction which breaks large **alkanes*** into smaller alkanes and **alkenes***. The smaller alkanes are used as **gasoline**. Cracking occurs at high temperatures, or with a **catalyst*** (**catalytic cracking** or **"cat cracking"**).

$$C_9H_{20} \rightarrow C_7H_{16} + C_2H_4$$

| Alkane (Nonane) | Alkane (Heptane) | Alkene (Ethene*) |

- **Reforming**. A process which produces **gasoline** from lighter **fractions** by breaking up **straight chain*** **alkanes*** and reassembling them as **branched chain*** molecules.

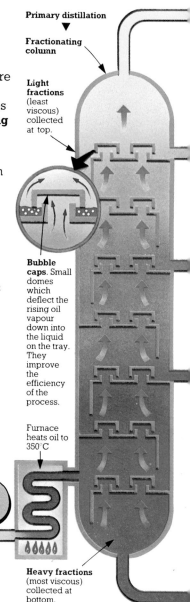

Primary distillation ▼

Fractionating column

Light fractions (least viscous) collected at top.

Bubble caps. Small domes which deflect the rising oil vapour down into the liquid on the tray. They improve the efficiency of the process.

Furnace heats oil to 350°C

Petroleum

Heavy fractions (most viscous) collected at bottom.

* Alkanes, 78; Alkenes, 79; Branched chain, 76; Catalyst, 47; Ethene, 79; Hydrocarbons, 77; Natural gas, 78 (Methane); Straight chain, 76.

- **Refinery gas**. A gas which consists mainly of **methane***. Other **light fractions** contain **propane** and **butane** (both **alkanes***) and are made into **liquefied petroleum gas** (**LPG**).

Liquefied petroleum gas (see **refinery gas**) is used as bottled gas.

- **Chemical feedstocks**. **Fractions** of petroleum which are used in the production of organic chemicals. These fractions are mainly **refinery gas** and **naptha**, a part of the **gasoline** fraction.

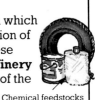

Chemical feedstocks

Refinery gas

- **Gasoline** or **petrol**. A liquid **fraction** obtained from **primary distillation**. It consists of **alkanes*** with 5 to 12 carbon atoms in their molecules and has a boiling point range of 40-150°C. See also **cracking** and **reforming**.

- **Octane rating**. A measure of how well **gasoline** burns, measured on a scale of 0 to 100. It is increased by using an **anti-knock agent** such as tetraethyl-lead ($Pb(OC_2H_5)_4$).

Gasoline used in cars has an **octane rating** of over 90. It consists mainly of **branched chain*** **alkanes***.

Gasoline

- **Kerosene** or **paraffin**. A liquid **fraction** obtained from **primary distillation**. Kerosene consists of **alkanes*** with about 9-15 carbon atoms in their molecules. It has a boiling point range of 150-250°C.

Kerosene is used as a **fuel*** in jet engines and domestic heaters.

Kerosene

- **Diesel oil** or **gas oil**. A liquid **fraction** obtained from **primary distillation**. It consists of **alkanes*** with about 12-25 or more carbon atoms in their molecules. It has a boiling point of 250°C and above.

Diesel oil is used as a **fuel*** in diesel engines.

Diesel oil

- **Residue**. The oil left after **primary distillation**. It consists of **hydrocarbons*** of very high **relative molecular masses***, their molecules containing up to 40 carbon atoms. Its boiling point is greater than 350°C. Some is used as **fuel oil**, the rest is re-distilled to form the substances on the right.

- **Lubricating oil**. A mixture of non-**volatile*** liquids obtained from the distillation of **residue** in a vacuum.

- **Hydrocarbon waxes** or **paraffin waxes**. Soft solids which are separated from **lubricating oil** after the distillation of **residue** in a vacuum.

Candles and polish

- **Bitumen** or **asphalt**. A liquid left after the distillation of **residue** under vacuum. It is a tarry, black semi-solid at room temperature.

Road surfaces and roofing

Residue

Polymers and plastics

Polymers are substances that consist of many **monomers** (small molecules) bonded together in a repeating sequence. They are very long molecules with a high **relative molecular mass***. Polymers occur naturally, e.g. **proteins***. There are also many **synthetic polymers**, e.g. **plastics**.

●**Monomers**. Relatively small molecules that react to form polymers. For example, **ethene*** molecules are monomers which react together to form **polythene** (see also equation for **homopolymer**).

▶

Simplified picture of a **polymerization reaction** – a reaction in which **monomers** bond to form a polymer.

Picture representing a **monomer**.

Picture representing a **polymer**.

●**Addition polymerization**. Polymerization reactions in which **monomers** bond to each other without losing any atoms. The polymer is the only product and has the same **empirical formula*** as the monomer. See also **addition reaction**, page 79.

Example of an **addition polymerization** reaction

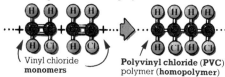

···+···▷

Vinyl chloride **monomers**

Polyvinyl chloride (**PVC**) polymer (**homopolymer**)

●**Condensation polymerization**. Polymerization reactions in which **monomers** form a polymer with the loss of small molecules such as water. (See **condensation reaction**, page 83.)

●**Homopolymer**. A polymer made from a single type of **monomer**.

Reaction to produce the **homopolymer polythene**.

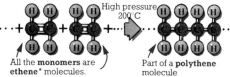

···+···+···▷···

All the **monomers** are ethene* molecules.
This is an **addition polymerization** reaction.

Part of a **polythene** molecule

●**Copolymer**. A polymer made from two or more different **monomers**. See **condensation polymerization** example below.

●**Depolymerization**. The breakdown of a polymer into its original **monomers**. It occurs for example when **acrylic** is heated.

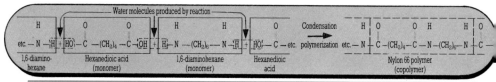

Water molecules produced by reaction

etc. — N —H + HO— C —(CH₂)₄—C—OH + H— N —(CH₂)₆— N —H + HO— C —etc. Condensation polymerization etc. — N — C —(CH₂)₄—C — N —(CH₂)₆— N — C —

1,6-diamino-hexane | Hexanedioic acid (monomer) | 1,6-diaminohexane (monomer) | Hexanedioic acid | Nylon 66 polymer (copolymer)

●**Synthetic** or **man-made polymers**. Polymers prepared in the laboratory or in industry (not natural polymers), e.g. **nylons**.

●**Plastics. Synthetic polymers** that are easily moulded. They are made from chemicals derived from **petroleum*** and are usually durable, light solids which are thermal and electrical insulators. They are often not **biodegradable*** and give off poisonous fumes when burnt. There are two types of plastic – **thermoplastics** which soften or melt on heating (e.g. **polythene**) and **thermosetting plastics** which harden on heating and do not remelt (e.g. plastic used in worktops).

Some uses of plastics

* **Biodegradable**, 96; **Empirical formula**, 26; **Ethene**, 79; **Petroleum**, 84; **Proteins**, 91; **Relative molecular mass**, 24.

- **Polyesters.**
Copolymers, formed by the **condensation polymerization** of **diol*** and **dicarboxylic acid*** monomers. The monomers are linked by **-COO- functional groups***, as found in **esters***.

Yachts have sails made of **polyesters**.

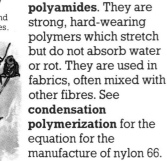

Some **polyesters** are produced as fibres which are used in clothing and furnishing materials.

- **Polystyrene** or **poly(phenylethene)**. A **homopolymer** formed by the **addition polymerization** of **styrene (phenylethene)**.

Nylons are used to make many things, e.g. parachutes and climbing ropes.

- **Nylons.** A family of **polyamides**. They are strong, hard-wearing polymers which stretch but do not absorb water or rot. They are used in fabrics, often mixed with other fibres. See **condensation polymerization** for the equation for the manufacture of nylon 66.

- **Polythene.** Also called **poly(ethene)** or **poly(ethylene)**. A **homopolymer** formed by the **addition polymerization** of **ethene*** (see **homopolymer**). Polythene is produced in two forms (depending on the method used) – a soft material of low density, and a hard, more rigid, material of high density. Polythene has a **relative molecular mass*** of between 10,000 and 40,000 and is used to make many things.

Polythene is used to make many kitchen utensils, e.g. washing-up bowls.

- **Polyamides. Copolymers** formed by the **condensation polymerization** of a **dicarboxylic acid*** monomer with a **diamine*** monomer, e.g. **nylons**.

Polystyrene is used to make disposable knives, forks and cups. Air-expanded sheets of polystyrene are used in packaging and insulation.

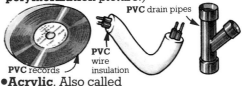

- **Polyvinyl chloride** (**PVC**) or **poly(chloroethene)**. A hard-wearing **homopolymer** used to make many things. Some examples are shown below. (See also **addition polymerization** picture.)

PVC drain pipes

PVC records

PVC wire insulation

- **Acrylic.** Also called **poly(methylmethacrylate)** or **poly ((1-methoxycarbonyl)-1-methylethene)**. A **homopolymer** formed by **addition polymerization**. It is often used as a glass substitute.

Methyl methacrylate, the acrylic monomer

$$H \underset{H}{\overset{}{\diagdown}} C = C \underset{COOCH_3}{\overset{CH_3}{\diagup}}$$

Acrylic is used to make outdoor signs.

- **Natural polymers** or **biopolymers.** Polymers that occur naturally, e.g. **starch** and **rubber**. Starch is made from **monomers** of **glucose***. For a picture of the starch polymer, see **starch**, page 90.

Part of a rubber polymer

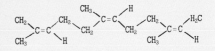

Rubber polymer is extracted from **latex*** tapped from the rubber tree. It is then **vulcanized*** to produce the rubber used in tyres, hoses etc.

---

*Carboxyl group, 81 (Carboxylic acids); Diamines, Dicarboxylic acids, 81; Diols, 83 (Polyhydric alcohols); Esters, 81; Ethene, 79; Functional group, 77; Glucose, 90; Latex, 115; Relative molecular mass, 24; Vulcanization, 115.

Detergents

Detergents are substances which, when added to water, enable it to remove dirt. They do this in three ways: by lowering the water's **surface tension*** so that it spreads evenly instead of forming droplets, by enabling grease molecules to dissolve in water, and also by keeping removed dirt suspended in the water. **Soap** is a type of detergent, but there are also many **soapless detergents**.

● **Detergent molecule.** A large molecule consisting of a long **hydrocarbon*** chain with a **functional group*** at one end (making that end **polar***). The **non-polar*** chain is **hydrophobic** (repelled by water) and the polar end is **hydrophilic** (attracted to water). In water, these molecules form **micelles**.

Simple representation of a **detergent molecule**.

Hydrophilic functional group* (head end of molecule)

Hydrophobic hydrocarbon* chain (tail end of molecule)

● **Soap.** A type of detergent. It is the sodium or potassium **salt*** of a long-chain **carboxylic acid*** such as octadecanoic acid, see equation. It is made by reacting animal fats or vegetable oils (**esters***) with sodium hydroxide or potassium hydroxide solution (soap made with potassium hydroxide is softer). The process of making soap is **saponification**. Soap molecules form **micelles** in water. Soap produces a scum in **hard water*** whereas **soapless detergents** do not.

Soap-making factory

Saponification (soap-making)

Measured amounts of **fats*** and sodium hydroxide or potassium hydroxide solutions are continuously fed into a large, hollow, column-like structure. The column is at high temperature and pressure. **Soap** and propane-1,2,3-triol are formed.

The propane-1,2,3-triol is dissolved in salt water. Then centrifuges used to separate **soap** from propane-1,2,3-triol in salt water.

The final part of the process is **fitting** or **finishing**. Any unreacted long-chain **carboxylic acids*** are **neutralized*** with alkali. Salt concentration is adjusted. Mixture is centrifuged to separate out **soap**.

Saponification equation ▼

$$\begin{array}{c} C_{17}H_{35}COOCH_2 \\ | \\ C_{17}H_{35}COOCH \\ | \\ C_{17}H_{35}COOCH_2 \end{array} \; + \; 3NaOH \; \xrightarrow{\text{Saponification}} \; 3C_{17}H_{35}COO^-Na^+ \; + \; \begin{array}{c} CH_2OH \\ | \\ CHOH \\ | \\ CH_2OH \end{array}$$

Ester (from mutton fat) — Sodium hydroxide — Sodium octadecanoate (sodium stearate) — Propane 1,2,3 triol

All **soap** molecules are sodium or potassium **salts*** of long-chain **carboxylic acids***. In this example, it is a salt of **octadecanoic acid.**

● **Micelle.** A spherical grouping of **detergent molecules** in water. Oils and greases dissolve in the **hydrophobic** centre of the micelle. The picture opposite right shows how micelles remove grease.

Washing powder is one type of detergent used to remove grease.

Grease stain

*Carboxylic acids, 81; Esters, 80; Fats, 90 (Lipids); Functional group, 77; Hard water, 93; Hydrocarbons, 77; Neutralization, 31; Non-polar molecule, 19 (Polar molecule); Salts, 39; Surface tension, 115.

- **Soapless detergents** or **synthetic detergents**. Types of detergent made from by-products of **refining*** crude oil. They are used to make many products, including **washing powders**, shampoos and hair conditioners, and are usually simply referred to as detergents. Soapless detergents do not form a scum in **hard water*** and lather better than **soaps**. If they are not **biodegradable** they pollute rivers.

Example of a **soapless detergent** molecule that does not have an **ionic*** part - used in washing-up liquid.

Non-polar* part of molecule

Polar* part of molecule

$\left(O(CH_2)_2\right)_n OH$

Benzene ring*

Example of an **ionic*** **soapless detergent** molecule – used in kitchen soap.

Long **hydrocarbon*** chain (**non-polar*** part of molecule)   **Ionic*** end (**polar*** part of molecule)

- **Washing powders. Soap** or **soapless detergents** used to wash clothes. They are better for fabrics than water alone, as they make it easier to remove dirt. There are two main types of washing powder - those used when hand-washing clothes (usually soap powders) and those used in washing machines. The latter are mostly **soapless detergents** with other substances added to keep the lather down and to brighten the appearance of the fabric. When they also contain **enzymes***, they are called **biological washing powders**, or **enzyme detergents**. Enzymes help to break down **proteins*** and loosen dirt.

- **Biodegradable detergents. Soapless detergents** that are broken down by bacteria (see **biodegradable**, page 96). Foams from **non-biodegradable detergents** cannot be broken down and cover the water, depriving life of oxygen.

Non-biodegradable foam kills creatures living in water as it stops oxygen dissolving in the water.

- **Surfactants**. Substances which lower the **surface tension*** of water. As a result of this property, detergents have many other uses, as well as removing dirt. They are used in:

Paints, to ensure the pigment is evenly mixed in, and the paint gives a smooth finish and does not drip.

Lubricating greases, to make them gel better.

Cosmetics, to make face powder cover well and evenly, and ensure cosmetic creams mix well with water and thicken properly.

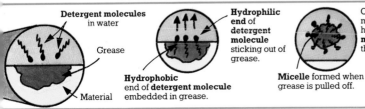

Detergent molecules in water

Grease

Material

Hydrophobic end of **detergent molecule** embedded in grease.

Hydrophilic end of **detergent molecule** sticking out of grease.

Micelle formed when grease is pulled off.

Constant motion of washing machine, and attraction of head end of **detergent molecules** to water pull off the detergent and grease.

Micelles tend to keep grease suspended in solution.

* Benzene ring, 76; Enzyme, 47; Hard water, 93; Hydrocarbons, 77; Ionic compound, 17; Non-polar molecule, 19 (Polar molecule); Proteins, 91; Refining, 84; Surface tension, 115.

Food

In order to survive and grow, living organisms must take in a number of different substances. These substances include water, minerals and **trace elements*** needed by both plants and animals, various **organic*** nutrients needed only by animals (plants make their own by **photosynthesis***) and **fibre**, or **roughage**, needed by many animals to help move food through the gut. Different animals need different amounts of substances for a healthy diet (the wrong amount of a substance causes illness). More information on **vitamins** and the organic nutrients – **proteins, carbohydrates** and **lipids** – can be found on the next two pages.

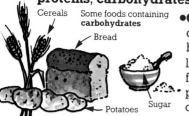

Cereals
Some foods containing **carbohydrates**
Bread
Potatoes
Sugar

●**Carbohydrates. Organic compounds*** that contain carbon, hydrogen and oxygen atoms only. They all have the **general formula*** $C_x(H_2O)_y$. Almost all living organisms use the simple carbohydrate **glucose** for energy. If there is not enough glucose available, it is produced from the **metabolism*** of more complex carbohydrates, or of **lipids** or **proteins**.

●**Sucrose.** A **carbohydrate** with the **molecular formula*** $C_{12}H_{22}O_{11}$. It is a **disaccharide** (a sugar containing two carbohydrate units), with one unit of each of the two **monosaccharides glucose** and **fructose**. It is a sweet-tasting carbohydrate, often used to sweeten food and commonly known as sugar. It is obtained from sugar cane and sugar beet.

●**Glucose.** A **carbohydrate** with the **molecular formula*** $C_6H_{12}O_6$. It is a **monosaccharide** (a sugar containing only one carbohydrate unit). Green plants make glucose by **photosynthesis***. Both plants and animals use glucose for energy. This energy is obtained as a result of a complex chain of reactions when glucose is broken down. Plants store glucose as **starch**, animals store it as the **polymer* glycogen**.

Low **carbohydrate** level means lack of energy.

Carbohydrate gained by eating chocolate (contains **sucrose**)

Sucrose broken down into **glucose** and **fructose**, which are broken down further to give energy.

Simplified equation showing energy released when **glucose** is broken down in the body.

$$C_6H_{12}O_6 + 6O_2 \rightarrow 6CO_2 + 6H_2O + 2830\,kJ$$

Glucose | Oxygen taken in by respiration | Carbon dioxide | Water | Energy released by reaction

●**Starch.** A complex **carbohydrate**, known as a **polysaccharide** (a sugar containing thousands of carbohydrate units – **glucose monosaccharides).** It is a **natural polymer*** (made of many glucose **monomers***). Plants make starch and store it as a food reserve. When animals eat starch they break it down into **glucose** which is then used to provide energy.

Part of a **starch** molecule ▼

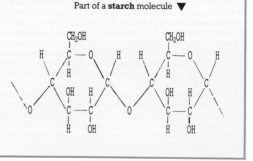

* **General formula**, 77 (Homologous series); **Metabolism**, 115; **Molecular formula**, 26; **Monomers**, 86; **Natural polymers**, 87; **Organic compounds** 76; **Photosynthesis**, 95; **Polymer**, 86; **Respiration**, 95; **Trace elements**, 115.

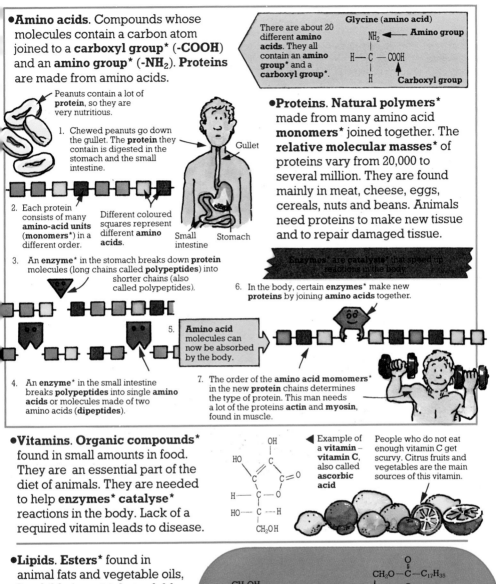

●**Amino acids**. Compounds whose molecules contain a carbon atom joined to a **carboxyl group*** (-COOH) and an **amino group*** (-NH$_2$). **Proteins** are made from amino acids.

Glycine (amino acid)

There are about 20 different **amino acids**. They all contain an **amino group*** and a **carboxyl group***.

Amino group → NH$_2$

H— C — COOH

H ← Carboxyl group

Peanuts contain a lot of **protein**, so they are very nutritious.

1. Chewed peanuts go down the gullet. The **protein** they contain is digested in the stomach and the small intestine.

Gullet

2. Each protein consists of many **amino-acid units** (**monomers***) in a different order.

Different coloured squares represent different **amino acids**.

Small intestine   Stomach

●**Proteins**. Natural polymers* made from many amino acid **monomers*** joined together. The **relative molecular masses*** of proteins vary from 20,000 to several million. They are found mainly in meat, cheese, eggs, cereals, nuts and beans. Animals need proteins to make new tissue and to repair damaged tissue.

Enzymes* are catalysts* that speed up reactions in the body.

3. An **enzyme*** in the stomach breaks down **protein** molecules (long chains called **polypeptides**) into shorter chains (also called polypeptides).

6. In the body, certain **enzymes*** make new **proteins** by joining **amino acids** together.

5. Amino acid molecules can now be absorbed by the body.

4. An **enzyme*** in the small intestine breaks **polypeptides** into single **amino acids** or molecules made of two amino acids (**dipeptides**).

7. The order of the **amino acid momomers*** in the new **protein** chains determines the type of protein. This man needs a lot of the proteins **actin** and **myosin**, found in muscle.

●**Vitamins. Organic compounds*** found in small amounts in food. They are an essential part of the diet of animals. They are needed to help **enzymes*** catalyse* reactions in the body. Lack of a required vitamin leads to disease.

◄ Example of a **vitamin** – **vitamin C**, also called **ascorbic acid**

People who do not eat enough vitamin C get scurvy. Citrus fruits and vegetables are the main sources of this vitamin.

●**Lipids. Esters*** found in animal fats and vegetable oils, Insoluble in water but soluble in **organic solvents***. **Fats** are solid or semi-solid lipids made from **saturated*** carboxylic acids*. **Oils** are liquid lipids mostly made from **unsaturated*** carboxylic acids*. Organisms use lipids as a reserve energy source.

CH$_2$OH
CHOH   + 3C$_{17}$H$_{35}$COOH →
CH$_2$OH
Propane-1,2,3-triol

Octadecanoic acid (or stearic acid), a long chained carboxylic acid

CH$_2$O—C—C$_{17}$H$_{35}$
CHO—C—C$_{17}$H$_{35}$ + 3H$_2$O
CH$_2$O—C—C$_{17}$H$_{35}$
An animal fat   Water

Example of a reaction to make a **fat**: ▲

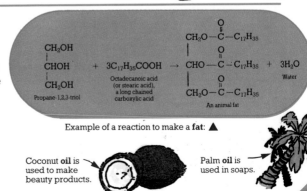

Coconut **oil** is used to make beauty products.

Palm **oil** is used in soaps.

Water

Water (H₂O) is the most important compound on earth. It is found on the surface, in the atmosphere, and is present in animals and plants. Vast amounts of water are used every day in the home and in industry, e.g. for manufacturing processes and the cooling of chemical plants. Water normally contains some dissolved gases, **salts*** and **pollutants***. See also page 53.

A molecule of water contains one oxygen atom and two hydrogen atoms.

The molecule is a **polar molecule***, which makes water a good **polar solvent***.

When water freezes and expands in pipes, they crack.

•**Ice**. The solid form of water. It has a **molecular lattice*** in which the molecules are further apart than in water. This is caused by **hydrogen bonds*** and means that ice is less dense than water, and that water expands when it freezes.

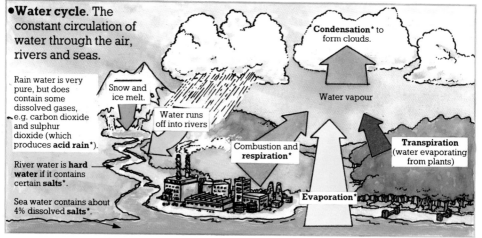

•**Water cycle**. The constant circulation of water through the air, rivers and seas.

Condensation* to form clouds.

Rain water is very pure, but does contain some dissolved gases, e.g. carbon dioxide and sulphur dioxide (which produces **acid rain***).

Snow and ice melt.

Water runs off into rivers

River water is **hard water** if it contains certain **salts***.

Sea water contains about 4% dissolved **salts***.

Combustion and **respiration***

Water vapour

Transpiration (water evaporating from plants)

Evaporation*

Atmospheric water

•**Humidity**. The amount of water vapour in the air. It depends on the temperature and is higher (up to 4% of the air) in warm air than cold air.

•**Hygroscopic**. Describes a substance which can absorb up to 70% of its own mass of water vapour. Such a substance becomes damp, but does not dissolve.

Sodium chloride absorbs water in a damp atmosphere.

•**Deliquescent**. Describes a substance which absorbs water vapour from the air and dissolves in it, forming a **concentrated*** solution.

Calcium chloride left open to the air

forms a **concentrated*** solution

•**Efflorescent**. Describes a crystal which loses part of its **water of crystallization*** to the air. A powdery coating is left on its surface.

A white powder forms on sodium carbonate crystals.

* Acid rain, 96; Concentrated, 30; Condensation, Evaporation, 7; Hydrogen bond, 20; Molecular lattice, 23; Polar molecule, 19; Polar solvent, 30; Pollutants, 96; Respiration, 95; Salts, 39; Water of crystallization, 21.

Water supply

●**Distilled water.** Water which has had **salts*** removed by **distillation***. It is very pure, but does contain some dissolved gases.

●**Desalination.** The treatment of sea water to remove dissolved **salts***. It is done by **distillation*** or **ion exchange**.

●**Purification.** The treatment of water to remove bacteria and other harmful substances, and produce pure water.

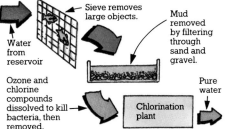

Sieve removes large objects.

Mud removed by filtering through sand and gravel.

Water from reservoir

Ozone and chlorine compounds dissolved to kill bacteria, then removed.

Chlorination plant

Pure water

●**Hard water.** Water which contains calcium and magnesium **salts*** that have dissolved from the rocks over which the water has flowed (see **calcium**, page 57). Water that does not contain these salts is called **soft water**. There are two types of hardness – **temporary hardness** (which can be removed relatively easily) and **permanent hardness** (which is more difficult to remove).

Hard water does not lather with soap and forms a **scum**.

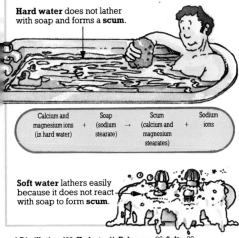

Calcium and magnesium ions (in hard water)	+	Soap (sodium stearate)	→	Scum (calcium and magnesium stearates)	+	Sodium ions

Soft water lathers easily because it does not react with soap to form **scum**.

●**Temporary hardness.** One type of water hardness, caused by the **salt*** calcium hydrogencarbonate dissolved in the water. It can be removed by boiling, producing an insoluble white solid (calcium carbonate or "scale").

"Scale" forms in kettles used to boil **hard water**.

●**Permanent hardness.** The more severe type of water hardness, caused by calcium and magnesium **salts*** (sulphates and chlorides) dissolved in the water. It cannot be removed by boiling, but can be removed by **distillation*** (producing **distilled water**) or by **water softening** (**ion exchange** or use of **water softeners**).

●**Ion exchange.** A method of **water softening** (see **permanent hardness**). Water is passed over a material such as **zeolite** (sodium aluminium silicate), which removes calcium and magnesium ions and replaces them with sodium ions. Some organic **polymers*** are also used as ion exchange materials.

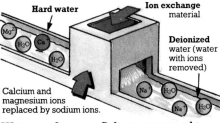

Hard water

Ion exchange material

Deionized water (water with ions removed)

Calcium and magnesium ions replaced by sodium ions.

●**Water softeners.** Substances used to remove **permanent hardness**. They react with the calcium and magnesium **salts*** to form compounds which do not react with soap.

●**Washing soda.** The common name for the **hydrate*** of sodium carbonate (see also page 55). It is used as a **water softener** in the home.

Washing soda

* **Distillation**, 106; **Hydrate**, 41; **Polymers**, 86; **Salts**, 39.

Air and burning

Air is a mixture of gases, including oxygen, carbon dioxide and nitrogen, which surrounds the earth and is essential for all forms of life. These gases can be separated by the **fractional distillation of liquid air***, and are used as raw materials in industry. Air also contains some water vapour and may contain **pollutants*** in some areas.

Composition of air

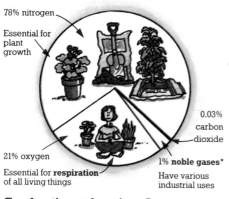

78% nitrogen

Essential for plant growth

0.03% carbon dioxide

21% oxygen

Essential for **respiration** of all living things

1% **noble gases***
Have various industrial uses

●**Slow combustion**. A form of **combustion** which takes place at low temperature. No **flames** occur. **Respiration** is slow combustion.

●**Flame**. A mixture of heat and light energy produced during **rapid combustion**.

A **non-luminous flame** is produced when there is enough oxygen for all of the substance to burn. ▶

A **luminous flame** is produced when there is not enough oxygen for complete **combustion**. ▶

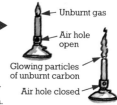

Unburnt gas

Air hole open

Glowing particles of unburnt carbon

Air hole closed

●**Combustion** or **burning**. An **exothermic reaction*** between a substance and a gas. Combustion usually takes place in air, when the substance which burns combines with oxygen. Substances can also burn in other gases, e.g. chlorine. Combustion does not normally happen spontaneously. It has to be started by heating (see **activation energy**, page 46).

Natural gas* (mainly **methane***) burns in gas cookers producing heat for cooking.

$$CH_4(g) + O_2(g) \rightarrow CO_2(g) + 2H_2O(g) + ENERGY$$

Methane | Oxygen from air | Carbon dioxide | Water vapour | for cooking

●**Rapid combustion**. **Combustion** in which a large amount of heat and light energy is given out.

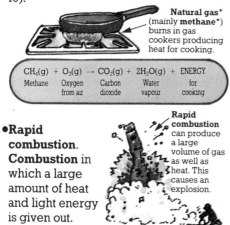

Rapid combustion can produce a large volume of gas as well as heat. This causes an explosion.

●**Fuel**. A substance which is burned to produce heat energy. Most fuels used today are **fossil fuels**, which were formed from the remains of prehistoric animal and plant life.

Wood is the oldest known **fuel**.

Fossil fuels are extracted from deep under the ground.

Petroleum*   Coal*

●**Calorific value**. A measure of the amount of heat energy produced by a specific amount of a **fuel**. The table below shows the different values for some common fuels.

Gasoline*
Natural gas*
Coal*
Coke*
Anthracite*
Wood

Heat energy in **kilojoules*** per gram

* **Anthracite**, 65 (**Coal**); **Coke**, 65; **Exothermic reaction**, 33; **Fractional distillation of liquid air**, 69; **Gasoline**, 85; **Kilojoule**, 32; **Natural gas**, 78 (**Methane**); **Noble gases**, 75; **Petroleum**, 84; **Pollutants**, 96.

- **Corrosion**. A reaction between a metal and the gases in air. The metal is **oxidized*** to form an oxide layer on the surface, usually weakening the metal, but sometimes forming a protective coat against further corrosion. Corrosion can be prevented by stopping oxygen reaching the metal or by preventing electrons from leaving it (see **sacrificial protection**, page 45). The corrosion of iron is called **rusting** (see also **rust**, page 60).

- **Respiration**. A form of **slow combustion** in animals. It produces energy from the reaction of **glucose*** with oxygen. It is chemically the opposite of **photosynthesis**.

Carbon dioxide released into air

Oxygen from air

Glucose* from food reacts with oxygen.

Food

$$C_6H_{12}O_6 + 6O_2 \rightarrow 6CO_2 + 6H_2O + ENERGY$$

Energy produced by reaction of glucose and oxygen

- **Photosynthesis**. A **photochemical reaction*** in green plants. It involves the production of **glucose*** from the combination of carbon dioxide and water, using the energy from sunlight. Photosynthesis is chemically the opposite of **respiration**.

Carbon dioxide

Oxygen

Energy from sun

Water

$$6CO_2 + 6H_2O \xrightarrow[\text{from sun}]{\text{Energy}} C_6H_{12}O_6 + 6O_2$$

Carbon dioxide reacts with water producing glucose.

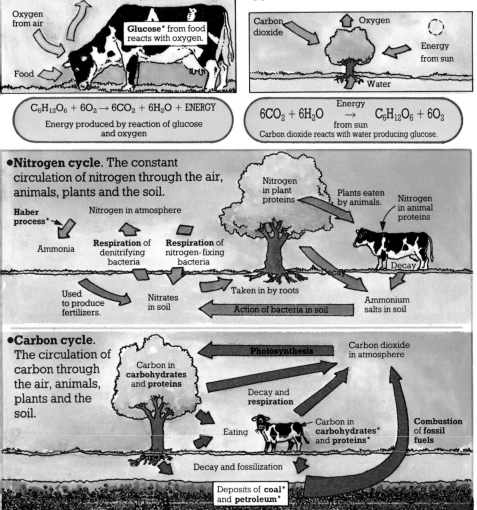

- **Nitrogen cycle**. The constant circulation of nitrogen through the air, animals, plants and the soil.

Nitrogen in plant proteins

Plants eaten by animals.

Nitrogen in animal proteins

Haber process*

Ammonia

Nitrogen in atmosphere

Respiration of denitrifying bacteria

Respiration of nitrogen-fixing bacteria

Decay

Decay

Used to produce fertilizers.

Nitrates in soil

Taken in by roots

Action of bacteria in soil

Ammonium salts in soil

- **Carbon cycle**. The circulation of carbon through the air, animals, plants and the soil.

Carbon in **carbohydrates** and **proteins**

Photosynthesis

Carbon dioxide in atmosphere

Decay and **respiration**

Eating

Carbon in **carbohydrates*** and **proteins***

Combustion of **fossil fuels**

Decay and fossilization

Deposits of **coal*** and **petroleum***

Pollution

Pollution is the release into the land, atmosphere, rivers and oceans, of undesirable substances which upset the natural processes of the Earth. These substances are known as **pollutants**. The major sources and types of pollution are shown below.

- **Biodegradable**. Describes a substance which is converted to simpler compounds by bacteria. Many **plastics*** are not biodegradable (see also **biodegradable detergents**, page 89).

- **Smog**. Fog mixed with dust and soot. It is acidic because of the sulphur dioxide produced when **fuels*** are burnt in industrial cities.

- **Acid rain**. Rain water which is more acidic than usual. Rain water normally has a **pH*** of between 5 and 6, due to dissolved carbon dioxide forming dilute carbonic acid. Sulphur dioxide and oxides of nitrogen, products of the combustion of **fuels***, react with water in the atmosphere to produce sulphuric and nitric acids with a pH of about 3.

- **Eutrophication**. An overgrowth of aquatic plants caused by an excess of nitrates, nitrites and phosphates from fertilizers in rivers. It results in a shortage of oxygen in the water, causing the death of fish.

- **Greenhouse effect**. The trapping of solar energy in the earth's atmosphere by carbon dioxide, causing an increase in the temperature of the air. The burning of **fuels*** produces more carbon dioxide and makes the problem worse.

- **Thermal pollution**. The effect of releasing warm water from factories and power stations into rivers and lakes. This causes a decrease in the oxygen dissolved in the water and affects aquatic life.

Oxides of nitrogen, produced by the combustion of **fuels***, contribute to **acid rain**. Sunlight makes nitrogen dioxide react with oxygen to produce poisonous **ozone*** gas.

The concentration in the atmosphere of carbon dioxide, a product of the combustion of **fuels***, is gradually increasing (see **greenhouse effect**).

Carbon monoxide, which is highly poisonous, is a product of incomplete combustion of **fuels*** in power stations and cars.

Sulphur dioxide, produced by impurities in **fuels***, is the major cause of **acid rain**.

Buried **radioactive*** waste will take thousands of years to become safe.

Smog over city

Poisonous lead compounds from cars which use petrol containing tetraethyl-lead, an **anti-knock agent***.

Plants are killed and buildings eroded by **acid rain**.

Fertilizers containing phosphates and nitrates washed into streams and rivers cause **eutrophication**.

Petroleum* spilt from ships causes pollution of water and seashores. A very small amount of oil can poison millions of gallons of water.

Purification* plant for cleaning water

Toxic (poisonous) heavy metals, such as mercury, leak into rivers and oceans from factories, killing life.

Thermal pollution from factories and power stations kills aquatic life.

* **Anti-knock agent**, 85 (**Octane rating**); **Fuel**, 94; **Ozone**, 69; **Petroleum**, 84; **pH**, 38; **Plastics**, 114; **Purification**, 93; **Radioactivity**, 114.

The reactivity series (showing ten metals – see also page 44)

Metal	Symbol	Reaction with air	Reaction with water	Reaction with dilute strong acids*	Displacement* reactions	Reaction of carbon with oxide	Reaction of hydrogen with oxide	Action of heat on oxide	Action of heat on carbonate	Action of heat on nitrate	Symbol
Potassium	K	Burn strongly to form oxides.	React with cold water to produce hydrogen gas and hydroxide. Hydroxide dissolves in water to form alkaline solution. React with decreasing vigour down the series.	Explosive reaction to give hydrogen gas and salt* solution.		No reaction	No reaction	No reaction	No reaction	Decompose to form nitrite and oxygen.	K
Sodium	Na										Na
Calcium	Ca	Burn, when heated, to form oxides. Burn with decreasing vigour down the series.	No reaction with cold water. React with steam to form hydrogen gas and oxide. React with decreasing vigour down the series.	React to give hydrogen gas and salt* solution with decreasing vigour down the series.	All metals displace ions of metals below them from solution.				Decompose to form oxide and carbon dioxide with increasing ease down the series.	Decompose to form oxide, oxygen and nitrogen dioxide with increasing ease down the series.	Ca
Magnesium	Mg										Mg
Aluminium	Al										Al
Zinc	Zn					Oxide reduced* to metal with increasing ease down the series. Carbon dioxide formed.	Oxide reduced* to metal with increasing ease down the series. Water is formed.				Zn
Iron	Fe										Fe
Lead	Pb	Do not burn when heated, but form an oxide layer on surface.	No reaction	No reaction							Pb
Copper	Cu										Cu
Silver	Ag	No reaction						Decomposes to form metal and oxygen only.	and carbon dioxide.	and nitrogen dioxide.	Ag

The properties of the elements

Below is a chart giving information on the physical properties of the elements in the periodic table (see pages 50-51). The last eight elements (**atomic numbers*** 96-103) are not listed, as there is very little known about them – they all have to be made under special laboratory conditions and only exist for a fraction of a second.

All the density measurements below are taken at room temperature except those of gases (marked with a †), which are measured at boiling point. A dash (–) at any place on the chart indicates that there is no known value.

Element	Symbol	Atomic number*	Approx. relative atomic mass*	Density* (g cm^{-3})	Melting point (°C)	Boiling point (°C) (brackets indicate approximations)
Actinium	Ac	89	227	10.1	1050	3200
Aluminium	Al	13	27	2.7	660	2470
Americium	Am	95	243	11.7	(1200)	(2600)
Antimony	Sb	51	122	6.62	630	1380
Argon	Ar	18	40	1.4 †	−189	−186
Arsenic	As	33	75	5.72	–	613 (**sublimes***)
Astatine	At	85	210	–	(302)	–
Barium	Ba	56	137	3.51	714	1640
Beryllium	Be	4	9	1.85	1280	2477
Bismuth	Bi	83	209	9.8	271	1560
Boron	B	5	11	2.34	2300	3930
Bromine	Br	35	80	3.12	−7.2	58.8
Cadmium	Cd	48	112	8.64	321	765
Caesium	Cs	55	133	1.9	28.7	690
Calcium	Ca	20	40	1.54	850	1487
Carbon	C	6	12	2.25 (**graphite***) 3.51 (**diamond***)	3730 (**sublimes***) 3750	4830 –
Cerium	Ce	58	140	6.78	795	3470
Chlorine	Cl	17	35.5	1.56†	−101	−34.7
Chromium	Cr	24	52	7.19	1890	2482
Cobalt	Co	27	59	8.9	1492	2900
Copper	Cu	29	64	8.92	1083	2595
Dysprosium	Dy	66	162	8.56	1410	2600
Erbium	Er	68	167	9.16	1500	2900
Europium	Eu	63	152	5.24	826	1440
Fluorine	F	9	19	1.11†	−220	−188
Francium	Fr	87	223	–	(27)	–
Gadolinium	Gd	64	157	7.95	1310	3000
Gallium	Ga	31	70	5.91	29.8	2400
Germanium	Ge	32	73	5.35	937	2830
Gold	Au	79	197	19.3	1063	2970
Hafnium	Hf	72	178.5	13.3	2220	5400
Helium	He	2	4	0.147†	−270	−269
Holmium	Ho	67	165	8.8	1460	2600
Hydrogen	H	1	1	0.07†	−259	−252
Indium	In	49	115	7.3	157	2000
Iodine	I	53	127	4.93	114	184
Iridium	Ir	77	192	22.5	2440	5300
Iron	Fe	26	56	7.86	1535	3000
Krypton	Kr	36	84	2.16†	−157	−152
Lanthanum	La	57	139	6.19	920	3470
Lead	Pb	82	207	11.3	327	1744
Lithium	Li	3	7	0.53	180	1330
Lutetium	Lu	71	175	9.84	1650	3330

* Atomic number, 13; Density, 114; Diamond, Graphite, 64; Relative atomic mass, 24; Sublimation, 7.

Element	Symbol	Atomic number*	Approx. relative atomic mass*	Density* (g cm^{-3})	Melting point (°C)	Boiling point (°C)
Magnesium	Mg	12	24	1.74	650	1110
Manganese	Mn	25	55	7.2	1240	2100
Mercury	Hg	80	201	13.6	−38.9	357
Molybdenum	Mo	42	96	10.2	2610	5560
Neodymium	Nd	60	144	7.0	1020	3030
Neon	Ne	10	20	1.2 †	−249	−246
Neptunium	Np	93	237	20.4	640	–
Nickel	Ni	28	59	8.9	1453	2730
Niobium	Nb	41	93	8.57	2470	3300
Nitrogen	N	7	14	0.808†	−210	−196
Osmium	Os	76	190	22.5	3000	5000
Oxygen	O	8	16	1.15†	−218	−183
Palladium	Pd	46	106	12	1550	3980
Phosphorus	P	15	31	1.82 (**white***)	44.2 (**white**)	280 (**white**)
				2.34 (**red***)	590 (**red**)	–
Platinum	Pt	78	195	21.4	1769	4530
Plutonium	Pu	94	242	19.8	640	3240
Polonium	Po	84	210	9.4	254	960
Potassium	K	19	39	0.86	63.7	774
Praseodymium	Pr	59	141	6.78	935	3130
Promethium	Pm	61	147	–	1030	2730
Protactinium	Pa	91	231	15.4	1230	–
Radium	Ra	88	226	5	700	1140
Radon	Rn	86	222	4.4†	−71	−61.8
Rhenium	Re	75	186	20.5	3180	5630
Rhodium	Rh	45	103	12.4	1970	4500
Rubidium	Rb	37	85	1.53	38.9	688
Ruthenium	Ru	44	101	12.3	2500	4900
Samarium	Sm	62	150	7.54	1070	1900
Scandium	Sc	21	45	2.99	1540	2730
Selenium	Se	34	79	4.81	217	685
Silicon	Si	14	28	2.33	1410	2360
Silver	Ag	47	108	10.5	961	2210
Sodium	Na	11	23	0.97	97.8	890
Strontium	Sr	38	88	2.62	768	1380
Sulphur	S	16	32	2.07 (**rhombic***)	113 (**rhombic**)	444
				1.96 (**monoclinic***)	119 (**monoclinic**)	
Tantalum	Ta	73	181	16.6	3000	5420
Technetium	Tc	43	99	11.5	2200	3500
Tellurium	Te	52	128	6.25	450	990
Terbium	Tb	65	159	8.27	1360	2800
Thallium	Tl	81	204	11.8	304	1460
Thorium	Th	90	232	11.7	1750	3850
Thulium	Tm	69	169	9.33	1540	1730
Tin	Sn	50	119	7.28	232	2270
Titanium	Ti	22	48	4.54	1675	3260
Tungsten	W	74	184	19.4	3410	5930
Uranium	U	92	238	19.1	1130	3820
Vanadium	V	23	51	5.96	1900	3000
Xenon	Xe	54	131	3.52†	−112	−108
Ytterbium	Yb	70	173	6.98	824	1430
Yttrium	Y	39	89	4.34	1500	2930
Zinc	Zn	30	65	7.14	420	907
Zirconium	Zr	40	91	6.49	1850	3580

* Atomic number, 13; Density, 114; Monoclinic sulphur, 70; Red phosphorus, 68 (**Phosphorus**); Relative atomic mass, 24; Rhombic sulphur, 70; White phosphorus, 68 (**Phosphorus**).

Naming simple organic compounds

Simple **organic compounds*** (those with one or no **functional group***) can be named by following Stages 1 and 2.

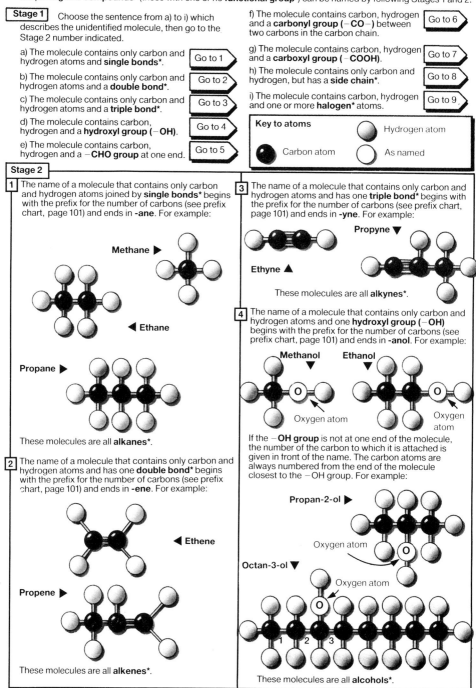

Stage 1 Choose the sentence from a) to i) which describes the unidentified molecule, then go to the Stage 2 number indicated.

a) The molecule contains only carbon and hydrogen atoms and **single bonds***. **Go to 1**

b) The molecule contains only carbon and hydrogen atoms and a **double bond***. **Go to 2**

c) The molecule contains only carbon and hydrogen atoms and a **triple bond***. **Go to 3**

d) The molecule contains carbon, hydrogen and a **hydroxyl group (−OH)**. **Go to 4**

e) The molecule contains carbon, hydrogen and a −**CHO group** at one end. **Go to 5**

f) The molecule contains carbon, hydrogen and a **carbonyl group (−CO−)** between two carbons in the carbon chain. **Go to 6**

g) The molecule contains carbon, hydrogen and a **carboxyl group (−COOH)**. **Go to 7**

h) The molecule contains only carbon and hydrogen, but has a **side chain***. **Go to 8**

i) The molecule contains carbon, hydrogen and one or more **halogen*** atoms. **Go to 9**

Key to atoms

○ Hydrogen atom

● Carbon atom

○ As named

Stage 2

1 The name of a molecule that contains only carbon and hydrogen atoms joined by **single bonds*** begins with the prefix for the number of carbons (see prefix chart, page 101) and ends in **-ane**. For example:

Methane ▶

◀ **Ethane**

Propane ▶

These molecules are all **alkanes***.

2 The name of a molecule that contains only carbon and hydrogen atoms and has one **double bond*** begins with the prefix for the number of carbons (see prefix chart, page 101) and ends in **-ene**. For example:

◀ **Ethene**

Propene ▶

These molecules are all **alkenes***.

3 The name of a molecule that contains only carbon and hydrogen atoms and has one **triple bond*** begins with the prefix for the number of carbons (see prefix chart, page 101) and ends in **-yne**. For example:

Propyne ▼

Ethyne ▲

These molecules are all **alkynes***.

4 The name of a molecule that contains only carbon and hydrogen atoms and one **hydroxyl group (−OH)** begins with the prefix for the number of carbons (see prefix chart, page 101) and ends in **-anol**. For example:

Methanol ▼   **Ethanol ▼**

Oxygen atom   Oxygen atom

If the −**OH group** is not at one end of the molecule, the number of the carbon to which it is attached is given in front of the name. The carbon atoms are always numbered from the end of the molecule closest to the −OH group. For example:

Propan-2-ol ▶

Oxygen atom

Octan-3-ol ▼

Oxygen atom

These molecules are all **alcohols***.

* Alcohols, 82, **Alkanes**, 78; **Alkenes**, 79; **Alkynes**, 80; **Double bond**, 18; **Functional group**, 77; **Halogens**, 72; **Organic compounds, Side chain**, 76; **Single bond, Triple bond**, 18.

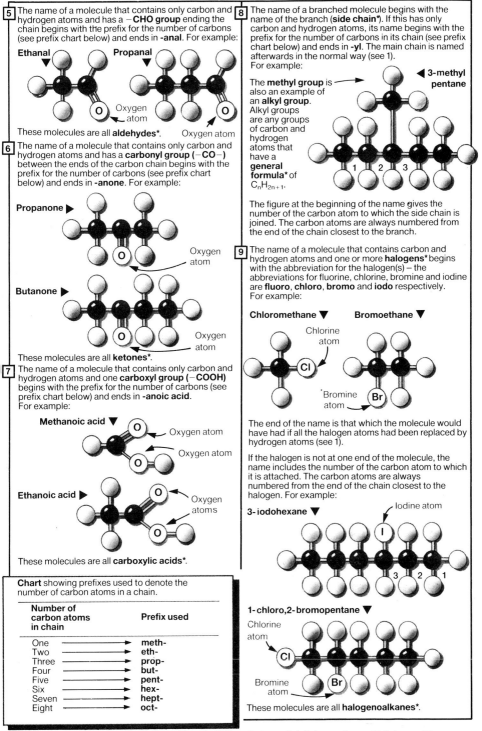

5 The name of a molecule that contains only carbon and hydrogen atoms and has a −**CHO** group ending the chain begins with the prefix for the number of carbons (see prefix chart below) and ends in **-anal**. For example:

Ethanal ▼   **Propanal** ▼

Oxygen atom

Oxygen atom

These molecules are all **aldehydes***.

6 The name of a molecule that contains only carbon and hydrogen atoms and has a **carbonyl group (−CO−)** between the ends of the carbon chain begins with the prefix for the number of carbons (see prefix chart below) and ends in **-anone**. For example:

Propanone ▶

Oxygen atom

Butanone ▶

Oxygen atom

These molecules are all **ketones***.

7 The name of a molecule that contains only carbon and hydrogen atoms and one **carboxyl group (−COOH)** begins with the prefix for the number of carbons (see prefix chart below) and ends in **-anoic acid**. For example:

Methanoic acid ▼

Oxygen atom

Oxygen atom

Ethanoic acid ▶

Oxygen atoms

These molecules are all **carboxylic acids***.

Chart showing prefixes used to denote the number of carbon atoms in a chain.

Number of carbon atoms in chain	Prefix used
One ⟶	meth-
Two ⟶	eth-
Three ⟶	prop-
Four ⟶	but-
Five ⟶	pent-
Six ⟶	hex-
Seven ⟶	hept-
Eight ⟶	oct-

8 The name of a branched molecule begins with the name of the branch (**side chain***). If this has only carbon and hydrogen atoms, its name begins with the prefix for the number of carbons in its chain (see prefix chart below) and ends in **-yl**. The main chain is named afterwards in the normal way (see 1). For example:

The **methyl group** is also an example of an **alkyl group**. Alkyl groups are any groups of carbon and hydrogen atoms that have a **general formula*** of C_nH_{2n+1}.

◀ **3-methyl pentane**

The figure at the beginning of the name gives the number of the carbon atom to which the side chain is joined. The carbon atoms are always numbered from the end of the chain closest to the branch.

9 The name of a molecule that contains carbon and hydrogen atoms and one or more **halogens*** begins with the abbreviation for the halogen(s) – the abbreviations for fluorine, chlorine, bromine and iodine are **fluoro**, **chloro**, **bromo** and **iodo** respectively. For example:

Chloromethane ▼   **Bromoethane** ▼

Chlorine atom

*Bromine atom

The end of the name is that which the molecule would have had if all the halogen atoms had been replaced by hydrogen atoms (see 1).

If the halogen is not at one end of the molecule, the name includes the number of the carbon atom to which it is attached. The carbon atoms are always numbered from the end of the chain closest to the halogen. For example:

3-iodohexane ▼

Iodine atom

1-chloro,2-bromopentane ▼

Chlorine atom

Bromine atom

These molecules are all **halogenoalkanes***.

***Aldehydes**, 80; **Carboxylic acids**, 81; **General formula**, 77 (**Homologous series**); **Halogenoalkanes**, 81; **Halogens**, 72; **Ketones**, 80; **Side chain**, 76.

The laboratory preparation of six gases

Methods for preparing six gases – **carbon dioxide**, **chlorine**, **hydrogen**, **ethene**, **nitrogen** and **oxygen** – are described below.

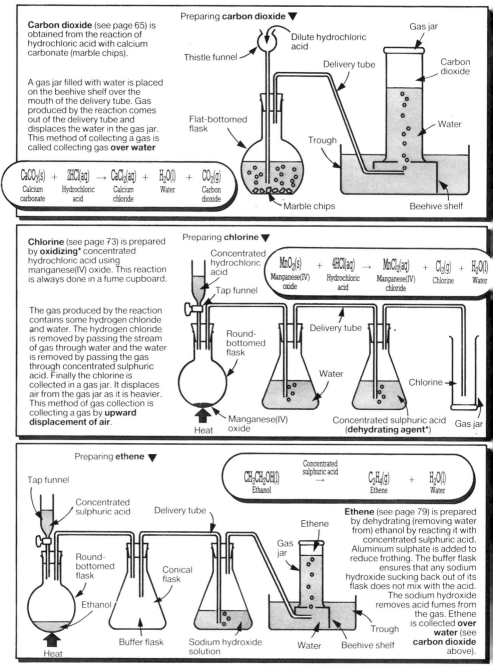

Carbon dioxide (see page 65) is obtained from the reaction of hydrochloric acid with calcium carbonate (marble chips).

A gas jar filled with water is placed on the beehive shelf over the mouth of the delivery tube. Gas produced by the reaction comes out of the delivery tube and displaces the water in the gas jar. This method of collecting a gas is called collecting gas **over water**

Preparing **carbon dioxide** ▼

Gas jar

Thistle funnel

Dilute hydrochloric acid

Delivery tube

Carbon dioxide

Flat-bottomed flask

Water

Trough

Marble chips

Beehive shelf

$$CaCO_3(s) + 2HCl(aq) \rightarrow CaCl_2(aq) + H_2O(l) + CO_2(g)$$
Calcium carbonate | Hydrochloric acid | Calcium chloride | Water | Carbon dioxide

Chlorine (see page 73) is prepared by **oxidizing*** concentrated hydrochloric acid using manganese(IV) oxide. This reaction is always done in a fume cupboard.

The gas produced by the reaction contains some hydrogen chloride and water. The hydrogen chloride is removed by passing the stream of gas through water and the water is removed by passing the gas through concentrated sulphuric acid. Finally the chlorine is collected in a gas jar. It displaces air from the gas jar as it is heavier. This method of gas collection is collecting a gas by **upward displacement of air**.

Preparing **chlorine** ▼

Concentrated hydrochloric acid

Tap funnel

$$MnO_2(s) + 4HCl(aq) \rightarrow MnCl_2(aq) + Cl_2(g) + H_2O(l)$$
Manganese(IV) oxide | Hydrochloric acid | Manganese(IV) chloride | Chlorine | Water

Delivery tube

Round-bottomed flask

Water

Chlorine

Heat

Manganese(IV) oxide

Concentrated sulphuric acid (**dehydrating agent***)

Gas jar

Preparing **ethene** ▼

Tap funnel

Concentrated sulphuric acid

Delivery tube

$$CH_3CH_2OH(l) \xrightarrow[\text{sulphuric acid}]{\text{Concentrated}} C_2H_4(g) + H_2O(l)$$
Ethanol | Ethene | Water

Ethene

Gas jar

Round-bottomed flask

Conical flask

Ethanol

Buffer flask

Sodium hydroxide solution

Water

Beehive shelf

Trough

Heat

Ethene (see page 79) is prepared by dehydrating (removing water from) ethanol by reacting it with concentrated sulphuric acid. Aluminium sulphate is added to reduce frothing. The buffer flask ensures that any sodium hydroxide sucking back out of its flask does not mix with the acid. The sodium hydroxide removes acid fumes from the gas. Ethene is collected **over water** (see **carbon dioxide** above).

Preparing **hydrogen** ▼

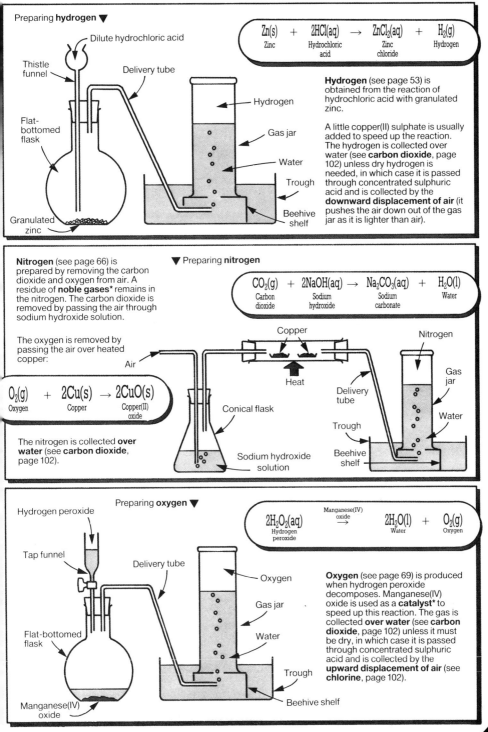

Dilute hydrochloric acid

Thistle funnel

Delivery tube

Flat-bottomed flask

Granulated zinc

Hydrogen

Gas jar

Water

Trough

Beehive shelf

$$Zn(s) \; + \; 2HCl(aq) \; \rightarrow \; ZnCl_2(aq) \; + \; H_2(g)$$
Zinc   Hydrochloric acid   Zinc chloride   Hydrogen

Hydrogen (see page 53) is obtained from the reaction of hydrochloric acid with granulated zinc.

A little copper(II) sulphate is usually added to speed up the reaction. The hydrogen is collected over water (see **carbon dioxide**, page 102) unless dry hydrogen is needed, in which case it is passed through concentrated sulphuric acid and is collected by the **downward displacement of air** (it pushes the air down out of the gas jar as it is lighter than air).

Nitrogen (see page 66) is prepared by removing the carbon dioxide and oxygen from air. A residue of **noble gases*** remains in the nitrogen. The carbon dioxide is removed by passing the air through sodium hydroxide solution.

The oxygen is removed by passing the air over heated copper:

$$O_2(g) \; + \; 2Cu(s) \; \rightarrow \; 2CuO(s)$$
Oxygen   Copper   Copper(II) oxide

The nitrogen is collected **over water** (see **carbon dioxide**, page 102).

▼ Preparing **nitrogen**

$$CO_2(g) \; + \; 2NaOH(aq) \; \rightarrow \; Na_2CO_3(aq) \; + \; H_2O(l)$$
Carbon dioxide   Sodium hydroxide   Sodium carbonate   Water

Copper

Air

Heat

Conical flask

Sodium hydroxide solution

Nitrogen

Gas jar

Delivery tube

Trough

Water

Beehive shelf

Preparing **oxygen** ▼

Hydrogen peroxide

Tap funnel

Delivery tube

Flat-bottomed flask

Manganese(IV) oxide

Oxygen

Gas jar

Water

Trough

Beehive shelf

$$2H_2O_2(aq) \; \xrightarrow{\text{Manganese(IV) oxide}} \; 2H_2O(l) \; + \; O_2(g)$$
Hydrogen peroxide   Water   Oxygen

Oxygen (see page 69) is produced when hydrogen peroxide decomposes. Manganese(IV) oxide is used as a **catalyst*** to speed up this reaction. The gas is collected **over water** (see **carbon dioxide**, page 102) unless it must be dry, in which case it is passed through concentrated sulphuric acid and is collected by the **upward displacement of air** (see **chlorine**, page 102).

---

* **Catalyst**, 47; **Noble gases**, 75.

Laboratory tests

Various different tests are used to identify substances. Some of the tests involve advanced machinery, others are simple laboratory tests and all are known collectively as **qualitative analysis**. Some of the more advanced tests are shown on page 108; these two pages cover simple laboratory tests leading to the identification of water, common gases, a selection of **anions*** and **cations*** (i.e. components of compounds) and some metals.

The appearance or smell of a substance often gives clues to its identity – these can be confirmed by testing. If there are no such clues, then it is a matter of progressing through the tests, gradually eliminating possibilities (it is often a good idea to start with a **flame test**). Often more than one test is needed to identify an ion (anion or cation), as only one particular combination of results can confirm its presence (compare the tests and results for **lead**, **zinc** and **magnesium**).

Tests for water (H_2O)

Test	Results
Add to **anhydrous*** copper(II) sulphate.	White copper sulphate powder turns blue.
Add to **anhydrous*** cobalt(II) chloride.	Blue cobalt(II) chloride turns pink.

Tests to identify gases

Gas	Symbol	Test	Results
Carbon dioxide	CO_2	Pass into **limewater** (calcium hydroxide solution).	Turns limewater cloudy.
Hydrogen	H_2	Put a lighted splint into a sample of the gas.	Burns with a "popping" noise.
Oxygen	O_2	Put a glowing splint into a sample of the gas.	Splint relights.

Tests for anions*

These tests are used to identify some of the **anions*** found in compounds.

Anion	Symbol	Test	Results
Bromide	Br^-	Add silver nitrate solution to a solution of substance in dilute nitric acid.	Pale yellow precipitate, dissolves slightly in ammonia solution.
Carbonate	CO_3^{2-}	a) Add dilute hydrochloric acid to the substance.	Carbon dioxide gas given off.
		b) Try to dissolve the substance in water containing **universal indicator*** solution.	Dissolves and turns the indicator purple. (Compare **hydrogencarbonate** test.)
Chloride	Cl^-	Add silver nitrate solution to a solution of substance in dilute nitric acid.	Thick white precipitate dissolves in ammonia solution.
Hydrogen-carbonate	HCO_3^-	a) Add dilute hydrochloric acid to the substance.	Carbon dioxide gas evolved.
		b) Try to dissolve the substance in water containing **universal indicator*** solution.	Dissolves and green indicator solution turns purple when boiled.
Iodide	I^-	Add silver nitrate solution to a solution of substance in dilute nitric acid.	Yellow precipitate, does not dissolve in ammonia solution.
Nitrate	NO_3^-	Add iron(II) sulphate solution followed by concentrated sulphuric acid to the solution.	Brown ring forms at the junction of the two liquids.
Sulphate	SO_4^{2-}	Add barium chloride solution to the solution.	White precipitate, does not dissolve in dilute hydrochloric acid.
Sulphite	SO_3^{2-}	Add barium chloride solution to the solution.	White precipitate, that dissolves in dilute hydrochloric acid.
Sulphide	S^{2-}	Add lead(II) ethanoate solution to the solution.	Black precipitate

*Anhydrous, 41 (Anhydrate); Anion, Cation, 16; Universal Indicator, 38.

Tests for cations*

Most **cations*** in compounds can be identified by the same **flame tests** which are used to identify pure metals (see page 108 for how to carry out a flame test). The chart on the right gives a selection of flame test results. Cations can also be identified by the results of certain reactions. A number of these reactions are listed in the chart below. They cannot be used to identify pure metals, since many metals are insoluble in water and hence cannot form solutions.

Flame tests

Metal	Symbol	Flame colour
Barium	Ba	Yellow-green
Calcium	Ca	Red
Copper	Cu	Green
Lead	Pb	Blue
Lithium	Li	Pink
Potassium	K	Lilac
Sodium	Na	Orange

Cation	Symbol	Test	Results
Aluminium	Al^{3+}	a) Add dilute sodium hydroxide solution to a solution of the substance.	White precipitate that dissolves as more sodium hydroxide solution is added
		b) Add dilute ammonia solution to a solution of the substance.	White precipitate that does not dissolve as more ammonia solution is added.
		c) Compare with **lead**, see tests below.	————————
Ammonium	NH_4^+	Add sodium hydroxide solution to a solution of the substance and heat gently.	Ammonia gas is given off, it has a distinctive choking smell.
Calcium	Ca^{2+}	a) See **flame test**	————————
		b) Add dilute sulphuric acid to a solution of the substance.	White precipitate formed.
Copper(II)	Cu^{2+}	a) See **flame test**	————————
		b) Add dilute sodium hydroxide solution to a solution of the substance.	Pale blue precipitate that dissolves as more sodium hydroxide is added.
		c) Add dilute ammonia solution to a solution the substance.	Pale blue precipitate, changing to deep blue solutions as more ammonia solution is added.
Iron(II)	Fe^{2+}	a) Add dilute sodium hydroxide solution to a solution of the substance.	Pale green precipitate formed.
		b) Add dilute ammonia solution to a solution of the substance.	Pale green precipitate formed.
Iron(III)	Fe^{3+}	a) Add dilute sodium hydroxide solution to a solution of the substance.	Red-brown precipitate formed.
		b) Add dilute ammonia solution to a solution of the substance.	Red-brown precipitate formed.
Lead(II)	Pb^{2+}	a) Add dilute sodium hydroxide solution to a solution of the substance.	White precipitate that dissolves as more sodium hydroxide solution is added.
		b) Add dilute ammonia solution to a solution of the substance.	White precipitate that does not dissolve as more ammonia solution is added.
		c) See also **flame test** to distinguish between lead and **aluminium**	————————
Magnesium	Mg^{2+}	a) Add dilute sodium hydroxide solution to a solution of the substance.	White precipitate that does not dissolve as more sodium hydroxide solution is added.
		b) Add dilute ammonia solution to a solution of the substance.	White precipitate that does not dissolve as more ammonia solution is added.
Zinc	Zn^{2+}	a) Add dilute sodium hydroxide solution to a solution of the substance.	White precipitate that dissolves as more sodium hydroxide solution is added.
		b) Add dilute ammonia solution to a solution of the substance.	White precipitate that dissolves as more ammonia solution is added.

Investigating substances

The investigation of chemical substances involves a variety of different techniques. The first step is often to obtain a pure sample of a substance (impurities affect experimental results). Some of the separating and purifying techniques used to achieve this are explained on these two pages. A variety of different methods are then used to find out the chemical composition and the chemical and physical properties of the substance (**qualitative analysis**), and how much of it is present (**quantitative analysis**). For more information, see also pages 104-105 and 108.

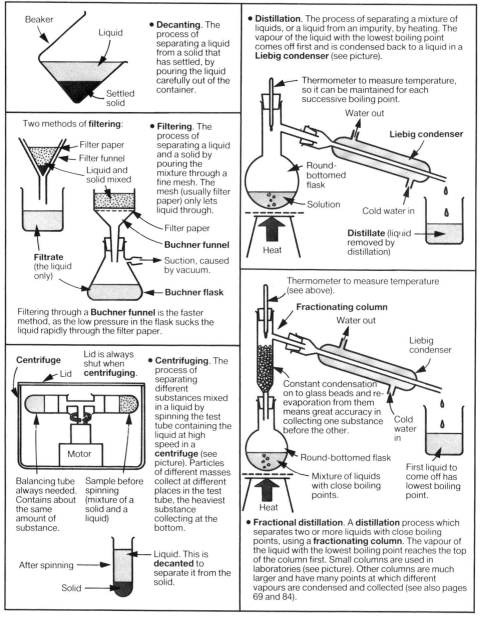

Beaker

Liquid

Settled solid

- **Decanting**. The process of separating a liquid from a solid that has settled, by pouring the liquid carefully out of the container.

Two methods of **filtering**:

Filter paper

Filter funnel

Liquid and solid mixed

Filter paper

Buchner funnel

Filtrate (the liquid only)

Suction, caused by vacuum.

Buchner flask

- **Filtering**. The process of separating a liquid and a solid by pouring the mixture through a fine mesh. The mesh (usually filter paper) only lets liquid through.

Filtering through a **Buchner funnel** is the faster method, as the low pressure in the flask sucks the liquid rapidly through the filter paper.

Centrifuge

Lid is always shut when **centrifuging**.

Lid

Motor

Balancing tube always needed. Contains about the same amount of substance.

Sample before spinning (mixture of a solid and a liquid)

- **Centrifuging**. The process of separating different substances mixed in a liquid by spinning the test tube containing the liquid at high speed in a **centrifuge** (see picture). Particles of different masses collect at different places in the test tube, the heaviest substance collecting at the bottom.

After spinning

Solid

Liquid. This is **decanted** to separate it from the solid.

- **Distillation**. The process of separating a mixture of liquids, or a liquid from an impurity, by heating. The vapour of the liquid with the lowest boiling point comes off first and is condensed back to a liquid in a **Liebig condenser** (see picture).

Thermometer to measure temperature, so it can be maintained for each successive boiling point.

Water out

Liebig condenser

Round-bottomed flask

Solution

Cold water in

Heat

Distillate (liquid removed by distillation)

Thermometer to measure temperature (see above).

Fractionating column

Water out

Liebig condenser

Constant condensation on to glass beads and re-evaporation from them means great accuracy in collecting one substance before the other.

Cold water in

Round-bottomed flask

Mixture of liquids with close boiling points.

Heat

First liquid to come off has lowest boiling point.

- **Fractional distillation**. A **distillation** process which separates two or more liquids with close boiling points, using a **fractionating column**. The vapour of the liquid with the lowest boiling point reaches the top of the column first. Small columns are used in laboratories (see picture). Other columns are much larger and have many points at which different vapours are condensed and collected (see also pages 69 and 84).

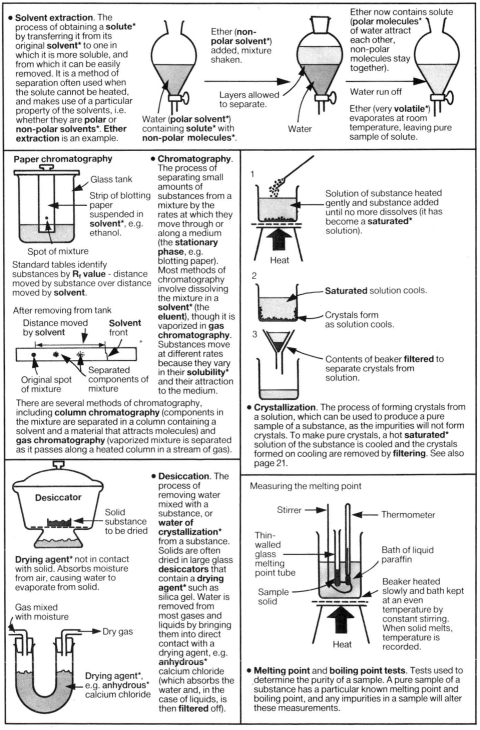

- **Solvent extraction**. The process of obtaining a **solute*** by transferring it from its original **solvent*** to one in which it is more soluble, and from which it can be easily removed. It is a method of separation often used when the solute cannot be heated, and makes use of a particular property of the solvents, i.e. whether they are **polar** or **non-polar solvents***. **Ether extraction** is an example.

Water (**polar solvent***) containing **solute*** with **non-polar molecules***.

Ether (**non-polar solvent***) added, mixture shaken.

Layers allowed to separate.

Water

Ether now contains solute (**polar molecules*** of water attract each other, non-polar molecules stay together).

Water run off

Ether (very **volatile***) evaporates at room temperature, leaving pure sample of solute.

Paper chromatography

Glass tank

Strip of blotting paper suspended in **solvent***, e.g. ethanol.

Spot of mixture

Standard tables identify substances by R_f **value** - distance moved by substance over distance moved by **solvent**.

After removing from tank

Distance moved by **solvent**

Solvent front

Separated components of mixture

Original spot of mixture

There are several methods of chromatography, including **column chromatography** (components in the mixture are separated in a column containing a solvent and a material that attracts molecules) and **gas chromatography** (vaporized mixture is separated as it passes along a heated column in a stream of gas).

- **Chromatography**. The process of separating small amounts of substances from a mixture by the rates at which they move through or along a medium (the **stationary phase**, e.g. blotting paper). Most methods of chromatography involve dissolving the mixture in a **solvent*** (the **eluent**), though it is vaporized in **gas chromatography**. Substances move at different rates because they vary in their **solubility*** and their attraction to the medium.

1
Solution of substance heated gently and substance added until no more dissolves (it has become a **saturated*** solution).

Heat

2
Saturated solution cools.

Crystals form as solution cools.

3
Contents of beaker **filtered** to separate crystals from solution.

- **Crystallization**. The process of forming crystals from a solution, which can be used to produce a pure sample of a substance, as the impurities will not form crystals. To make pure crystals, a hot **saturated*** solution of the substance is cooled and the crystals formed on cooling are removed by **filtering**. See also page 21.

Desiccator

Solid substance to be dried

Drying agent* not in contact with solid. Absorbs moisture from air, causing water to evaporate from solid.

Gas mixed with moisture

Dry gas

Drying agent*, e.g. **anhydrous*** calcium chloride

- **Desiccation**. The process of removing water mixed with a substance, or **water of crystallization*** from a substance. Solids are often dried in large glass **desiccators** that contain a **drying agent*** such as silica gel. Water is removed from most gases and liquids by bringing them into direct contact with a drying agent, e.g. **anhydrous*** calcium chloride (which absorbs the water and, in the case of liquids, is then **filtered** off).

Measuring the melting point

Stirrer

Thermometer

Thin-walled glass melting point tube

Sample solid

Bath of liquid paraffin

Beaker heated slowly and bath kept at an even temperature by constant stirring. When solid melts, temperature is recorded.

Heat

- **Melting point** and **boiling point tests**. Tests used to determine the purity of a sample. A pure sample of a substance has a particular known melting point and boiling point, and any impurities in a sample will alter these measurements.

Qualitative and quantitative analysis

There are two types of analysis used to investigate substances: **qualitative analysis** – any method used to study chemical composition – and **quantitative analysis** – any method used to discover how much of a substance is present in a sample. Below are some examples of both types of analysis.

Qualitative analysis

Below are some examples of qualitative analysis. The **flame test** and the tests on pages 104-105 are examples of qualitative analysis used in schools. The other methods described are more advanced.

- **Flame test**. Used to identify metals. A substance is collected on the tip of a clean platinum or nichrome wire. This is held in the flame to observe the colour with which the substance burns (see also page 105). Between tests, the wire is cleaned by dipping it in concentrated hydrochloric acid and then heating strongly.

Hot bunsen flame

Change of flame colour where substance burning

Clean platinum wire

- **Mass spectroscopy**. A method of investigating the composition of a substance, in particular the **isotopes*** it contains. It is also used as a method of quantitative analysis as it involves measuring the relative proportions of isotopes or molecules in the substance. The apparatus used is called a **mass spectrometer**.

▼ **Mass spectrometer**

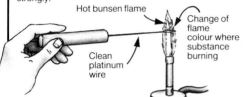

Vaporized sample of substance

High energy electrons produced to **ionize*** the substance. The positive ions pass into an electric field which accelerates them.

Electron gun

Magnet
A magnetic field deflects the ions of different masses by different amounts.

Ion detector

- **Nuclear magnetic resonance (n.m.r.) spectroscopy**. A method used for investigating the position of atoms in a molecule. Radio waves are passed through a sample of a substance held between the poles of a magnet. The amount of absorption reveals the positions of particular atoms within a molecule. This information is presented on a graph called a **nuclear magnetic resonance (n.m.r.) spectrum**. ▼

Nuclear magnetic resonance spectrum of ethanol*
(CH_3CH_2OH)

Degree of absorption

Peak showing an -OH group

Peaks showing a -CH_2- group

Peaks showing a -CH_3 group

Quantitative analysis

Below are some examples of quantitative analysis. See also **mass spectroscopy**.

- **Volumetric analysis**. A method of determining the concentration of a solution using **titration**. This is the addition of one solution into another, using a **burette***. The concentration of one solution is known. The first solution is added from the burette until the **end point**, when all the second solution has reacted. The volume of solution from the burette needed to reach the end point is called the **titre**. This, the volume of solution in the flask and the known concentration of one solution are used to calculate the concentration of the second solution. ▶

Burette*

Solution A

Tap

Conical flask containing measured volume of solution B.

Apparatus used for **titrations**

- **Gravimetric analysis**. A method of determining the amount of a substance present by converting it into another substance of known chemical composition that is easily purified and weighed. ▼

Gravimetric analysis can be used to measure the amount of lead in a sample of water containing a lead salt.

Potassium dichromate ($K_2Cr_2O_7$) is added to a known volume of water.

A yellow **precipitate*** is formed. This is removed by **filtering***.

The precipitate is then washed, dried and weighed accurately.

The concentration of the lead in the sample of water is calculated from the volume of water, the weight of lead chromate and the **relative atomic mass*** of lead.

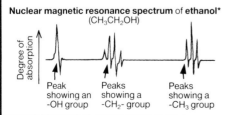

Apparatus

Apparatus is chemical equipment. The most common items are described and illustrated below and on pages 110-111. Simple 2-D diagrams used to represent them are also shown, together with approximate ranges of sizes.

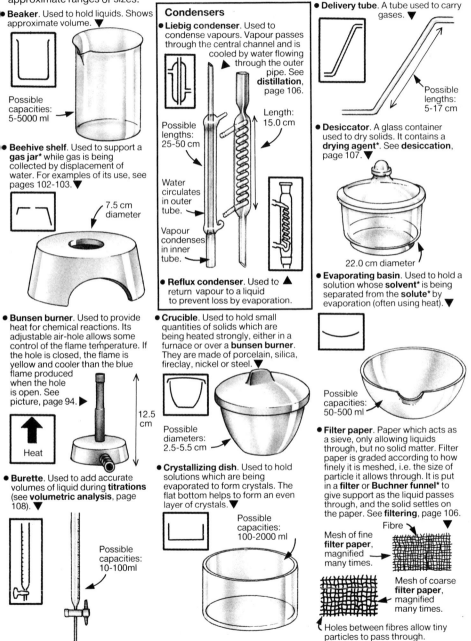

● **Beaker**. Used to hold liquids. Shows approximate volume. ▼

Possible capacities: 5-5000 ml

● **Beehive shelf**. Used to support a **gas jar*** while gas is being collected by displacement of water. For examples of its use, see pages 102-103. ▼

7.5 cm diameter

● **Bunsen burner**. Used to provide heat for chemical reactions. Its adjustable air-hole allows some control of the flame temperature. If the hole is closed, the flame is yellow and cooler than the blue flame produced when the hole is open. See picture, page 94. ▶

12.5 cm

Heat

● **Burette**. Used to add accurate volumes of liquid during **titrations** (see **volumetric analysis**, page 108). ▼

Possible capacities: 10-100ml

Condensers

● **Liebig condenser**. Used to condense vapours. Vapour passes through the central channel and is cooled by water flowing through the outer pipe. See **distillation**, page 106.

Possible lengths: 25-50 cm

Water circulates in outer tube.

Vapour condenses in inner tube.

Length: 15.0 cm

● **Reflux condenser**. Used to ▲ return vapour to a liquid to prevent loss by evaporation.

● **Crucible**. Used to hold small quantities of solids which are being heated strongly, either in a furnace or over a **bunsen burner**. They are made of porcelain, silica, fireclay, nickel or steel. ▼

Possible diameters: 2.5-5.5 cm

● **Crystallizing dish**. Used to hold solutions which are being evaporated to form crystals. The flat bottom helps to form an even layer of crystals. ▼

Possible capacities: 100-2000 ml

● **Delivery tube**. A tube used to carry gases. ▼

Possible lengths: 5-17 cm

● **Desiccator**. A glass container used to dry solids. It contains a **drying agent***. See **desiccation**, page 107. ▼

22.0 cm diameter

● **Evaporating basin**. Used to hold a solution whose **solvent*** is being separated from the **solute*** by evaporation (often using heat). ▼

Possible capacities: 50-500 ml

● **Filter paper**. Paper which acts as a sieve, only allowing liquids through, but no solid matter. Filter paper is graded according to how finely it is meshed, i.e. the size of particle it allows through. It is put in a **filter** or **Buchner funnel*** to give support as the liquid passes through, and the solid settles on the paper. See **filtering**, page 106.

Mesh of fine **filter paper**, magnified many times.

Fibre ▼

Mesh of coarse **filter paper**, magnified many times.

Holes between fibres allow tiny particles to pass through.

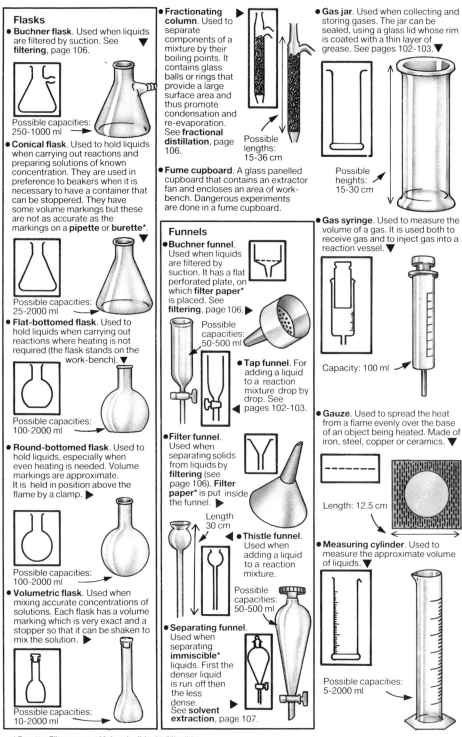

Flasks

- **Buchner flask.** Used when liquids are filtered by suction. See **filtering**, page 106. ▼

Possible capacities: 250-1000 ml ➡

- **Conical flask.** Used to hold liquids when carrying out reactions and preparing solutions of known concentration. They are used in preference to beakers when it is necessary to have a container that can be stoppered. They have some volume markings but these are not as accurate as the markings on a **pipette** or **burette***. ▼

Possible capacities: 25-2000 ml ➡

- **Flat-bottomed flask.** Used to hold liquids when carrying out reactions where heating is not required (the flask stands on the work-bench). ▼

Possible capacities: 100-2000 ml ➡

- **Round-bottomed flask.** Used to hold liquids, especially when even heating is needed. Volume markings are approximate. It is held in position above the flame by a clamp. ▶

Possible capacities: 100-2000 ml ➡

- **Volumetric flask.** Used when mixing accurate concentrations of solutions. Each flask has a volume marking which is very exact and a stopper so that it can be shaken to mix the solution. ▶

Possible capacities: 10-2000 ml ➡

- **Fractionating column.** Used to separate components of a mixture by their boiling points. It contains glass balls or rings that provide a large surface area and thus promote condensation and re-evaporation. See **fractional distillation**, page 106.

Possible lengths: 15-36 cm

- **Fume cupboard.** A glass panelled cupboard that contains an extractor fan and encloses an area of work-bench. Dangerous experiments are done in a fume cupboard.

Funnels

- **Buchner funnel.** Used when liquids are filtered by suction. It has a flat perforated plate, on which **filter paper*** is placed. See **filtering**, page 106. ▶

Possible capacities: 50-500 ml

- **Tap funnel.** For adding a liquid to a reaction mixture drop by drop. See pages 102-103. ◀

- **Filter funnel.** Used when separating solids from liquids by **filtering** (see page 106). **Filter paper*** is put inside the funnel. ▼

Length 30 cm

- **Thistle funnel.** Used when adding a liquid to a reaction mixture. ▶

Possible capacities: 50-500 ml

- **Separating funnel.** Used when separating **immiscible*** liquids. First the denser liquid is run off then the less dense. See **solvent extraction**, page 107. ▶

- **Gas jar.** Used when collecting and storing gases. The jar can be sealed, using a glass lid whose rim is coated with a thin layer of grease. See pages 102-103. ▼

Possible heights: 15-30 cm

- **Gas syringe.** Used to measure the volume of a gas. It is used both to receive gas and to inject gas into a reaction vessel. ▼

Capacity: 100 ml ➡

- **Gauze.** Used to spread the heat from a flame evenly over the base of an object being heated. Made of iron, steel, copper or ceramics. ▼

Length: 12.5 cm

- **Measuring cylinder.** Used to measure the approximate volume of liquids. ▼

Possible capacities: 5-2000 ml ➡

● **Pipeclay triangle**. Used to support **crucibles*** on **tripods** when they are being heated. They are made of iron or nickel-chromium wire enclosed in pipeclay tubes. ▼

Length: 21 cm

Pipettes

● **Pipette**. Used to dispense accurate volumes of liquid. They come in different sizes for different volumes. The liquid is run out of the pipette until its level has dropped from one volume marking to the next. ►

Possible capacities: 1-100 ml

Possible capacities: 1-2 ml

●◄ **Dropping pipette** or **teat pipette**. Used to dispense small volumes or drops of liquid. It does not provide an accurate measurement.

● **Stands and clamps**. Used to hold apparatus in position, e.g. **round-bottomed flasks**. ▼

Possible lengths: 50-100 cm

● **Spatula**. Used to pick up small quantities of a solid. ▼

Possible lengths: 10-20 cm

● **Test tube holder**. Used to hold a test tube, e.g. when heating it in a flame, creating a chemical reaction within it, or transferring it from one place to another. ▼

●**Test tube rack**. Used to hold many test tubes upright. ▼

●**Thermometer**. Used to measure temperature. They are filled either with alcohol or with mercury, depending on the temperature range for which they are intended. ▼

Large temperature range: -10 to 400'C

Small temperature range: -10 to 50'C

● **Tongs**. Used to move hot objects. ▼

● **Top pan balances**. Used for quick, accurate weighing. ▼

● **Trough**. Used when collecting gas **over water** (see **carbon dioxide**, page 102). The water contained in a gas jar inverted in the trough is displaced into the trough. Troughs are also used when substances such as potassium are reacted (see picture, page 55). ▼

Possible diameters: 20-30 cm

● **Tripod**. Used with a **pipeclay triangle** or **gauze** when heating **crucibles***, **flasks**, etc. ▼

Length: 21 cm

Tubes

● **Boiling tube**. A thick-walled tube used to hold substances being heated strongly. ►

Possible length: 12.5 cm

● **Test tube**. A tube used to hold substances for simple chemical reactions not involving strong heating. ►

Possible length: 7.5 cm

● **Ignition tube**. A disposable tube used to hold small quantities of substances being melted or boiled. ►

Possible length: 5.0 cm

● **Watch glass**. Used when evaporating small quantities.

Possible diameters: 5-15 cm

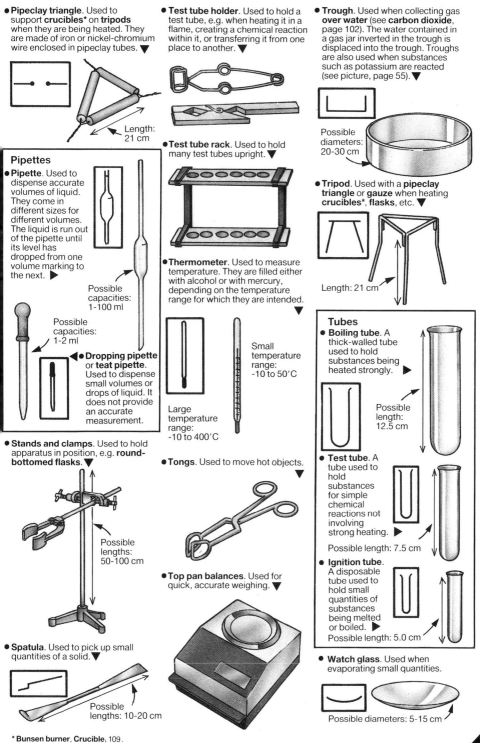

Units

A **unit** is the measure used as the standard for a quantity, e.g. the standard unit of mass is the **kilogram** (so all masses are measured in kilograms, or units that are multiples of the kilogram). Below are the seven basic **System International (SI) units**. These definitions are very complicated but they show how one standard unit of a quantity is determined.

- **Ampere (amp – A)**. The intensity of a constant current of electrons flowing through parallel, straight wires (that are infinitely long and have a negligible cross section) in a vacuum that produces a force between the wires of 2×10^{-7} N m^{-1}. This unit is used to measure electric current.

- **Candela (cd)**. The strength of the light coming perpendicularly from 1/600 000 square metres of the surface of a totally black object which is at the temperature of freezing platinum under a pressure of 101,325 N m^{-2}. This unit is used to measure the intensity of light.

- **Kelvin (K)**. The fraction 1/273.16 of the thermodynamic temperature of the **triple point*** of water. This unit is used to measure temperature. See also page 29.

- **Metre (m)**. The length equal to 1,650,763.73 wavelengths of a certain type of radiation emitted by the krypton-86 atom. This unit is used to measure length.

- **Mole (mol)**. The amount of substance that contains a number of particles (whether atoms, molecules, electrons or ions) equal to the Avogadro's constant (6.02×10^{23}). See also page 25. This unit is used to measure the amount of a substance.

- **Second (s)**. The duration of 9,192,631,770 periods of a certain type of radiation emitted by the caesium-133 atom. This unit is used to measure time.

- **Kilogram (kg)**. The mass of the international prototype of the kilogram, kept at Sèvres, near Paris. This unit is used to measure mass.

• Derived units

Some units that have been worked out (or derived) from the seven basic **SI units**. Where the unit of measurement is very complicated it is given a name and a symbol.

Quantity	Units of measurement			Derivation
	Units	Name of unit	Symbol of unit	
Velocity	m s^{-1}			distance/time
Acceleration	m s^{-2}			velocity/time
Force	kg m s^{-2}	newton	N	mass x acceleration
Energy	kg m^2 s^{-2}	joule	J	force x distance
Pressure	kg m^{-1} s^{-2}	pascal	Pa	force/unit area
Volume	dm^3			cubic decimetre
Density	kg m^{-3}			kilogram/cubic metre
Concentration	mol dm^{-3}		M	moles/cubic metre
Electric charge	A s	coulomb	C	amperes x time
Electric potential	kg m^2 s^{-3} A^{-1}	volt	V	joule/coulomb

Prefixes for units

Prefixes and powers of ten are often used to write numbers more concisely e.g. 8,000 m can be written as 8 x 10^3 m or 8 km.

Power of ten	Figure	Prefix	Symbol
10^9	1,000,000,000	giga	G
10^6	1,000,000	mega	M
10^3	1,000	kilo	k
10^2	100	hecto	h
10^1	10	deca	da
10^{-1}	.1	deci	d
10^{-2}	.01	centi	c
10^{-3}	.001	milli	m
10^{-6}	.000 001	micro	μ
10^{-9}	.000 000 001	nano	n

* Triple point. 115.

Famous chemists

The first chemical experimentation, known as **alchemy**, began in Greece over 2,000 years ago. The aim of alchemists was to find a way of turning metals into gold by rearranging what they thought were the four elements - earth, fire, air and water. Although they never succeeded in this impossible task, alchemists added a great deal to chemical knowledge by their experiments. Gradually alchemy developed into the science of chemistry, based on experiment, observation and deduction. In the seventeenth century, the old idea of the four elements was challenged, and the modern era of chemistry began. The list below shows some of the chemists whose influence was vital in the centuries that followed.

- **Robert Boyle** (1627-91). The Irishman Robert Boyle was the founder of modern chemistry and came from an aristocratic background. After he moved to England, he published his book "The Sceptical Chymist". In it he insisted on the use of scientific methods of experiment, observation and deduction, and he destroyed the old belief in four basic elements (see also **Boyle's law**, page 28).

- **Henry Cavendish** (1731-1810). Henry Cavendish was educated at Cambridge University, England, but left without a degree and devoted the rest of his life to science. He inherited a vast fortune, which he used to finance his experiments. He was one of the first chemists to study gas reactions, and among his most important work was the discovery that water was not an element but a compound. He was an eccentric recluse and much of his work was only published after his death.

- **Joseph Priestley** (1733-1804). Joseph Priestley had no scientific training, but as a child he lived near a brewery in Leeds, England. Watching the beer-making processes fired his enthusiasm for experiments. He identified most of the common gases, discovering oxygen in 1774. As well as a chemist, Priestley was a minister, schoolmaster, writer and politician. His radical views on the French revolution made him very unpopular in England, so he emigrated to America and settled in Pennsylvania until his death.

- **Antoine Lavoisier** (1743-94). This French scientist and reformer contributed vital information on the elements, and distinguished between chemical and physical changes (see page 5 and also **Law of conservation of mass**, page 11). He was trained as a lawyer, and worked for the tax corporation of the French government. In 1775 he took charge of French gunpowder factories. But during the French revolution he was attacked for his government work, and guillotined

- **John Dalton** (1766-1844). John Dalton was the son of a Quaker weaver. He made a living as a schoolmaster in Cumbria, England, until he could afford to devote himself wholly to science. His great achievement was to prove the existence of the **atom**, the foundation stone of modern chemistry. He also worked on the behaviour of gases (see **Dalton's law of partial pressures**, page 29), helped to develop the new science of weather study, and proved that humans could be colour-blind - a condition he suffered from.

- **Johann Wolfgang Döbereiner** (1780-1849). Johann Döbereiner was born in Germany, the son of a coachman. He had little formal education, but got a job as an apothecary's assistant at the age of 14. He taught himself chemistry and was eventually appointed Assistant Professor of chemistry at Jena University. His observations of regular increments of atomic weight in elements with similar properties was a vital step on the way to **Mendeléev's periodic table** (see pages 50-51).

- **Dmitri Ivanovich Mendeléev** (1834-1907). This Russian scientist was the youngest child of a large Siberian family. His father was blind, and to support the family his mother ran a glass factory. As a young man, Mendeléev learnt science from a brother-in-law. He went to St. Petersburg to study, and eventually became a Professor at the University there. In 1869 he published his **periodic table** (see pages 50-51). Element 101 is named **mendelevium** in his honour.

- **Antoine Becquerel** (1852-1908). Antoine Becquerel came from a distinguished family of French scientists. In 1896 he discovered that some materials give out invisible rays - **radioactivity** (see pages 14-15). He wrapped a piece of photographic paper in black paper and shut it in a drawer below some aluminium sprinkled with a chemical containing uranium. When the film was developed it was marked with a shadow caused by the uranium's radioactive rays.

- **Sir Joseph John Thomson** (1856-1940). J.J. Thomson studied at Manchester University, England, and became a Professor at Cambridge University at the age of only 28. His brilliant experimental work led to the discovery of the **electron** (see page 12). He also discovered that gases could be made to conduct electricity, paving the way for radio, television and radar. He was a great teacher, and some of his pupils went on to win Nobel prizes.

- **Marie Curie**, née **Marja Sklodowska** (1867-1934). Marie Curie was born in Warsaw, Poland. Polish girls were not allowed further education at this time, so Marie had to study secretly. She left for Paris at the age of 24 and went to the Sorbonne, where she met and married a young Professor, Pierre Curie. Together they discovered radium, which they extracted from pitchblende through patient and tiring experiment. From this discovery scientists were able to learn more about **radioactivity** (see pages 14-15). Pierre died in a tragic street accident, and Marie herself eventually died of radiation sickness after a brilliant career.

- **Fritz Haber** (1868-1934). Fritz Haber was born in Germany, the son of a merchant. He discovered how to synthesize ammonia (see **Haber process**, page 66), initially to use in making fertilizer. His process was developed on an industrial scale by Carl Bosch. After World War I, Haber tried unsuccessfully to repay Germany's war debts by a process of extracting gold from seawater.

- **Lord Ernest Rutherford** (1871-1937). New Zealander Ernest Rutherford finally established the science of **radioactivity** (see pages 14-15). He revealed the structure of the atom, and was the first to split it. He worked with **J.J. Thomson** at Cambridge University, England, and succeeded him as a Professor. He gained many honours for his work, and is buried alongside great world scientists in Westminster Abbey, London.

Glossary

Abrasive. A material which wears away the surface of another material.

Adhesive. A substance which sticks to one or more other substances.

Alloy. A mixture of two or more metals, or of a metal and a non-metal. It has its own properties, independent of those of its constituents.

Amalgam. An **alloy** of mercury with other metals. It is usually soft and may even be liquid.

Antacid. A substance which counteracts excess stomach acidity by **neutralizing*** the acid.

Bleach. A substance used to remove colour from a material or solution. Sunlight and most strong **oxidizing** and **reducing agents*** are good bleaches. The most common household bleach is a solution of sodium hypochlorite, which is also a highly effective **germicide.**

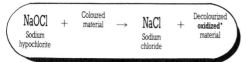

Calorie. A unit of heat energy. One calorie (1 cal) is the amount of heat needed to raise the temperature of one gram (1 g) of water by one degree **Celsius** (1°C).

Calorimetry. The measurement of heat change during a chemical reaction. There are a variety of methods of calorimetry, many of which involve the measurement of temperature change in a known mass of water, e.g. when a known amount of a substance is cooled down in the water (the heat change being a loss of heat energy from the substance and a gain by the water). Change of water temperature may also be used to measure the heat given off when a known amount of a substance is burnt (see **bomb calorimeter** diagram, page 32).

Celsius temperature or **Centigrade temperature.** Temperature measured on the **Celsius** (**Centigrade**) **scale**, where zero degrees (0°C) is set at the freezing point of water and one hundred degrees (100°C) at the boiling point of water.

Conductor. A material through which electric current or heat can flow (it has the property of **conductivity**). An **electrical conductor** is a substance which allows an electric current to flow through it. Metals, solutions which contain ions, and molten **ionic compounds*** are all electrical conductors. A **thermal conductor** is a substance which allows heat to flow through it. Metals are good thermal conductors. See also **semiconductors** and **insulators.**

Constant. A numerical quantity that does not vary, e.g. the **Avogadro constant*** or the **gas constant**, which is 8.314 J k^{-1} mol^{-1} (joules per kelvin per mole).

Control rods. Part of the control system of a nuclear reactor. They are rods or tubes which are moved up or down to alter the rate of the reaction inside the reactor. They are made of steel or aluminium containing boron, cadmium or some other strong absorber of **neutrons*.**

Coolant. A fluid used for cooling in industry or in the home (see also **refrigerant**). The fluid usually extracts heat from one source and transfers it to another. In a nuclear power station, the coolant transfers the heat from the nuclear reaction to the steam generator, where the heat is used to produce steam. This turns turbines and generates electricity.

Dehydrating agent. A substance used to absorb moisture from another substance, removing water molecules if present, but also, importantly, hydrogen and oxygen atoms from the molecules of the substance. This leaves a different substance plus water (see also **drying agent**). Concentrated sulphuric acid is an example:

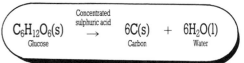

Concentrated sulphuric acid can also be used as a **drying agent** if it does not react with the substance added to it. For example, it is used to dry samples of chlorine gas, i.e. remove surrounding molecules of water vapour (see page 102).

Density. A measurement of the **mass** of a unit **volume** of a substance, or that of a body of given volume. It is calculated by dividing the mass of the substance by its volume and is measured in kilograms per cubic metre (kg m^{-3}).

Drying agent. A substance used to absorb moisture from another substance, but which only removes water molecules from in and around the substance, not separate hydrogen and oxygen atoms from its molecules. The substance itself is not changed (see also **desiccation**, page 107 and **dehydrating agent**). **Phosphorus pentoxide (P_2O_5)** is an example:

Ductile. Describes a substance which can be stretched. In chemistry, it is normally used of metals which can be drawn out into thin wire, e.g. copper. Different substances show varying degrees of **ductility** (see page 51).

Friction. The force, caused by contact between two objects, which opposes the movement of the touching surfaces over each other. The force trying to make one object move, or both objects move in opposing directions, must be strong enough to overcome friction in order to cause movement.

Fumigation. The killing of bacteria, insects and other pests by poisonous gas or smoke.

Fungicide. A substance used to destroy harmful fungi, e.g. moulds and mildews growing on crops.

Germicide. A substance used to destroy bacteria, especially those carrying disease (germs).

*Anhydrous, 41 (Anhydrate); Avogadro constant, 25; Hydrated, 41 (Hydrate); Ionic compound, 17; Neutralization, 37; Neutron, 12; Oxidation, Oxidizing agent, Reducing agent, 34.

- **Graduations**. Equally-spaced marks used for measurement, e.g. those on a measuring cylinder, which are used to measure the **volume** of liquid.

- **Inert**. Describes an unreactive substance. Such substances do not easily take part in chemical reactions, e.g. the **noble** (or **inert**) **gases***.

- **Insulator**. A poor **conductor** of heat or electricity. Non-metallic elements and their compounds are usually insulators, e.g. sulphur and rubber.

- **Latex**. A milky fluid produced by plants, particularly that produced by the rubber tree, from which raw natural rubber is extracted (and which also forms the basis of some **adhesives**). Also certain similar synthetic **polymers***.

- **Malleable**. Describes a substance which can be moulded into different shapes. In chemistry, it is normally used of substances which can be hammered out into thin sheets, in particular many metals and **alloys** of metals. Different substances show varying degrees of **malleability** (see page 51).

- **Mass**. A measurement of the amount of matter in a body. It is measured in kilograms by "weighing", but is not the same as **weight**. Weighing scales convert the downward force exerted by an object (its weight) into a measurement of the mass of the object.

- **Metabolism**. A term for the chemical processes which occur within a living organism, under the control of **enzymes***. It involves both the breaking down of complex substances into simple forms for energy and the building up of simple substances into more complex ones for storage and tissue-building.

- **Mineral**. A natural inorganic substance which does not come from animals or plants, e.g. **rock salt***. Different minerals have different chemical compositions and properties (see also **ore**).

- **Ore**. A naturally occurring **mineral** from which an element (usually a metal) is extracted, e.g. bauxite, which yields aluminium.

- **Organic solvent**. An organic liquid in which substances will dissolve.

- **Photocell** or **photoelectric cell**. A device used for the detection and measurement of light.

- **Pigments**. Substances which give colour to plants and animals. Pigments are used as insoluble powders to give colour to paints, plastics, etc.

- **Raw material**. A material obtained from natural sources for use in industry, e.g. iron **ore**, coke and limestone are the raw materials used to produce iron.

- **Refrigerant**. A type of **coolant** used in refrigerators. It must be a liquid which **evaporates*** at low temperatures. The substances commonly used nowadays are the **chlorofluorocarbons**, or **freons**, although ammonia was widely used in the past.

- **Resins**. Substances used as **adhesives**. They are often insoluble in water. **Natural resins** are organic compounds secreted by certain plants and insects. **Synthetic resins** are plastic materials produced by **polymerization***.

- **Semiconductor**. An **electrical conductor** (see **conductor**) that contains special impurities and has a resistance to current flow that decreases as the temperature rises (the resistance of normal conductors increases as temperature rises). Semiconductors are usually **metalloids***, such as germanium or silicon. Their properties are altered by adding controlled amounts of impurities.

- **Superheated steam**. Steam above a temperature of 100°C (see also **Celsius temperature**). It is obtained by heating water under pressure.

- **Surface tension**. The tendency of the surface of a liquid to behave as though covered by a skin, owing to the force of attraction between the surface molecules. An isolated drop of liquid occupies the smallest space possible (usually by taking the shape of a ball) because of surface tension.

- **System**. A set of connected parts which have an effect on each other and form a whole unit, e.g. the substances involved in a reaction at **chemical equilibrium***.

- **Tarnish**. To lose or partially lose shine due to the formation of a dull surface layer, e.g. silver sulphide on silver or lithium oxide on lithium. Tarnishing is a type of **corrosion***.

- **Trace elements**. Elements such as copper or iodine which are vital, although only in tiny amounts, to the life of many organisms. They often form part of **enzymes*** or **vitamins***.

- **Triple point**. The point at which the gaseous, liquid and solid **phases*** of a substance all exist. This occurs at a specific temperature, pressure and volume.

- **Viscous**. Describes a fluid that moves in a treacle-like manner, e.g. engine oil. **Viscosity** is due to the movement of different layers of a fluid at different rates, causing resistant forces to operate which try to slow down the faster-moving layers and speed up those moving more slowly.

- **Volatile**. Describes a liquid that **evaporates*** or **sublimes*** easily, e.g. petrol.

- **Volume**. A measurement of the amount of space occupied by a body. With regular-shaped objects, it can be calculated by simple measurement. With irregular-shaped objects, a common way of calculating volume is by measuring the volume of water displaced by such an object. Volume is measured in cubic decimetres (dm^3).

- **Vulcanization**. The process of heating raw natural rubber (extracted from **latex**) with sulphur. Vulcanized rubber is harder, tougher and less temperature-sensitive than raw rubber (the more sulphur used, the greater the difference). This is because the sulphur atoms form cross-links between the chains of rubber molecules (see picture, page 87).

- **Weight**. A measurement of the force with which a body is attracted to the earth. It is calculated by multiplying the **mass** of an object by the acceleration due to gravity and is measured in newtons. The weight of an object can vary with latitude or altitude, but its mass will always stay the same.

* **Chemical equilibrium**, 49; **Corrosion**, 95; **Enzyme**, 47; **Evaporation**, 7; **Metalloids**, 51 (**Metal**); **Noble gases**, 75; **Phase**, 6; **Polymerization**, **Polymers**, 86; **Rock salt**, 54 (**Sodium**); **Sublimation**, 7; **Vitamins**, 91.

Index of substances, symbols and formulae

This index is an index of all the substances which are either defined in the book or used as examples to illustrate particular terms or chemical reactions. It begins with a list which identifies all the chemical symbols and formulae used in the book, giving the name of the relevant substance in each case. Capital letters come alphabetically before small ones in this list, i.e. each element is kept together with its relevant compounds. For example, **CH₃OH** (methanol - a carbon compound) is found in an alphabetical list after **C** (carbon); but before the **Ca** (calcium) list begins. The page entries for the substances themselves are given in the index of names which follows (beginning on page 118).

The page numbers listed in the index are of three different types. Those printed in bold type (e.g. **79**) indicate in each case where the main definition of a substance can be found. Those in lighter type (e.g. 82) refer to supplementary entries. Page numbers printed in italics (e.g. *34*) indicate pages where the name of a substance can be found in a small print label to a picture, or where the substance is used in an equation.

If a page number is followed by a word in brackets, it means that the indexed word can be found inside the text of the definition indicated. If it is followed by (I), the indexed word can be found in the introductory text on the page given. Synonyms are indicated by the word "see" , or by an oblique stroke (/), if they fall together alphabetically.

Symbols and formulae

3Ca₃(PO₄)₂.CaF₂, see **Apatite**

Ac, see **Actinium**

Ag, see **Silver**
AgBr, see **Silver bromide**
AgCl, see **Silver chloride**
AgI, see **Silver iodide**
AgNO₃, see **Silver nitrate**

Al, see **Aluminium**
Al(OH)₃, see **Aluminium hydroxide**
Al₂O₃, see **Aluminium oxide/ Corundum**
Al₂O₃.2H₂O, see **Bauxite**
Al₂(SO₄)₃, see **Aluminium sulphate**

Am, see **Americium**
Ar, see **Argon**
As, see **Arsenic**
At, see **Astatine**
Au, see **Gold**

B, see **Boron**
B₂O₃, see **Boron oxide**
BCl₃, see **Boron trichloride**
Ba, see **Barium**
BaCl₂, see **Barium chloride**
Be, see **Beryllium**
Bi, see **Bismuth**
Bk, see **Berkelium**
Br/Br₂, see **Bromine**
-**Br**, see **Bromo group**

C, see **Carbon**
C₂H₂, see **Ethyne**
C₂H₄, see **Ethene**
C₂H₅Br, see **Bromoethane**
C₂H₅CHO, see **Propanal**
C₂H₅Cl, see **Chloroethane**
C₂H₅COOH, see **Propanoic acid**
C₂H₅OH, see **Ethanol**
C₂H₆, see **Ethane**
C₃H₄, see **Propyne**
C₃H₆, see **Propene**
C₃H₆O, see **Propanone**
C₃H₇OH, see **Propan-1-ol**

C₃H₈, see **Propane**
C₄H₆, see **But-1-yne**
C₄H₈, see **But-1-ene**
C₄H₉OH, see **Butan-1-ol**
C₄H₁₀, see **Butane**
C₅H₁₀, see **Pent-1-ene**
C₅H₁₂, see **Pentane**
C₆H₈O₆, see **Ascorbic acid**
C₆H₁₂O₆, see **Glucose**
C₆H₁₄, see **Hexane**
C₇H₁₆, see **Heptane**
C₈H₁₈, see **Octane**
C₉H₂₀, see **Nonane**
C₁₂H₂₂O₁₁, see **Sucrose**
C₁₇H₃₅COOH, see **Octadecanoic acid**
CCl₄, see **Tetrachloromethane**
CH₂BrCH₂Br, see **1,2-dibromoethane**
CH₂CHCl, see **Vinyl chloride**
-**CH₃**, see **Methyl group**
CH₃CCH, see **Propyne**
CH₃CH₂CCH, see **But-1-yne**
CH₃CH₂CH₂CH₂OH, see **Butan-1-ol**
CH₃CH₂CH₂OH, see **Propan-1-ol**
CH₃CH₂CHO, see **Propanal**
CH₃CH₂Cl, see **Chloroethane**
CH₃CH₂CH₃, see **Butanone**
CH₃CH₂COOH, see **Propanoic acid**
CH₃CH₂OH, see **Ethanol**
CH₃CH₂ONa, see **Sodium ethoxide**
CH₃CHO, see **Ethanal**
CH₃CHOHCH₃, see **Propan-2-ol**
CH₃Cl, see **Chloromethane**
CH₃COCH₃, see **Propanone**
CH₃COOCH₂CH₃, see **Ethyl ethanoate**
CH₃COOH, see **Ethanoic acid**
CH₃NH₂, see **Methyl amine**
CH₃OCH₃, see **Methoxymethane**
CH₃OH, see **Methanol**
CH₄, see **Methane**
CHCH, see **Ethyne**
-**CHO** (functional group), 80 (Aldehydes), 100 (e), 101 (5)
CO, see **Carbon monoxide**

-**CO**-, see **Carbonyl group**
CO₂, see **Carbon dioxide**
-**COO**- (functional group), 81 (Esters), 87 (Polyesters)
-**COOH**, see **Carboxyl group**
(COOH)₂, see **Ethanedioic acid**
COOH(CH₂)₄COOH, see **Hexanedioic acid**

Ca, see **Calcium**
Ca₃(PO₄)₂, see **Calcium phosphate**
CaCl₂, see **Calcium chloride**
CaCO₃, see **Calcium carbonate**
CaCO₃.MgCO₃, see **Dolomite**
CaF₂, see **Fluorospar**
Ca(HCO₃)₂, see **Calcium hydrogencarbonate**
CaO, see **Calcium oxide**
Ca(OH)₂, see **Calcium hydroxide**
CaSiO₃, see **Calcium metasilicate**
CaSO₄, see **Calcium sulphate**
CaSO₄.2H₂O, see **Gypsum**

Cd, see **Cadmium**
Ce, see **Cerium**
Cf, see **Californium**
Cl/Cl₂, see **Chlorine**
-**Cl**, see **Chloro group**
Cm, see **Curium**
Co, see **Cobalt**
CoCl₂, see **Cobalt(II) chloride**
Cr, see **Chromium**
Cs, see **Caesium**

Cu, see **Copper**
Cu₂O, see **Copper(I) oxide**
CuCl, see **Copper(I) chloride**
CuCl₂, see **Copper(II) chloride**
CuCO₃.Cu(OH)₂, see **Malachite**
(CuFe)S₂, see **Copper pyrites**
(Cu(NH₃)₄)SO₄, see **Tetraammine copper(II) sulphate**
Cu(NO₃)₂, see **Copper(II) nitrate**
CuO, see **Copper(II) oxide**
CuSO₄, see **Copper(II) sulphate**
CuSO₄.3Cu(OH)₂, see **Basic copper sulphate**

D, see **Deuterium**
D$_2$O, see **Deuterium oxide**

Dy, see **Dysprosium**

Er, see **Erbium**
Es, see **Einsteinium**
Eu, see **Europium**

F/F$_2$, see **Fluorine**
-F, see **Fluoro group**

Fe, see **Iron**
Fe$_2$O$_3$, see **Haematite**
Fe$_2$O$_3$.xH$_2$O, see **Rust**
FeCl$_2$, see **Iron(II) chloride**
FeCl$_3$, see **Iron(III) chloride**
Fe(OH)$_3$, see **Iron(III) hydroxide**
FeS, see **Iron(II) sulphide**
FeSO$_4$, see **Iron(II) sulphate**

Fm, see **Fermium**
Fr, see **Francium**

Ga, see **Gallium**
Gd, see **Gadolinium**
Ge, see **Germanium**

H/H$_2$, see **Hydrogen**
H$_2$CO$_3$, see **Carbonic acid**
H$_2$O, see **Water**
H$_2$O$_2$, see **Hydrogen peroxide**
H$_2$S, see **Hydrogen sulphide**
H$_2$S$_2$O$_7$, see
　　Fuming sulphuric acid
H$_2$SO$_3$, see **Sulphurous acid**
H$_2$SO$_4$, see **Sulphuric acid**
H$_3$PO$_4$, see **Phosphoric acid**
HBr, see **Hydrogen bromide**
HCl, see **Hydrogen chloride/**
　　Hydrochloric acid
HCHO, see **Methanal**
HCOOH, see **Methanoic acid**
HI, see **Hydrogen iodide**
HNO$_2$, see **Nitrous acid**
HNO$_3$, see **Nitric acid**

He, see **Helium**
Hf, see **Hafnium**
Hg, see **Mercury**
HgS, see **Cinnabar**
Ho, see **Holmium**

I/I$_2$, see **Iodine**
In, see **Indium**
Ir, see **Iridium**

K, see **Potassium**
K$_2$CO$_3$, see
　　Potassium carbonate
K$_2$Cr$_2$O$_7$, see
　　Potassium dichromate
K$_2$SO$_4$, see **Potassium sulphate**
K$_2$SO$_4$.Al$_2$(SO$_4$)$_3$, see **Aluminium**
　　potassium sulphate-
　　12-water
KBr, see **Potassium bromide**
KCl, see **Potassium chloride**
KI, see **Potassium iodide**
KMnO$_4$, see
　　Potassium permanganate
KNO$_3$, see **Potassium nitrate**
KOH, see **Potassium hydroxide**

Kr, see **Krypton**
KrF$_2$, see **Krypton fluoride**

La, see **Lanthanum**
La$_2$O$_3$, see **Lanthanum oxide**
Li, see **Lithium**
Li$_3$N, see **Lithium nitride**
LiCl, see **Lithium chloride**
LiOH, see **Lithium hydroxide**
Lr, see **Lawrencium**
Lu, see **Lutetium**
Lw, see **Lawrencium**

Md, see **Mendelevium**

Mg, see **Magnesium**
MgCl$_2$, see **Magnesium chloride**
MgCO$_3$, see **Magnesium**
　　carbonate
MgO, see **Magnesium oxide**
Mg(OH)$_2$, see **Magnesium**
　　hydroxide
MgSO$_4$, see **Magnesium**
　　sulphate

Mn, see **Manganese**
MnCl$_2$, see **Manganese(IV) chloride**
MnO$_2$, see **Pyrolusite/**
　　Manganese(IV) oxide
Mo, see **Molybdenum**

N/N$_2$, see **Nitrogen**
N$_2$O, see **Dinitrogen oxide**
N$_2$O$_4$, see **Dinitrogen tetraoxide**
-NH$_2$, see **Amino group**
NH$_2$(CH$_2$)$_6$NH$_2$, see
　　1,6-diaminohexane
NH$_3$, see **Ammonia**
(NH$_4$)$_2$SO$_4$, see
　　Ammonium sulphate
NH$_4$Cl, see **Ammonium chloride**
NH$_4$OH, see **Ammonia solution**
NH$_4$NO$_3$, see **Ammonium nitrate**
NO, see **Nitrogen monoxide**
NO$_2$, see **Nitrogen dioxide**

Na, see **Sodium**
Na$_2$CO$_3$, see **Sodium carbonate**
Na$_2$CO$_3$.10H$_2$O, see
　　Washing soda
Na$_2$SO$_3$, see **Sodium sulphite**
Na$_2$SO$_4$, see **Sodium sulphate**
Na$_3$AlF$_6$, see **Cryolite**
NaAl(OH)$_4$, see
　　Sodium aluminate
NaBr, see **Sodium bromide**
NaCl, see **Sodium chloride**
NaClO$_3$, see **Sodium chlorate**
NaHCO$_3$, see
　　Sodium hydrogencarbonate
NaHSO$_4$, see
　　Sodium hydrogensulphate
NaIO$_3$, see **Sodium iodate**
NaNO$_2$, see **Sodium nitrite**
NaNO$_3$, see **Sodium nitrate**
NaOCl, see **Sodium hypochlorite**
NaOH, see **Sodium hydroxide**

Nb, see **Niobium**
Nd, see **Neodymium**
Ne, see **Neon**
Ni, see **Nickel**
NiS, see **Nickel sulphide**
No, see **Nobelium**
Np, see **Neptunium**

O/O$_2$, see **Oxygen**
O$_3$, see **Ozone**
-OH (functional group), see
　　Hydroxyl group

Os, see **Osmium**
OsO$_4$, see **Osmium tetroxide**

P, see **Phosphorus**
P$_2$O$_5$, see **Phosphorus pentoxide**
Pa, see **Protactinium**

Pb, see **Lead**
PbI$_2$, see **Lead(II) iodide**
Pb(NO$_3$)$_2$, see **Lead(II) nitrate**
PbO, see **Lead(II) oxide**
PbO$_2$, see **Lead(IV) oxide**
Pb(OC$_2$H$_5$)$_4$, see **Tetraethyl-lead**
Pb(OH)$_2$, see **Lead(II) hydroxide**
PbS, see **Galena**

Pd, see **Palladium**
Pm, see **Promethium**
Po, see **Polonium**
Pr, see **Praseodymium**
Pt, see **Platinum**
Pu, see **Plutonium**

Ra, see **Radium**
Rb, see **Rubidium**
Re, see **Rhenium**
Rh, see **Rhodium**
Rn, see **Radon**
Ru, see **Ruthenium**

S, see **Sulphur**
SO$_2$, see **Sulphur dioxide**
SO$_3$, see **Sulphur trioxide**

Sb, see **Antimony**
Sc, see **Scandium**
Se, see **Selenium**
Si, see **Silicon**
SiO$_2$, see **Silicon dioxide**
Sm, see **Samarium**
Sn, see **Tin**
Sr, see **Strontium**

T, see **Tritium**
Ta, see **Tantalum**
Tb, see **Terbium**
Tc, see **Technetium**
Te, see **Tellurium**
Th, see **Thorium**
Ti, see **Titanium**
Tl, see **Thallium**
Tm, see **Thulium**

U, see **Uranium**

V, see **Vanadium**
V$_2$O$_5$, see **Vanadium pentoxide**

W, see **Tungsten**

Xe, see **Xenon**
XeF$_4$, see **Xenon tetrafluoride**

Y, see **Yttrium**
Yb, see **Ytterbium**

Zn, see **Zinc**
ZnCl$_2$, see **Zinc chloride**
ZnCO$_3$, see **Calamine**
ZnO, see **Zincite/Zinc oxide**
Zn(OH)$_2$, see **Zinc hydroxide**
Zn(OH)Cl, see
　　Basic zinc chloride
ZnS, see **Zinc blende**
ZnSO$_4$, see **Zinc sulphate**

Zr, see **Zirconium**

Substances

α–sulphur, see Alpha sulphur
β–sulphur, see Beta sulphur

1,2-dibromoethane
(CH₂BrCH₂Br), 74 (Bromine),
79
1,6-diaminohexane
(NH₂(CH₂)₆NH₂), *86*
1-bromo,1-chloro,
2,2,2-trifluoroethane,
see Halothane
1-chloro,2-bromopentane, *101* (9)
2-methyl propan-2-ol, 83
3-iodohexane, *101* (9)
3-methyl pentane, *76*, *101* (8)

Acetic acid, see Ethanoic acid
Acetone, see Propanone
Acetylene, see Ethyne
Acetylenes, see Alkynes
Acrylic, *80*, 87
Actin, *91*
Actinium (Ac), 50, 98
Activated charcoal, *65*
Air, *69*, 94 (I), *97*, 102, 103
Alcohol, see Ethanol
Alcohols, 82-83, *100* (4)
Aldehydes, 80, *101* (5)
Alkali metals, 51, 54-55
Alkaline-earth metals, 51, 56-57
Alkanes, 78, *100* (1)
Alkenes, 79, *100* (2)
Alkyl group, 101 (8)
Alkyl halides, see
Halogenoalkanes
Alkynes, 80, *100* (3)
Alpha sulphur (α–sulphur), see
Rhombic sulphur
Alum, see Aluminium potassium
sulphate-12-water
Alumina, see Aluminium oxide
Aluminium (Al), *37*, 51, 62, *97*, 98,
105 (Cations)
Aluminium hydroxide (Al(OH)₃),
62
Aluminium oxide (Al₂O₃), 62,
69 (Oxides)
Aluminium potassium sulphate-
12-water (K₂SO₄.Al₂(SO₄)₃,
40
Aluminium sulphate (Al₂(SO₄)₃),
62, 102 (Ethene)
Americium (Am), 50, 98
Amino acids, *91*
Amino group (-NH₂), 81 (Primary
amines, Diamines),
91 (Amino acids)
Ammonia (NH₃), *18*, 19, *29*, 37
(Base), *38*, 39 (I), *48*, *49*, 66
(Haber process), 67, *68*, *95*,
105 (Cations)
Ammonia solution (NH₄OH),
67 (Ammonia), 104 (Anions),
105 (Cations)
Ammonium chloride (NH₄Cl), *29*,
39, *48*, 67
Ammonium hydroxide, see
Ammonia solution
Ammonium nitrate (NH₄NO₃), *39*,
67, *68* (Nitrates)
Ammonium sulphate
((NH₄)₂SO₄), 67

Anhydrite calcium sulphate
(CaSO₄), 57 (Calcium
sulphate)
Anthracite, 65 (Coal), *94*
Antimony (Sb), 51, 66, 98
Apatite (3Ca₃(PO₄)₂.CaF₂),
68 (Phosphorus)
Aqua regia, *68*
Argon (Ar), 51, *69*, 75, 98
Arsenic (As), 51, 66, 98
Ascorbic acid (C₆H₈O₆), *36*, *91*
Asphalt, see Bitumen
Astatine (At), 51, 72, 98

Barium (Ba), 50, 56, 98,
105 (Flame tests)
Barium chloride (BaCl₂),
104 (Anions)
Basic copper sulphate
(CuSO₄.3Cu(OH)₂),
61 (Copper)
Basic zinc chloride (Zn(OH)Cl), *40*
Bauxite (Al₂O₃.2H₂O),
62 (Aluminium oxide)
Berkelium (Bk), 51
Beryllium (Be), 50, 56, 98
Beta sulphur (β–sulphur), see
Monoclinic sulphur
Bicarbonate of soda, see
Sodium hydrogencarbonate
Biodegradable detergents, 89
Biopolymers, see
Natural polymers
Bismuth (Bi), 51, 66, 98
Bitumen, 85
Bituminous coal, 65 (Coal)
Bordeaux mixture, *61*
Boron (B), 51, 62, 98
Boron oxide (B₂O₃), 62
Boron trichloride (BCl₃), *19*
Brass, *61*
Brine, 55 (Sodium chloride)
Bromides, 72 (I), 74, 104 (Anions)
Bromine (Br/Br₂), 51, 72, 74, *79*,
98, *101* (9)
Bromine water, 74 (Bromine)
Bromoethane (C₂H₅Br), *101* (9)
Bromo group (-Br), *81*, *101* (9)
Bromothymol blue, *38*
Bronze, *61*
But-1-ene (C₄H₈), *79*
But-1-yne (C₄H₆), 80
Butan-1-ol (CH₃CH₂CH₂CH₂OH),
76, 82, 83
Butan-2-ol, 83
Butane (C₄H₁₀), 78,
85 (Refinery gas)
Butanone, *101* (6)

Cadmium (Cd), 51, 59, 98
Caesium (Cs), 50, 52, 54, 98
Calamine (ZnCO₃), 61 (Zinc)
Calcite, 57 (Calcium carbonate)
Calcium (Ca), 50, 56, 57, 93, *97*,
98, 105 (Flame tests, Cations)
Calcium carbonate (CaCO₃),
27 (Trivial name), 57,
65 (Carbonates),
93 (Temporary hardness),
102 (Carbon dioxide)
Calcium chloride (CaCl₂), 24, *35*,
57, *92*, *102*, 107 (Desiccation)

Calcium hydrogencarbonate
(Ca(HCO₃)₂), *57*,
93 (Temporary hardness)
Calcium hydroxide (Ca(OH)₂), 57
Calcium metasilicate (CaSiO₃),
63 (Silicates)
Calcium oxide (CaO), 57, *60*,
69 (Oxides)
Calcium phosphate (Ca₃(PO₄)₂),
68
Calcium stearate, *93*
Calcium sulphate (CaSO₄), *39*,
57, 71 (Sulphates)
Californium (Cf), 51
Carbohydrates, 90, *95*
Carbon (C), *13*, 24, *34*, 51,
60 (Steel), 63, 64, *95* (Carbon
cycle), *97*, 98, 100-101
Carbonates, 36 (Acid),
40 (method 2), 65, *97*,
104 (Anions)
Carbon dioxide (CO₂), 19, *26*, *34*,
36 (Acid), *55*, 57, *60*, 64, 65,
69 (Oxides), *83*, *90*, *94*,
95 (Photosynthesis), 96, *97*,
102, 103 (Nitrogen), 104
(Gases, Anions)
Carbon fibres, 65
Carbonic acid (H₂CO₃),
65 (Carbon dioxide),
96 (Acid rain)
Carbon monoxide (CO), *60*, 64,
65, *96*
Carbonyl group (-CO-),
80 (Ketones), 100 (f), 101 (6)
Carboxyl group (-COOH),
81 (Carboxylic acids), *91*
(Amino acids), 100 (g), 101 (7)
Carboxylic acids, 81, 88 (Soap),
91 (Lipids), *101* (7)
Cast iron, 60 (Iron)
Caustic potash, see
Potassium hydroxide
Caustic soda, see
Sodium hydroxide
Cerium (Ce), 50, 98
Chalk, 27 (Trivial name),
57 (Calcium carbonate)
Charcoal, 65
Chile saltpetre, see
Sodium nitrate
Chlorides, *16*, *17*, *40*, 73,
104 (Anions)
Chlorine (Cl/Cl₂), *17*, *18*, 24, *33*,
34, 46, 51, *56*, 73, *78*, *93*, 98,
101 (9), 102, 104 (Anions)
Chloroethane (CH₃CH₂Cl), *81*
Chlorofluorocarbons,
115 (Refrigerant)
Chloro group (-Cl), *81*, 101 (9)
Chloromethane (CH₃Cl), *78*, *101* (9)
Chlorophyll, *56*
Chrome iron ore, 58 (Chromium)
Chromium (Cr), 51, 58, 98
Cinnabar (HgS), 59 (Mercury)
Cis but-2-ene, *77*
Coal, 65, *94*, *95*
Coal gas, 65 (Carbon monoxide)
Coal tar, *65*
Cobalt (Co), 51, 59, 98
Cobalt(II) chloride (CoCl₂),
59 (Cobalt), 104 (Water)

120

Index of terms

As with the index of substances, the page numbers used in this index are of three different types. Those printed in bold type (e.g. **79**) indicate in each case where the main definition of a word (or words) can be found. Those in lighter type (e.g. 82) refer to supplementary entries. Page numbers printed in italics (e.g. *34*) indicate pages where a word (or words) can be found as a small print label to a picture.

If a page number is followed by a word in brackets, it means that the indexed word can be found inside the text of the definition indicated. If it is followed by (I), the indexed word can be found in the introductory text on the page given.

Bracketed singulars and plurals are given where relevant after indexed words. Synonyms are indicated by the word "see", or by an oblique stroke (/), if the synonyms fall together alphabetically.

Extract from BS 1986 reproduced
by permission of the British
Standards Institution.

With grateful thanks to Cécile
Landau.